THE
WANTED

ALSO BY ROBERT CRAIS

The Promise

Suspect

Taken

The Sentry

The First Rule

Chasing Darkness

The Watchmen

The Two Minute Rule

The Forgotten Man

The Last Detective

Hostage

Demolition Angel

L.A. Requiem

Indigo Slam

Sunset Express

Voodoo River

Free Fall

Lullaby Town

Stalking the Angel

The Monkey's Raincoat

THE
WANTED

ROBERT CRAIS

**SIMON &
SCHUSTER**

London · New York · Sydney · Toronto · New Delhi

A CBS COMPANY

First published in Great Britain by Simon & Schuster UK Ltd, 2018
A CBS COMPANY

1 3 5 7 9 10 8 6 4 2

Simon & Schuster UK Ltd
1st Floor
222 Gray's Inn Road
London WC1X 8HB

Simon & Schuster Australia, Sydney
Simon & Schuster India, New Delhi

www.simonandschuster.co.uk
www.simonandschuster.com.au
www.simonandschuster.co.in

A CIP catalogue record for this book is available from the British Library.

Hardback ISBN: 978 1 4711 5748 6
Trade Paperback ISBN: 978 1 4711 5750 9
eBook ISBN: 978 1 4711 5751 6

Printed and bound by CPI Group (UK) Ltd, Croydon, CR0 4YY

MIX
Paper from
responsible sources
FSC® C020471

Simon & Schuster UK Ltd are committed to sourcing paper that is made from wood
grown in sustainable forests and support the Forest Stewardship Council, the leading
international forest certification organisation. Our books displaying the FSC logo are
printed on FSC certified paper.

FOR MY FRIEND
OTTO PENZLER
A STEADY HAND IN AN UNSTEADY WORLD

THE
WANTED

PROLOGUE

THE BUSBOY

HARVEY AND STEMMS

HARVEY AND STEMMS were making progress, but they couldn't just blow into the club and flash the picture. The photograph of Unknown Male Subject Number One was dangerous. The picture connected Harvey and Stemms to the person in the picture, and the girl who threw up on the actor, and to everything that would soon happen. Stemms and Harvey were careful to avoid a connection. A connection could get them both killed.

Harvey frowned at the long line of people outside the dance club.

"This is crazy, Stemms. You really wanna mingle with hundreds of people?"

"Only your busboy, Harvey."

"He might not be working tonight. My source didn't know."

The busboy was a twenty-two-year-old parolee named Jesse Guzman. They needed to know if the girl's story was true, so Harvey made a few calls and came up with Guzman. The busboy had a history of misdemeanor arrests, substance abuse, and terrible luck, which was about to turn worse when he met Harvey and Stemms.

Stemms shrugged.

"If he's not here, we'll catch him at home. Either way, let's hope he remembers."

Harvey rolled his eyes.

"Remembers what, a barfer? A place like this, nobody can tell one barfing chick from the next. They mop up chick-barf every night."

Stemms hated Harvey's negativity.

"It isn't like she puked in the bathroom, Harvey. She threw up on a TV star."

Harvey sighed, and shook his head.

"There is nothing to remember, Stemms. She made it up."

"She didn't lie. The lady told us the truth."

"Not the old lady. The barfer. I don't doubt the girl said it, but criminals lie all the time, especially about themselves. It's what we call a fanciful life construction. Also known as baloney."

"Harvey."

"What?"

"You're right. The girl probably made it up, but we still have to check."

Harvey gave in with a nod.

Earlier that day, Stemms and Harvey back-traced a stolen SLR camera to a Santa Monica flea market. They located a flea market regular, this older woman with sun-scorched skin and liver spots, who remembered the young couple who sold the camera. The woman described a slender girl with green eyes and a scar on her wrist, and a good-looking boy with dimples. The girl was a lush. She slurped vodka from a pink plastic cup, and told outlandish stories, like how she'd thrown up on a has-been actor at a fancy Hollywood club, the Jade Horse or Gay Horse, a place she went to a lot. Stemms grew excited. He flashed the picture, and was surprised when the woman said, no, this wasn't the boy with the girl. Stemms felt bad for flashing the picture, but their progress was worth it. The SLR had led to the barfer, and the barfer was linked to a dance club in Hollywood. Harvey was a buzz kill, but if they found the girl, they'd find the Unknown Male Subjects, and everything else they'd been hired to find.

Jade House was one of those celebutante clubs with a squad of paparazzi camped at the door, three-hundred-pound guards, and a line of sexed-up women and nervous men begging a doorman to let them in. Stemms parked their stolen Chrysler around the corner, and slipped a doorman a thousand, cash, to buy their way past the line.

Stemms hated the place. The crowd was a sweaty press of hipsters, drunks, pretenders, and wealthy foreign nationals, all pounded by the sonic hammer of a Swedish DJ spinning a hip-hop dance mix. Stemms and Harvey split up to find the busboy, hiding their search in jokes and banter. The employees they questioned did not realize they were being questioned. None of them knew they were being asked about the busboy. Stemms and Harvey were good.

An hour into their search, Harvey slipped past two women sheathed in shimmering blue, and whispered.

"I found him. That bitch told the truth."

Stemms was shocked.

"You're kidding? For real?"

"He's going on break. Meet us. The next block, in the alley."

"Don't let anyone see you."

"No one sees me, Stemms. Ever."

Stemms hurried back to their car, and drove to the alley on the next block. Two minutes later, Harvey walked up with a trim, nice-looking guy with caramel skin.

Harvey told the busboy to sit up front, and slid into the backseat.

Harvey said, "Jesse, this is Detective Munson. Rich, Jesse Guzman."

Guzman offered his hand, but Stemms ignored it.

"He's high."

The kid's eyes flitted like a couple of June bugs bouncing off a light. Scared.

"Hey, no. No, sir. I'm doing the program."

"If I had you tested, think you'd show clean?"

Harvey's hand floated out of the darkness in back, and patted Guzman's shoulder.

"Stop grinding him, Rich. He was working the night she hurled on the actor. He saw it."

Guzman's head bobbed.

"She's here a lot. She gets sick a lot, too."

"Okay. What's her name?"

"I don't know her like that. I don't have conversations with these people. I'm a busboy."

Stemms sniffed the air loudly, like a dog catching a scent.

"I'm smelling bullshit."

Harvey spoke again, voice mellow and calm, like a jazz man at two in the morning.

"Relax, Jesse. What does she look like? Describe her."

"Really pretty. Like a model. Green eyes. She has a scar on her wrist."

Stemms glanced at Harvey. Guzman's description matched with the flea market. Stemms settled back, and studied the busboy.

"Okay, Jesse, I'm liking you better. Sounds like our girl. She comes here a lot?"

"Yes, sir."

"Is she here now?"

"I don't know. I don't think so, but it's a big club."

"Boyfriends?"

The kid flashed a nervous grin.

"She's hot. She always has boys."

Harvey spoke from the shadows.

"Show him."

Stemms hesitated, so Harvey said it again.

"Show him the picture."

Stemms took out his phone. The image he carried was taken from a high-quality residential surveillance video. The video was captured at night, and showed three figures creeping alongside a house. They moved in single file, one after another, and knew the camera was watching. All three wore hoodies and hats to cover their faces, and kept their heads down. The second figure blew it. The second figure, dubbed Unknown Male Number One, glanced up at the camera as he stepped out of frame. The image had to be enhanced and refined, but it turned out okay. A ball cap and hoodie masked a third of the face, but his features were readable. Now Harvey and Stemms needed a name.

Stemms held out the phone.

"What about this guy? You see him with the girl?"

Guzman studied the picture.

"I'm pretty sure I've seen him, but she's with another boy, more."

Stemms put away his phone, and repeated the old woman's description.

"Tall guy. Good-looking. Dimples."

Guzman's eyes lit up.

"Yeah. Alec."

Stemms glanced at Harvey, and tried not to smile. Harvey's hand appeared, and squeezed Guzman's shoulder. Encouraging.

"That's right. You know Alec's last name?"

Guzman squinted, as if he thought he should know, but didn't.

"Some of the staff know him. He's a waiter. Up in the Valley."

Stemms glanced at Harvey again.

"Alec the waiter. Up in the Valley."

He turned back to the busboy.

"You know this how?"

"They give him free drinks. They talk. Alec is here more than the girl."

"Yeah? So who in the club here knows Alec?"

"Crystal. There's Crystal, and Paul. Paul is a bartender. Crystal is a server. I can ask them. I can find out his last name."

Stemms ignored his offer.

"Has anyone else been asking about this?"

"Policemen?"

"Anyone."

"Not me. I don't know if anyone else been asked."

Harvey said, "The girl, Alec, their friends? Nobody's asking about them?"

Guzman again tried to turn, but Harvey's touch stopped him.

"No, sir. What did they do?"

Stemms ignored him again, and stared at Harvey.

"What do you think?"

Harvey's voice was a shadow.

"I think Jesse's been a big help. Thank you, Jesse."

Stemms smiled at the busboy.

"Yeah, dude. We owe you."

"Can I go?"

"Sure."

Stemms offered his hand.

Guzman was surprised. He beamed, and took the hand.

Harvey looped a rope across Guzman's throat as they shook. Stemms held tight, and hooked a hard left to the boy's temple. The busboy arched and thrashed and kicked the dashboard. Stemms hooked lefts as hard as he could, and Harvey strained against the rope. The kicking slowed, and finally stopped. Stemms made sure the busboy was dead, and pushed his body under the dash. Harvey said nothing. Stemms fired up the Chrysler, and pulled away. He listened to Harvey breathe, somewhere in the darkness behind him.

"He saw the picture."

Harvey said, "That's right."

Stemms and Harvey drove through Hollywood, looking for a place to dump the body. The image of Unknown Male Number One was captured sixteen days earlier. Stemms and Harvey had been on the hunt since before the image was captured. They were ahead of the police, the insurance investigators, and the private security firms. Now they were even further ahead. Stemms and Harvey were the best in the business.

Stemms glanced in the mirror.

"Hey, Harvey?"

Harvey was a shadow within a shadow. Silent.

Stemms glanced again.

"We're really bad people."

Stemms laughed. His laughter grew as they glided across the night, but Harvey didn't laugh with him.

PART I

RICH PEOPLE

1

ELVIS COLE

JAMES TYSON CONNOR walked out of his home on a chill fall morning, climbed into a twelve-year-old Volvo, and left for school an hour late. Tyson was a seventeen-year-old junior at an alternative school in the San Fernando Valley. He was thin, nervous, and cursed with soft features and gentle eyes that made him look like a freshman. Nothing about him suggested that Tyson was one of the most wanted felons in Los Angeles.

Tyson and his mother lived in a modest, one-story ranch house not far from his school. I was a block away, waiting for Tyson to leave. His mother had warned me he would be late. Tyson suffered from anxiety issues, and hated going to school. Two prior schools had expelled him for absenteeism and failing grades, so his mother enrolled him at the alternative school to keep him from dropping out. This was a decision she regretted.

His mother called as Tyson drove away.

"Mr. Cole? Are you here?"

"I've been here almost two hours, Ms. Connor. The sunrise was lovely."

"He's gone. You can come in now."

Tyson's mother worked as an office manager for a law firm in Encino. She appeared neat, trim, and ready for work when she opened the door, but carried herself with so much tension she might have been wrapped with duct tape.

I walked up the drive, and offered my hand.

"Elvis Cole."

"Devon Connor. Thanks so much for coming, Mr. Cole. I'm sorry he took so long."

I stepped into her living room, and watched her lock the door. The house smelled of pancakes and fish, and something I didn't place. A glowing aquarium bubbled beside a couch.

"The new school doesn't mind, him being so late?"

"With what they charge, they should send a limo."

She stopped herself, and closed her eyes.

"Sorry. I sound like a bitch."

"He's your son. You're worried."

"Beyond worried. I moved mountains to get him into this school, and now I feel like I've fed him to animals."

Devon had found money and valuables in Tyson's room. She believed her son had gotten involved with drug dealers and gangsters, and wanted me to find out what he was doing. I wasn't sure I wanted the job.

I tried to sound reassuring.

"It probably isn't as bad as you think, Ms. Connor. These things usually aren't."

She studied me like I was stupid, and abruptly turned away.

"Follow me. I'll show you how bad."

Tyson's bedroom was small, and looked like a typical middle-class, teenage boy's bedroom. A dresser sat opposite a walk-in closet, an unmade bed filled the corner, and his nightstand bristled with soda cans, chip bags, and crumbs. Special Forces operators with glowing green eyes watched us from a recruitment poster above the bed. A desk beneath his window was crowded with a desktop computer, a laptop, three monitors, and an impressive tangle of game controllers.

I said, "He must be a serious gamer."

"He can't sit still in school, but he can sit in front of these things for hours."

She went to the desk, opened the middle side drawer, and took something from the back of it.

"*This* is how bad it is."

She held out a watch with a bright white face, three dials, and three knobs on the rim. The distinctive Rolex crown was obvious.

"A Rolex?"

"A Rolex Cosmograph Daytona, made with eighteen-carat white gold. A watch like this sells for forty thousand dollars, new. Even used, they sell for more than twenty. He came home wearing it. I said, this is a Rolex, where'd you get a watch like this?"

Small nicks marred the rim and crystal, but the watch appeared otherwise perfect.

"What did he say?"

She rolled her eyes, and looked disgusted.

"A flea market, can you imagine? He says it's a knockoff, but I don't believe it. Does this look like a knockoff to you?"

She pushed the watch closer, so I took it. The body felt heavy and substantial. The hands showed the correct time, and the second hand swept the face with silent precision, but I wasn't an expert.

"Could it be a gift, and he doesn't want you to know?"

"Who would give him a gift like this?"

"His father? A grandparent?"

She frowned again, and gave me the 'you're stupid' eyes.

"His father left before Tyson was born, and everyone else is dead. My son should not have this watch. He shouldn't have *anything* this expensive, and we have to stop him before he gets himself killed or arrested."

We.

I tried to tone down the drama.

"Maybe we're getting ahead of ourselves. If the watch is real, then he shouldn't have it, but this is the kind of thing a kid might lift if he saw it at a friend's house. You don't need a detective if Tyson has sticky fingers."

The reasonable detective offered a reasonable explanation, but she seemed disappointed.

"There's so much more than the watch."

She went to the closet, and reached inside.

"It started with shirts. He didn't even bother to hide them, like with the watch."

I said, "Shirts."

She came out with a sleek black sport coat trimmed with velvet lapels.

"*New* shirts. Then new shoes turned up, and another new shirt, and this jacket, all from Barneys in Beverly Hills. We can't afford Barneys."

Her phone chirped with an incoming text. She checked the message, and slipped the phone back into her pocket.

"Sorry. The school. I text when he leaves, they text when he arrives. It's how we keep track."

Alternative.

I fingered the jacket. The fabric felt soft and creamy, like very fine wool. Expensive.

I glanced up, and found her watching me. Waiting.

"Did the clothes come from the same flea market?"

"No, this time a friend's father runs the wardrobe department at a studio. They get so many free clothes, Tyson can have whatever he wants."

I didn't say anything. Devon went on without my prompting.

"I called Barneys. This jacket? Tyson bought it. The salesman remembered because Tyson paid cash. Three thousand dollars, and Tyson paid *cash*."

She put the jacket back in the closet, and went to his bed.

"After I found out about Barneys, I searched his room."

She slid a plastic storage container from under the bed. The container was filled with keyboards, Game Boy and Xbox gear, and action figures. She moved a keyboard, took out a box, and opened it. The box contained a thick roll of cash wrapped by a blue rubber band.

"Four thousand, two hundred dollars. I counted. The first time, he had twenty-three hundred dollars. I found over seven thousand dollars here once. The amount changes."

I sat back and stared at her. Devon was describing an income stream.

"Did you ask him about the money?"

"If I ask, he'll lie, just like he lied about the clothes and the watch. I want to know what he's doing and who he's doing it with before I confront him."

"I can ask him."

"If we ask, he'll know I snoop, and he'll still lie. Don't detectives follow people? You could follow him and see what he does."

"Following someone is expensive. Asking is cheaper."

Her mouth pinched, and she glanced away. Worried.

"We should discuss your fee. I have a good job, but I'm not wealthy."

"Okay. What would you like to know?"

"How much would it cost to follow him?"

"Two cars minimum, one op per car, ready to go twenty-four/seven. Call it three thousand a day."

"Oh."

She wet her lips, and her eyes lost focus. She was trying to figure out how to come up with the money, and all her options were bad. I had met a hundred parents like Devon, and seen the same fearful confusion in their eyes. Like people who didn't know how to swim, watching their children drown.

I changed the subject.

"How long has this been going on?"

"Since the beginning of school."

"And whatever he's doing, you believe he's doing it with students from school."

Her eyes snapped into hard focus.

"Tyson's never been in trouble. Tyson's a sweetheart! He stayed home all the time, he never went out, he was afraid of everything, but then he started changing. He met a girl."

"Ah."

"I was thrilled. Tyson doesn't meet girls. Tyson's afraid of girls."

"Have you met her?"

"He wouldn't tell me her name. He made friends with a boy named Alec. They go to the mall. I ask questions, but he's evasive and vague, or makes up more lies. Tyson was never like this. He never used to go to the mall, and now he's never home."

Tyson sounded like any other teenage boy, except for the parts about money and watches.

"He met Alec at school?"

"I think so, but I checked the roster."

She took a slim red booklet from Tyson's desk. The cover was emblazoned with a soaring bird and the name of the school. Cal-Matrix Alternative Education. *Where students soar.*

"I didn't find anyone named Alec or Alexander."

We weren't exactly drowning in clues.

I jiggled the watch. An authentic Rolex had serial and model numbers cut into the head behind the bracelet, or on the inner rim below the crystal. High-end fakes often had numbers, too, but fake numbers didn't appear in the manufacturer's records.

"Tell you what. I have a friend who knows watches. She can tell us if the watch is real. She might even be able to tell us who owns it."

"You can't take it. Tyson might notice."

I told her about the numbers.

"I'll take off the bracelet, and copy the numbers. The watch can stay."

"You won't have to follow him?"

"We'll start small to keep the costs down, and see what develops. Sound good?"

Her face brightened, and split with a smile.

"Perfect."

I thought about the money and the watch she'd found, and wondered if Tyson had hidden anything else.

"You searched his room, but what about his car?"

"Only twice. When the car's home, he's home."

"If you have a spare key, I'd like it. I'll check his car after I call in the watch."

She started away for the key, then hesitated.

"I saw on your website, The Elvis Cole Detective Agency. The website says your work is confidential."

"That's right."

"Meaning, when we find out what Tyson's doing, you won't tell the police?"

"It depends."

"The website doesn't say anything about depends."

"If I find a human head in his trunk, I might feel the urge to report it."

She smiled again, and turned away.

"No human heads, Mr. Cole. Not yet."

I didn't like the way she said 'yet.'

Devon gave me the key and watched me copy the numbers. When the bracelet was back on the watch, she put the watch in the drawer, and we left the house together.

Devon Connor drove away first. She had a long drive in bad traffic ahead, and was already late for work. Alternative schools were expensive, and so were detectives.

I started my car, but I didn't leave. I pictured the skinny kid with gentle eyes who looked like a freshman. I pictured him sneaking cash into his room, and hiding it under his bed. There were many ways he could have gotten the cash, but none of the ways were good.

Devon's pleasant, middle-class street was peaceful. No one was trying to murder her, or Tyson, or me, but this was about to change.

2

SHERRI TOYODA AND HER FAMILY owned a watch shop in Santa Monica. The Toyodas sold moderately priced timepieces almost anyone could afford, but their restoration of antique and vintage collectibles had made them legends. Photographs of Sherri's parents with dignitaries, politicians, and movie stars covered the walls. Three U.S. presidents, eleven senators, and four Supreme Court justices were among their clients.

I checked the numbers from the watch, and called her.

"Guess who?"

"Yesterday's bad news?"

Sherri and I used to date.

"I need help with a Rolex."

"I'll help if I can, but we're not an authorized dealer."

"I'm not shopping. This is a specific Cosmograph Daytona."

"Sweet! If you can afford a Cosmo, I might date you again."

Everyone thinks they're a riot.

"I need to know if it's genuine."

"Bring it in. I can tell if it's real in five seconds."

"I don't have the watch. I have the serial and model numbers."

"Do you have the chronometer certification that came with it?"

"If I knew what a chronometer certification was, the answer would be no. All I have are the numbers."

She was silent for a moment.

"Okay, listen. I can check your numbers with a friend at the corporate office. If your numbers match his numbers, the watch is authentic."

"Great."

"Not so great if it's stolen. He'll want to know how I have the numbers, and why I'm asking. Is it?"

"Could be. How would he know?"

"Dude. You buy a watch like this, you're walking around with twenty or thirty thousand dollars on your wrist. Guess what?"

"They get stolen."

"Or lost, so the company keeps a list of AWOL watches for their clients. If you lose your watch, you give them the numbers. If your watch turns up, they know you're the rightful owner, and give you a shout."

"Meaning, you could find out who owns it?"

"Not necessarily. People sell watches. They give them as gifts. The company doesn't know."

"Oh."

"Are you trying to find the owner?"

"Maybe."

She thought some more.

"I still might be able to help. Stores activate the warranty when someone buys a watch like this. The original buyer might be in the warranty files. Want me to check?"

"You're the best, Sherri. Thanks."

I read off the numbers, and lowered my phone, but I still didn't leave. Devon had searched Tyson's room, but she was his mom, and almost certainly missed something. I was a trained professional, and knew where to look. Or maybe I'd get lucky.

I turned off my car, and walked up Devon's drive for the second time that morning. The side gate squealed, I passed Tyson's window, and let myself in through the kitchen.

The Connor residence held three bedrooms and two baths. Tyson probably wouldn't hide something in his mother's bedroom or bath, so I skipped them, and started in Tyson's bathroom.

Green streaks of toothpaste highlighted the sink, and the counter was forested with deodorant, mouthwash, zit cream, and all the usual bathroom items. A frazzled toothbrush and disposable razor stood sentry in a plastic X-Men cup. Tyson's medications were lined up beneath the mirror. The scripts bore Tyson's name, and were written for medicines commonly used to treat depression, anxiety, and attention deficit disorder. I found nothing out of the ordinary in the cabinets, behind the towels, or in the toilet tank.

The third bedroom was set up as an office, but Devon used it as a catch-all room. Mirrored sliders filled a wall opposite a desk, a file cabinet, and a bookcase jammed with law books, paperback thrillers, and titles like *The Unhappy Child*, *Coping with Fear*, and *The Single Mother's Rule Book*. Cardboard boxes of Christmas decorations were stacked on a treadmill between the desk and a window, and the desk was heavy with bills, unread magazines, and a file devoted to Tyson's school. The file contained promotional brochures, articles, and another copy of the roster. I took a brochure and the roster, and moved on to Tyson's room.

His closet and dresser were evidence free. No additional clues were wedged under his mattress, behind the headboard, or in, under, or around his nightstand. I found a pizza crust, a dead mayfly, six silverfish, and enough tortilla chip crumbs to fill a sandbox between his bed and the nightstand. Private detection was glamorous.

I was hoping his desk would contain a receipt, a note, a clue, or a photo of Tyson's friends, but I found nothing. If Tyson had pix of the girl or his friends, they were on his phone and computers.

I rolled the chair aside, crawled under the desk, and found more crumbs and dust bunnies. I opened the top drawer, detached the drawer from its slides, and removed the drawer from the desk. Devon had looked inside the drawers, but not outside. A plain white envelope was taped to the back of the drawer. The envelope was sealed, and taped well. I felt the contents, and decided the envelope contained cash. I didn't remove the envelope or open it. I photographed the envelope attached to the drawer, slipped the drawer back on its slides, and closed it. A second envelope was taped behind the middle drawer. Each envelope was thick, and probably held thousands.

Depressing.

I wandered back to the kitchen, and saw pictures dotting the fridge. Devon holding Tyson when he was a baby. Toddler Tyson with his mother at Disneyland, both wearing Mickey Mouse ears. Eight-year-old Spider-Man Tyson posing with an eight-year-old Incredible Hulk Halloween friend. Teenage Tyson locked in video game combat with a chunky gaming friend. The pictures were held to the door by magnets.

Finding the envelopes left me sad. I felt bad for Devon, and also for Tyson. She wanted me to find out what he was doing, but she wasn't going to like what I found. I wouldn't like it, either.

I let myself out, and went to find Tyson's car.

THE CAL-MATRIX ALTERNATIVE HIGH SCHOOL was eighteen minutes away. Online trolls described a gulag for drama queen celebrity offspring, where rich people hid their crash-and-burn children from bad influences, bad behavior, and drugs. Former students and parents presented a different image. They described caring teachers and a safe environment where teenagers with learning and social disorders were able to flourish. The only point everyone agreed on was the money. The tuition cost a fortune.

I was disappointed when I arrived. After all the talk about celebrities and rich people, Cal-Matrix was a small, flat building on a commercial street in Reseda. It looked like a dental office.

I cruised past twice. Tyson wasn't out front with drug-dealing gangsters, but his Volvo was in a parking lot adjoining the school. The lot was small, fenced, and held fewer than thirty cars. Tyson's Volvo was the oldest.

I parked across the street and considered the layout. A fence surrounded the school and the parking lot. Signs on the fence warned against unauthorized trespassers, and asked visitors to check in at the office. I would have to pass the school's entrance to reach the parking lot, but no guards were present and the parking lot was empty. I got out of my car, and immediately got back in. A girl came out of the school. She was thin, and wispy, and appeared to be fifteen or sixteen. She stopped outside the doors, lit a cigarette, and inhaled hard enough to inflate her body. I watched her smoke, and waited. Sooner or later, she would finish the cigarette or smoke herself to death.

She finally crushed the butt, and went back into the school. Alternative.

I hurried to Tyson's Volvo, and opened the trunk. It held a pair of flip-flops, two bottles of coolant, a quart of motor oil, and a dirty towel. No human heads were present. I checked to make sure no one was coming, and slid in behind the wheel.

Tyson's car was a rolling garbage can. Straws, wadded napkins, and take-out menus jammed a map holder built in the door. More napkins, plastic forks, and candy wrappers were wedged between the seat and the center console, and the console was crowded with open bags of Gummy Bears, M&M's, and tortilla chips. Crumpled fast-food containers and soda cans were thick beneath the seat.

The backseat was even worse. Taco wrappers, drive-thru cups, and greasy napkins covered the floor. I dug through most of it, but the only evidence I found was evidence of tooth decay. Tyson was an eating machine. He probably turned to crime to pay for a junk food habit.

I finished searching the rear, and climbed into the passenger seat. The smoker appeared again as I closed the door.

I ducked low, and watched her over the dash.

She resumed her position outside the double doors, and fired up another cigarette. A volcanic plume arced skyward and she stared into space.

I stayed low, and found a sunglass case beneath the seat. The case was new, and cleaner than anything else in Tyson's car. Inlaid black beads spelled a name across the mother-of-pearl case in swirling script. Amber. The sunglasses inside were sleek, black, and trimmed with an elegant spray of crystal. I didn't need to recognize the designer's emblem to know they were expensive.

Gucci.

The glasses were small, and sized for a woman. I studied the name again.

Amber.

I photographed the glasses and the case, then put the case back under the seat.

The smoker still smoked. She drew deep on the cigarette, held it, then tipped back her head and spouted a plume like a surfacing whale. She did this again and again. Inhaled, held it, exhaled. She seemed determined to smoke forever, and I was stuck in a Dumpster. Tyson's car smelled like taco sauce and pickles.

The smoker was still smoking when my phone buzzed. I checked the Caller ID, and smiled. Hess.

"Elvis Cole Detective Agency, where the client is always satisfied."

"Yes, she is. Where are you?"

"Hiding in a car in a parking lot. I'm watching an underage girl."

"Not one more word, or I'll arrest you."

"She's smoking."

"Stop. I'm inviting myself to dinner. Feel like cooking?"

"Sure. Whatever you want."

"You. I'll see you tonight."

Hess hung up, and I smiled even wider.

Janet Hess and I bumped heads on a difficult case, and began dating when the case resolved. Hess was a cop, but not an ordinary cop. She was Special Agent in Charge at the Los Angeles field office of the ATF. She was smart, interesting, and way over my pay grade. Also, she laughed at my jokes. I liked her a lot.

The smoker seemed content to keep smoking forever, but the longer I stayed in Tyson's car, the more likely it became that a student or teacher would see me. The smoker was facing the street, so I decided to go for it.

I eased out of the Volvo, quietly closed the door, and stepped away as the smoker saw me. Her expression didn't change. If she'd seen me leave Tyson's car, she gave no reaction.

I walked.

The smoker drew deep, exhaled, and vanished behind a cloud.

My phone buzzed again as I reached my car. Sherri.

I climbed inside, pulled the door, and answered.

Sherri said, "You knew it was stolen, you bastard. What's going on?"

"I don't know. That's why I called *you*."

"That watch is so far beyond stolen I should be furious. It's part of a major investigation."

I took a breath, and listened.

3

THE MID-MORNING TRAFFIC made Sherri difficult to hear.

"The original buyer was a Richard Slauson. He bought the watch sixteen years ago, here in L.A. Slauson notified the company thirty-two days ago. His watch was stolen, so he asked them to put it on the list. You want his info?"

"It was stolen thirty-two days ago?"

"He *reported* it thirty-two days ago. Do you want the man's contact info or not?"

Sherri was angry.

I said, "Please."

She spelled Slauson's name, and read off a phone number and an address in Beverly Hills.

I said, "You sound mad. What's wrong?"

"I'm annoyed. I told you what would happen if this thing was on the list. He knew the watch as soon as I mentioned the model. He was all over me."

Her friend.

"All over you, wanting to know why you were asking?"

"All over me, as in *demanding* and *threatening*. You don't have to worry. I didn't mention your name."

"I'm not worried. I'm wondering why the big deal."

"The police. The police showed up a few days after Slauson put his watch on the list. My friend has been in the business for *years*, and this was the first time the police have been to his office. They were all over this watch. They told him to call, twenty-four/seven, if the numbers turned up."

I didn't get it.

"For a watch?"

"He's never seen the police this hot to recover a timepiece. Ever."

"Is Slauson someone important?"

"I don't know, and I didn't ask. He wasn't anxious to share."

I thought about what she had told me, and understood why she was angry.

"Is your friend going to tell the police you asked?"

She hesitated.

"I don't know. I think so."

"Put it on me, Sherri. If the police call, tell them the truth. I don't want you to get in trouble."

Her voice softened, and lost the annoyance.

"You've been warned. Worry about yourself."

Sherri hung up.

Nothing about Slauson's name was familiar, so I searched his name and address on the Internet. Pictures and information were easy to find.

Richard, seventy-two, and Margaret, seventy-one, were retired dermatologists. Dr. and Dr. Slauson had two daughters and five grandchildren. They were active in charities, volunteered at a downtown mission, and appeared to be wonderful people. A voice mail answered my call, but I hung up before the beep. A personal visit would be more appropriate, especially since I wanted Tyson to personally return Dr. Slauson's watch.

The Doctors Slauson lived in a hillside Beverly Hills neighborhood called Trousdale Estates. Their home was set behind a wrought-iron gate and bird-of-paradise plants, with a motor court stretching from the gate to an older, well-kept Spanish Revival the color of peaches. I liked the color. Peaches were friendly.

A call box with a camera dome as black as a shark's eye topped a post at the gate. I parked across the street, and walked to the call box. The shark's eye watched me approach. I pressed the call button, and heard a buzz inside the house. The ringer buzzed for almost a minute, and finally quit. The Slausons weren't home.

I took out a card, and wrote a note asking the Slausons to call. I was about to put the card into their mailbox when a balding man in bad shorts and a T-shirt called from behind me.

"Are you one of the real estate people?"

His voice was deep, and didn't go with the rest of him.

"No, sir. Elvis Cole. I'm looking for Richard Slauson."

"George Wilcox. I live across the street."

I gave him the card, and watched him frown.

"Detective. You here about the burglary?"

Burglary.

"I'm looking into it. Do you know when the Slausons will be home?"

He flexed the card.

"They moved. Margie doesn't feel safe anymore, so they moved to the Palm Springs house."

"Because of the burglary?"

"She couldn't sleep. Had nightmares about people standing over the bed. Still has them, from what Rich tells me. Been over a month."

I glanced at the house. If Tyson could help the police identify the thief, even better.

"Were they home when it happened?"

"Uh-uh. Palm Springs. Came home, and found the house looted. You should've seen the police. We had police everywhere, asking if we saw anything."

We stepped aside to make way for a pickup truck. Construction workers, on their way to a job site. Wilcox scowled as they passed.

"You watch. It'll turn out to be one of these guys. All this construction, hundreds of workmen, half of them casing our homes."

I said, "Did you?"

"Did I what?"

"See anything."

He shook his head and waved at the call box.

"Not me, but the cameras got'm. Big, nasty mothers in masks. I told Rich, good thing you and Margie weren't home. They would've raped her."

Rich and Margie probably moved to get away from him.

A small sign stood in the ivy at the edge of the drive. FIRST TIER SECURITY. First Tier was a full-service, twenty-four-hour security company. Most of the homes in Beverly Hills had similar signs from other companies, but First Tier signs were common. I had helped one of the First Tier founders with a personal matter, and worked with them several times.

"Did you hear the alarm?"

Wilcox sneered.

"What alarm? These guys were hard-core professionals. They've robbed houses from Beverly Hills to Encino."

I nodded at the sign.

"Must be good if they beat the alarm. First Tier is as good as it gets."

Wilcox sneered again.

"Money wasted, for all the good. Now my wife wants a German shepherd. A man-eater the size of a horse."

He wasn't thrilled about picking up horse-sized dog poop.

"Rich loves this house, but Margie can't sleep. He says they'll probably sell, so now we're crawling with real estate people. One damned thing after another."

Wilcox was complaining about the real estate people when a brown sedan cruised past. The driver was a burly man in his forties with a broad face and cheap sunglasses. His female passenger had hard eyes, and raven hair pinned in a bun. They slowed as they passed, and gave Wilcox another reason to scowl.

"Look at these two. Lookie-loos."

I gestured at my card.

"When you speak to Dr. Slauson, would you please ask him to call? It's important."

He trudged up his drive without answering.

I said, "Thank you."

I took out a new card, and wrote the same note. The sedan reappeared as I dropped the card into the mailbox. The couple inside saw me, and saw me see them. The woman spoke to the man, and the man looked at my car.

I waited until they were gone, fished my card from the mailbox, and returned to my car. I called First Tier, and asked for Dave Deitman. Dave was one of the founders.

Dave said, "Hey, brudda man, long time. What's doing?"

"A house in Trousdale. The Slausons."

I started to give the address, but he didn't need to hear it.

"Yeah, sure, I know it. You in on the action?"

"What action?"

"You kidding me? All these high-end burglaries? Insurance investigators are having a feeding frenzy."

"I'm on something that might be connected. Has LAPD made an arrest?"

"Not yet, but it's coming. We pulled a good face off Slauson, and these kids leave prints and DNA everywhere."

The world slowed when I heard him.

I said, "Kids."

"They're kids. Three morons."

I said it again, just to be sure.

"Kids."

"Teenagers, young adults, whatever. A female and two males. I'm not saying they're little children."

I stared out the window. Wilcox described big nasty mothers and multiple burglaries.

"How many burglaries are we talking about?"

"Seventeen, eighteen, something like that. The number's in play. The task force is playing connect-the-dots with fingerprints."

"A task force has the case?"

"This is big, brudda man. You mess with rich people, you get the full-court press."

"They have prints and DNA, but no IDs."

"It happens. Never been busted, so they aren't in the system. They hood up, they're good about ducking the cameras, but the one kid, he finally screwed up. Unknown Male Numero Uno. We got him. First Tier got his face."

Dave was so proud of himself he laughed.

"Can I see his picture?"

"Sure. On the way."

My phone chimed when the picture arrived.

I knew who I'd see even before I opened Dave's email. The image was pixelated, and green with infrared glare. A ball cap and hoodie stole part of the subject's face, but his remaining features were clear.

I noted the time, and did the math. Three hours and seven minutes had passed since I left Devon Connor, and now her case was solved. Impressive. This was probably a record for high-speed detection, but being the World's Fastest Detective didn't make me feel better.

I looked at the picture, and Tyson looked back.

Dave was speaking, but his voice was lost.

I thought about Devon. She would have questions I couldn't answer. She would need help I wasn't sure I could give.

4

HARVEY AND STEMMS

PAUL THE BARTENDER'S true name was Charles Paul Skleener. Once they had his name, Stemms obtained a copy of his DMV photo and last known address, which was a two-story courtyard apartment building in the mid-Wilshire area, not far from K-Town.

Skleener's building was old, needed paint, and the ground-floor windows and entrance were protected by rusty security bars.

Harvey eyed the entry with disgust.

"You know what they call places like this?"

"Don't start."

"A shitbox. A shitbox like this doesn't have air-conditioning. I wouldn't live in a place, it didn't have air."

Stemms wanted to confirm that Skleener still lived at this address, so Harvey got out. Stemms waited in the Chrysler. Engine running. Air on. Tired. He popped an Adderall and half a Ritalin.

Harvey was back a few minutes later.

"No answer, but his name's on the box. What do you want to do?"

"He's sleeping. Bartenders get home late."

"I rang the bell five times."

"Earplugs."

"Whatever, Stemms. You want to wait, see if he comes home?"

They were moving too fast to wait. Paul the bartender could give them

Alec the waiter, and keep them out front, but only if they found the bartender quickly.

Stemms took out his phone.

"Hang on."

"Who are you calling?"

"Shh."

Stemms called Jade House, and asked for the manager. The manager wasn't available, but an assistant named Walder came on the line. Walder pronounced his name like it was spelled with a *V*.

He said, "This is Valder. May I help you?"

Harvey shook his head, and stared out the window.

Stemms made his pitch.

"Hey, Valder, Jerry Leach, over at Paramount. Listen, man, I'm calling with rave kudos for one of your bartenders, a guy named Paul, mm, his last name might be Skleener? Anyway, listen, I took a few buyers to your place the other night, and, man, your guy Paul rolled out the red. He could *not* have treated us better, so I'm sending a little something-something, know what I mean? Would you do me a favor? Would you pretty please make sure he gets it?"

Harvey rolled his eyes.

Stemms gave him the finger.

Walder said, "Of course. It vould be my pleasure."

"Thanks, brother, really. Now, listen, is Paul working tonight? If he works tonight, I'll have my assistant send it right over."

Walder had to check the schedule.

"No, I am sorry, Paul is not scheduled until the day after tomorrow."

"Oh, bum! What's up with that? Is he working a second gig somewhere?"

Harvey sat up, interested in the answer.

Walder said, "He has the acting. The school. Rehearsals. The auditions."

"Got it. Thanks, Valder. I'll call back in two days."

Stemms lowered the phone.

"Actor."

Harvey smirked.

"Actor, my ass. He's a bartender."

"Auditions. Rehearsals. Actor shit. If we knew where he was, we wouldn't have to sit here all day."

Harvey slumped low in the seat, and closed his eyes.

"He's a bartender."

Stemms studied the building.

"Anyone see you?"

"Nobody sees me. Ever."

"Cameras?"

"Are we seeing the same building?"

Stemms opened his door to get out, but Harvey's hand flicked like a striking cobra across the width of the car, and stopped him.

"I'll go. Make sure the guy doesn't surprise me."

Harvey got out, and returned to the building. Twenty-six minutes passed, during which Stemms became antsy, then irritated, then angry. He was five heartbeats from getting out of the Chrysler when Harvey swaggered across the street. Stemms couldn't tell from the swagger if Harvey felt smug or sour.

Harvey slid inside, and pulled the door hard.

"Nobody home."

Stemms frowned.

"You were gone all this time, and that's all you've got?"

"I was looking around. That's why I went in, right?"

"Well? Did you find something?"

"Scripts. Scripts everywhere. Scripts, plays, all these pictures of himself. This dude has almost as many pictures of himself as you do."

Stemms wondered if this was a joke.

Harvey suddenly grinned, and waved a slip bearing an address.

"*Yes*, I found something. Actor's workshop in Valley Village. Noon until four. He's doing a scene."

Stemms checked the address, and fired up the Chrysler.

"He'll be inside by the time we get there. We'll get him on the way out."

"Of course we will, Stemms."

Harvey settled back, and closed his eyes.

"Harold Pinter."

Harvey smiled.

"A bartender."

Stemms glanced at Harvey, and smiled along with him.

Stemms felt like a surfer riding the peak of domino waves, skimming his board from wave to wave as each behemoth toppled the next, picking up more and more speed, building up more and more energy, each wave joining the next until they became an unstoppable force.

Paul would lead to Alec, and Alec would lead to the barfing girl. The barfer would give them the boy in the picture, and everyone and everything they wanted to find.

They were ahead of the curve again, and pulling further away. They were so far in front of everyone else, Stemms could smell the kill.

5

ELVIS COLE

THE IMAGE HAD BEEN ENHANCED and enlarged, yielding a close-up indictment. His pupils glowed like the eyes of a coyote, trapped by oncoming headlights. Devon had to be told quickly, but I didn't know the charges Tyson would face, or how close the police were to making an arrest.

Dave was still talking, so I interrupted.

"Is LAPD close to making an arrest?"

"Why, you getting interested?"

"You said it yourself. If there's a feeding frenzy, I might be late for the banquet, but I still want something to eat."

Dave laughed.

"Tell you what, c'mon down, and talk to my guy. He'll help you catch up."

I thanked him, and went to catch up.

First Tier Security was located in Culver City at the edge of Marina del Rey. Metal siding, sharp angles, and pastel paint gave their building a look more suited to an Internet start-up, but Dave's company monitored more than six thousand subscribers across Los Angeles County.

Deitman greeted me with a firm handshake, and steered me toward a conference room.

A thin, wiry man stood when we entered. Tim Benson was the head of the First Tier technical staff. He wore a white, short-sleeved shirt with a narrow black tie and khaki cargo pants. His arms were striped with tribal tattoos, and his eyes were angry black dots.

Dave said, "Timmy cut the vid, and worked on the face with SID. He's our Slauson expert."

The strength of his grip surprised me.

I said, "Eighteen is a serious run. Dave says they're kids."

Benson shrugged like eighteen was nothing.

"We're talking cold-house entries, not banks."

This was good news. A cold entry meant the burglars only entered unoccupied homes.

Dave told me to sit, and took a seat beside me. We sat at a table facing a flat-screen TV. Benson sat with a wireless keyboard and a can of Mountain Dew.

Dave leaned back, and crossed his arms.

"Give'm an overview."

Benson's gaze flicked my way.

"As of now, we've got eighteen rez-burgs scattered through Brentwood, Bel Air, Holmby, and Beverly Hills, all occurring north of Sunset Boulevard. The Slausons were—"

I interrupted.

"As of now?"

"The perps are active, and the task force is checking prints against older cases. The number's probably gonna go up."

I nodded along, but was thinking ahead.

"Did the same three subjects pull all eighteen?"

"Doubtful. Cassett says a duo took some of the earlier scores."

"Who's Cassett?"

Dave said, "Dani Cassett and Mike Rivera. Robbery Special. Cassett runs the task force."

Benson pulled the keyboard closer, and continued.

"We've got one female and two males, so far unknown. They entered the Slauson residence through an unlocked glass door. How they did it at the Slausons is pretty much what they do every time. Their pattern doesn't change."

If Tyson was Unknown Male Subject Number One, I wondered if Alec was Unknown Male Number Two, and the female was Amber.

I glanced at Dave.

"A neighbor told me they beat the alarm?"

Benson spoke quickly, eyes even darker.

"Uh-uh. The Slausons didn't arm the system. Plus, the slider wasn't locked. Dr. Slauson thought he locked it, but the latch is fussy. I checked. You have to wiggle it."

Dave gave a sorrowful nod.

"People spend all this money on security, but get in a rush."

Benson glanced at Dave.

"You ready?"

"Let's do it."

Benson tapped a key. The flat-screen split into six frozen views of the Slausons' house. A time code was visible in the lower right corner of each image.

"The Slausons have six cameras, so we have six views. I added a time code for the police."

The camera locations were obvious, but he ticked them off anyway.

"Top left, the call box. Camera two, we see from the front door down the drive to the street. Then we have side-of-the-house three, and opposite side four. Five and six cover the back."

He pointed out the time code.

"The time is now eleven twenty-two P.M. Approach to exit, the crime takes forty-six minutes."

Surveillance cameras recorded continuously, which meant six cameras recorded six hours of video during a single one-hour period. Benson had cherry-picked shots from each camera, and cut together a narrative.

He tapped a key, and the entry cam's view filled the screen. The driveway gate was in the background, with a murky glimpse of the street beyond the gate. I wondered if Tyson's Volvo would pass.

Benson said, "The light sucks, but watch the street. They enter from the right."

He tapped again, and the time counter spun. Two grainy figures appeared beyond the gate, and stopped when they reached the drive.

"The female is on our left, Unknown Male One on the right."

The lack of light and the distance made them look like smudges.

"How can you tell which is which?"

"The female and Male One are about the same size. Unknown Male Two is taller. And I've seen this damned thing a hundred times."

Dave laughed.

I said, "They arrived on foot?"

"Assumption is, they parked a house or two away, but the police haven't confirmed it. They could've been dropped, and picked up after, but nobody knows."

A taller smudge joined the first two, and they drifted toward the gate. The angle cut to the call box camera, showing its view of the street. The frame was otherwise empty until a hand reached past the camera.

Benson froze the image.

"She's pressing the call button. Every caper they pull, they check to see if someone's home. If nobody answers, they jump the fence or whatever, and look for an unlocked entrance. They never break windows, or force an entry. If an alarm goes off, they split. A dog, they split. The same way every time."

"How do you know it's the girl?"

"You'll see."

Dave said, "She rings the damn bell four or five times. Let's skip the ringing."

Benson advanced the video.

"Okay. Now watch."

Lights flashed in the background as a car approached. The screen went dark as someone blocked the camera, and remained dark for almost ten seconds. Then someone walked directly away from the camera, letting us see their back.

Benson spoke over the action.

"See her legs? She's wearing leggings, not pants."

A second figure hurried after the first, also showing his back. Benson froze the screen.

"Unknown Male Number One. He's wearing pants. They always wear dark clothes. Hoodies and caps. Always the same."

Benson started the video. Tyson caught up to the girl, and bumped her from behind. The girl spun around, but the hoodie still hid her face. She launched a playful kick to ward Tyson off, and Benson froze the image with her foot in the air.

"Check out her sneaker. The midsole. See how it shines?"

The midsole shimmered like a strip of reflective tape.

"SID identified the brand. Japanese. They make'm for teenage girls, hence she's a girl. Keep watching."

Benson touched the key. Tyson jumped away from the kick, and the taller male raced forward. He lifted Tyson off his feet.

Benson arched his eyebrows.

"This is how we know they're kids. These morons are playing."

The female disappeared in the background. The taller kid lowered Tyson, and they raced after the girl.

The picture cut to a high-angle view of a side yard service walk, showing the length of the walk from the back of the house to a service gate in the distance. A figure hovered at the top of the gate.

"The girl comes over first. This chick is running the show."

The figure dropped, and came toward us. She reached a door, and tried the knob. The door didn't open, so she continued along the walk, coming toward the camera. The hoodie masked her face, but she kept her head down. Smart. She appeared calm, experienced, and unafraid.

Benson nudged me.

"Check her hands. No gloves. They hide their faces, but they leave fingerprints everywhere."

Maybe not so smart.

Tyson climbed over the gate next, and Alec came over last. Tyson wore a cap under his hoodie, and Alec's hoodie was drawn so tight he looked like an aardvark.

Benson leaned forward.

"Here it comes. Wait for it."

The girl passed beneath the camera, and out of frame. Tyson reached the camera next, and glanced up before he moved out of the frame. He only looked at the camera for a second, but a second was more than enough.

Benson slapped the table.

"Money shot! We got him."

I paid little attention after the money shot.

The view cut to the back of the Slausons' home. The female subject reached a sliding glass door, gripped the handle, and pulled. The door slid open easily.

Benson nudged me.

"Wasn't locked."

Tyson and Alec followed her into the house. The glass doors and glass walls framed an interior stage. We watched them open drawers, go into closets, and bounce on a bed. I felt bad for the Slausons, and sad for Devon.

I left when the video ended. Devon wanted to know how Tyson was getting money, and now I knew what to tell her.

The evidence against Tyson was overwhelming. He would be identified, arrested, and convicted, and Devon needed to know.

It was time to share the news.

6

DEVON WORKED at a small law firm in a three-story building on the far side of Encino. I didn't warn her I was coming. I called when I reached the building, and told her I was outside.

She said, "Wait. You're outside right now?"

"In a red zone. You'll see me."

"What's he doing? How much trouble is he in?"

"Come out."

"Is it drugs? Is he a drug dealer?"

"Come out. I'm in the red zone."

"I'll kill him. I swear to God I'm going to kill him."

She came out a few minutes later, and hurried into my car.

"Okay, what? What's he doing?"

I showed her the picture of the sunglass case.

"I found this in Tyson's car. Familiar?"

"Amber? Is Amber the girl?"

"I'm guessing yes, but I don't know. I won't be able to answer a lot of your questions, but there isn't much time."

"Time for what?"

I showed her the screen grab of Tyson. She frowned, and took my phone to look closely.

"He's green. What kind of picture is this?"

"A screen capture from a home surveillance video. He looks weird because the police enhanced and enlarged the image."

She settled against the door like a deflating balloon.

"This isn't starting well."

"A couple named Slauson owns the home. The Rolex belongs to them. On the night this picture was taken, they were in Palm Springs. Tyson and two friends entered their home, and stole sixty-eight thousand dollars in property and cash."

Devon's eyes widened, and she shriveled even more.

"Oh. My. God."

"The people with him were a taller male and a female."

"Alec and Amber?"

"I'm guessing yes. As of now, Tyson and his friends haven't been identified. The police have his picture and fingerprints, but not his name. That's the good news."

She closed her eyes.

"How could he be so stupid?"

"It gets worse. The police have linked these kids to seventeen other burglaries. Eighteen burglaries in total."

She opened her eyes, and stared.

"Tyson robbed eighteen homes?"

"It's possible he didn't participate in all eighteen, but this is how he's getting the money."

She glanced away. Her mouth hardened and dimples cratered the corners.

"A thief. He breaks into homes, and steals."

"I'm sorry. It's a lot to get your head around."

Her eyes suddenly softened.

"Have they hurt anyone?"

I liked her for asking.

"So far as I know, they haven't."

"I feel like I'm going to throw up."

I turned the vents toward her face.

"Deep breaths."

"I'm going to throw up. I mean it."

"Breathe."

She took my phone. Her hands quivered as she stared at his picture. Green. She gave back the phone, and stared out the window. His name exploded out of her without warning.

"TYSON!"

She slapped her thighs three times, and shouted again.

"TYSON!"

I waited. Sometimes, all you can do is wait. She finally took a breath, and came back to me.

"I have to ask. Are you sure?"

"I'm sure."

She straightened, and gathered herself.

"All right. Thank you. I knew he was in trouble, but I never thought it was something like this. I appreciate what you've done."

"I'm not finished."

She looked at me.

"Once they put a name to his face, he'll be arrested. If you want to help him, you have a window, but the window is closing."

"Help him how? Buy him a ticket to China?"

"He needs to turn himself in. It's called a voluntary surrender. If Tyson cooperates, he might even get a pretty good deal."

She chewed at her lips, thinking, then glanced at her watch. Tyson was still at school, but the school day was ending.

"I'd need a lawyer."

"Yes. A criminal attorney. I can recommend several."

She nodded to herself, and glanced at her building.

"My boss can refer me. I have to tell him about Tyson, anyway. The burglar."

"You understand what I mean about the window closing?"

She glanced again, and now her eyes were sharp.

"I'm only an office manager, Mr. Cole, but I pay attention. Once the police know who he is, they won't need us to surrender. They'll simply arrest him, and we won't have any leverage."

"So you have to move quickly."

"I understand. I'll get a lawyer as fast as I can."

"And Tyson has to cooperate."

The sharp eyes flashed.

"He'll cooperate or I'll kill him."

"This will blindside him. He'll be upset, and scared. I can be with you when you talk to him."

"Thank you, but it'll go better without a stranger present. I'll call Dr. Rossi. Rossi will want to help. We'll talk to Tyson tonight."

I remembered Rossi's name from Tyson's prescription bottles.

"Okay. One last thing. Your lawyer will want to speak with me. Give them my number. If you'd like me on calls when you interview people, I'll be on the calls. Whatever you want."

She studied me for a moment, and made a nice smile.

"You're really something."

"So I've been told."

Her smile deepened, and she opened the door to go.

"I'll let you know what happens. I'd better get started."

I said, "What about you? How are you?"

She hesitated, and glanced back for a last time.

"I'm sad."

Devon slid out, and returned to her office. I pulled away from the curb, and pointed my car toward home. Tyson Connor's arrest was inevitable. He, or the tall boy, or the girl, would flaunt their cash or brag to a friend, and a ripple of gossip would spread. A waitress would overhear, and share what she'd heard with a parolee boyfriend, who would pass along her gossip to curry a parole officer's favor. Fences got popped and gave up thieves, criminals bragged about crimes on Facebook, and backstabbing friends dropped revealing hints on Twitter. Always the same, and always inevitable.

The window was closing, but not closed.

7

DEVON WORKED QUICKLY. I was pulling into a market in Studio City when she called and introduced me to an attorney named Leslie Sanger. Sanger sounded smart, experienced, and had spent nine years as a Deputy District Attorney. I parked, and spent twenty minutes describing what I knew of the Slauson burglary, and how I knew it. I did not name Dave Deitman and Sherri Toyoda as sources. Sanger assured me their names and mine would not be necessary. Tyson would have to supply a detailed statement as proof of his involvement, but even Tyson would remain nameless until an agreement was reached. Then, Devon and Sanger would deliver Tyson to the agreed-upon agency, and complete his voluntary sur-render. Weighing his age, lack of a prior criminal history, and willingness to cooperate, Sanger felt confident the District Attorney's office and the court would be receptive and lenient. My part was finished, over and out.

When the call ended, I felt relieved. I also felt hungry, and wanted to celebrate. I picked up extra thick veal chops and a bottle of Roca Patrón tequila. Hess liked both, but the Roca was her favorite. Par-tay.

Shopping complete, I left the Valley behind.

Home was a redwood A-frame perched on a narrow road off Wood-row Wilson Drive near the top of Laurel Canyon. The house came with two bedrooms, a deck with a fine view of the canyon, and a cat. The cat was black, surly, and scarred from too many fights. He liked me okay, but he didn't care much for Hess. She didn't take it personally. He didn't like anyone except me and my partner, Joe Pike. Everyone else, he wanted to gut.

I parked in the carport, and carried the groceries into the kitchen. The cat was sitting by his bowl. Sullen.

I said, "Give me a minute, okay?"

He stared at the floor.

I put the chops in the fridge, and found the remains of a roast chicken. I took out the chicken and a bottle of Pacífico. The cat dish was crusted with the remains of breakfast, so I set out a clean dish.

I said, "Beer or chicken?"

His nose worked.

I sat on the floor with the beer and the chicken, and poured a little beer. He watched the foam, then lowered his nose, and lapped.

"Not too much. You might have to drive."

When you live with a cat, you talk to the cat.

When he finished the beer he looked at me.

I tore off bits of the chicken, and put them in his dish.

"Hess is coming. Knock off all the growling and hissing, okay? It gets old."

I drank some beer, then got up and went out onto my deck. The thick-cut chops screamed for the grill, so I scraped the grate and set fresh charcoal. When the grill was ready, I showered, put on fresh clothes, and went to work in the kitchen.

I trimmed the chops, then smashed some garlic and chopped fresh rosemary. I put the garlic and rosemary in a bowl, and mixed it with olive oil, salt, and pepper, until I had a nice paste. Fragrant. I added a squeeze of lemon juice. Better.

I glanced at the cat.

"What do you think, mint?"

He didn't look up from the chicken.

"Just kidding. We don't have mint."

I slathered the chops with the paste, wrapped them in plastic, and set them aside. I found some veggies in the fridge, and went to work on an eggplant. I cut it into lengthwise steaks, brushed both sides with olive oil, hit it with salt, pepper, and garlic powder, then panned the steaks, and shoved them into the oven. Low.

I smirked at the cat.

"Am I amazing or what?"

He gakked up a hairball and the chicken, blinked, and left. He could be difficult.

I cleaned his mess, then went outside and fired the coal. The flames were rising nicely when Hess called.

I said, "Hey! We're having veal."

She hesitated for half a heartbeat.

"I am so sorry."

Her tone told me everything.

"What's up?"

"TSA issue. I am so sorry, babe. One of those deals."

Hess was the SAC. The top-of-the-ATF-food-chain boss of her bureau in the SoCal region. When the SAC's phone rang, she had to answer.

"No problem. Don't sweat it."

I tried to sound cheerier than I felt.

"You know I sweat it. I hate when this happens."

"I'm fine, Janet. Really."

"Believe me, I'd rather be eating your veal."

"I've got plenty you can eat."

Hess giggled. She was a tough-as-nails, hard-core ATF agent, but she could still giggle. I liked that about her.

She said, "How'd it work out with your underage girl?"

"Smokin'."

She didn't get it, but no reason she should.

"Gotta go. Kiss."

"Kiss."

I finished the beer, opened another, and wandered out to the deck. Purple shadows were filling the canyon below, and the sky was a deepening blue. The coals were an angry bright orange. Too hot for the chops, but they'd cool.

I checked the time, and thought about Devon and Tyson. I wondered if Devon had confronted him, or if she'd gotten cold feet, and needed to work up her nerve. Maybe it was already over and they'd live happily ever after, or maybe she chickened out, and was putting it off until tomorrow. I felt bad for her. Being a parent wasn't easy.

I went inside for the chops, scraped the excess paste, and put the chops on the grill. The sound of the sear when they hit the heat was perfect.

The cat came to the door and blinked at me.

"How's the tum?"

He walked to the edge of the deck, and stared at something I could not see.

I flipped the chops, went in for the eggplant, and brought the egg- plant out.

I liked kids, and thought I'd make a pretty good father, but I didn't have children. I liked the idea of having a child with someone special, but find- ing someone special had proven elusive. I came close with a woman named Lucy Chenier, who had a son named Ben. They lived in Louisiana when we fell in love, and moved to Los Angeles to be near me, but Lucy's ex did terrible things to punish her, and by the time it was over the harm was done. Lucy and Ben returned to Louisiana. Safer, she said. A place he can heal.

Okay.

I loved Ben like a son, and I missed him. We stayed in touch. I wish I had killed his father.

I moved the chops to a cooler place, added the eggplant, and drank more beer. Tyson's father left before he was born.

What an asshole.

I poked a chop. You can tell the doneness by the give in the meat. Felt like medium. Perfect. I put the chops on a plate.

I didn't know my father. Never met the man, and knew nothing about him. My mother never told me his name, and may not have known, so it's possible he never knew she was pregnant. She was like that. I tried to find him a few times, but after a while my interest waned.

When I imagined myself as a father, my imaginary child's gender didn't matter. I would build Lego castles and play with dolls, read *Good-Night Moon* at bedtime, and stand in lines at Disneyland. Boy or girl, I would teach them to cook. We would hike in Runyon Canyon, make silly faces, and watch horror movies. I would worry when my son got his driver's license, and glare at boys who dated my daughter, and cry when their hearts were broken. I guess I imagined myself as the father I would have wanted. I thought about Devon. Being a parent was difficult.

The cat came over and licked his lips.

"Almost."

The eggplant was crisping at the edges, and showed nice grill marks. I put the eggplant on the plate with the chops, grabbed a knife and fork, and sat on the deck.

The cat came closer, and sat beside me.

I sliced off a piece of veal, cut it into smaller pieces, and held out a piece. He touched his nose to the piece, licked, and took the bit of meat from my fingers as gently as a kiss.

I didn't have kids. I had a cat.

8

HARVEY AND STEMMS

PAUL THE BARTENDER knew Alec Rickey from a workshop production in Toluca Lake. Paul had played Slim, a cowboy from Wyoming who wanted to be a stuntman, but ended up being a movie star. Alec understudied the role of Lewis, a wannabe actor who ran errands for a coke fiend who made slasher flicks. Only problem was, the ham who played Lewis never missed a performance, so Alec quit, and took a gig waiting tables at Brasserie Le Jean in Sherman Oaks. Listening to all this bullshit gave Harvey a headache, but at least they learned where to find Alec.

Harvey and Stemms parked across from Le Jean at seven forty-one. They didn't know if Rickey was working that night, so Harvey went in. He returned a few minutes later, and hit Stemms with the grin.

"It's him. Over and out."

"You sure?"

"No doubt. Alec."

Harvey tapped his chest.

"Has a name tag. Tall, good-looking, the dimples. Looks like his DMV photo."

Stemms eyeballed the restaurant. They were close, and he wanted to end it.

"How many diners?"

"Full house. Mostly older."

Stemms decided to see for himself. A valet seated on a folding chair by the entrance jumped up and opened the door.

The restaurant was dark, and tables were shoehorned together. A hall leading to the kitchen and restrooms passed a bar at the back of the room. Waiters and busboys flowed in and out of the kitchen, and walked on tightropes between the tables. Stemms didn't see anyone who looked like Rickey.

A small man with a trim mustache greeted him.

"Did you have a reservation, sir?"

"I'm meeting a friend. Mind if I peek at a menu?"

A menu appeared in the man's hand, but he gave an officious sniff.

"With no reservation, the wait will be at least thirty minutes."

"I understand. Thanks."

Prick.

A tall, thin kid carried an oval tray out of the kitchen. A middle-aged waiter set up a folding stand next to a table, and the kid placed the tray on the stand. After the salads were served, the kid took the tray and the stand back to the kitchen.

Stemms handed the menu to the man with the mustache.

"I'll phone ahead next time. Thanks."

Stemms returned to the car.

"It's him."

"You couldn't trust me?"

"Harvey, stop."

"Let me ask you a question. Why is this kid lugging trays?"

"I'm begging you, Harvey."

"These kids are taking good scores. What's the gross, three-point-two, three-point-three million?"

"Maybe he likes the job."

"Bullshit."

Stemms started the Chrysler, and circled the block. A long, poorly lit alley ran behind the restaurant, stretching from one residential cross street to the next. They cruised past the restaurant, rounded the block, and parked in the alley behind a knitting shop. They settled in, and watched the restaurant's back door.

Every ten or fifteen minutes, a kitchen worker came out to grab a smoke. Stemms and Harvey watched the smokers in silence. They had watched people and buildings for countless hours together, and neither had much left to say.

The restaurant staff began leaving at ten-thirty. Two men with knapsacks came out, walked to the far end of the alley, and turned toward Ventura.

Harvey said, "Bus riders."

Stemms started the Chrysler, but left it dark.

A singleton came next, followed by two more guys, and a woman. Alec Rickey appeared at eleven-oh-five, but he wasn't alone.

Harvey said, "Couldn't be easy."

Rickey was with two blonde women. Stemms had seen one of the women behind the bar.

"Relax. They'll split up."

The taller blonde lit a cigarette, and they stood around yukking it up before they finally headed toward the street.

Harvey said, "Ten bucks, left or right."

"Left."

When they reached the end of the alley, Rickey and the women turned left.

Harvey said, "Shit."

"Get out, Harvey. Go."

Harvey got out, and hurried after them. Stemms waited until Harvey was gone, then idled forward. His phone rang when he reached the end of the alley.

Harvey's voice was a whisper.

"Left, then left again at the stop sign. Park on the right. Slow."

Stemms guided the Chrysler through a lace of moonshadows cast by jacaranda trees. A car came toward him, and flashed its lights, signaling his were off. He turned on his lights, but killed them as the car passed.

Harvey said, "They're in the street, halfway down. I'm to the right, on the sidewalk. Wait, hang on—"

Stemms turned at the stop sign, and pulled to the right.

"Say something, Harvey. I don't see you."

"They stopped. Hang on—"

An alarm chirped a block ahead as a car unlocked.

Harvey whispered, "That's him. Back up, Stemms. Turn around. He's coming toward you."

Stemms backed around the corner and into a driveway. Six seconds later, Harvey jumped in as headlights approached.

"This is him. Easy, now."

A black two-door Nissan rolled through the stop sign, and turned toward Ventura.

Stemms counted to ten, then snapped on his lights, and followed.

"Are the women with him?"

"Uh-uh. He's alone."

They followed the Nissan along Ventura through Sherman Oaks and into Studio City. Stemms hoped Rickey was going home, but the kid drifted along like he had nowhere to go. Traffic wasn't bad, but when they reached Sushi Row, cars crowded together like salmon chasing toro and uni. The Nissan slowed at one restaurant, then another, then a third, as if Rickey couldn't decide where to eat.

Stemms jumped lights to stay close.

Harvey said, "This kid is pissing me off."

Two cars ahead, the Nissan edged into the center lane, and stopped. Rickey got out of his car in the middle of traffic, and studied the cars behind him.

Stemms said, "Damnit, Harvey, he made us. He saw you."

"Uh-uh. No way."

The kid looked nervous, but his eyes skipped over the Chrysler without recognition. Horns blared, so Stemms leaned on the Chrysler's horn.

"Look at him. He's freaked."

"Maybe one of his friends got popped. Maybe they called. We're not the only people after these turds."

Rickey stared over their heads a few more seconds, then climbed into his car, and traffic bumped forward.

"Harvey. I got a feeling."

"I'm on it."

The Nissan swung hard across the oncoming lanes into a parking lot, and gunned for an exit. Brakes screeched and more horns screamed. Stemms jerked the Chrysler across the lanes, punched through the parking lot, and swerved out the other side. Harvey leaned forward, searching for Rickey's car.

"Got him. The freeway."

Once they had eyes on the Nissan, Stemms backed off.

The kid settled down once he was on the freeway, as if he felt safe in the stream of red lights. They trailed him down into Hollywood. Stemms hoped the little shit was going to meet his friends, but Rickey didn't stop. He made a slow, meandering pass through Hollywood, and drifted back to the freeway.

Stemms glanced at Harvey.

"What do you think?"

Harvey shrugged.

"What I said. Something happened. He's probably trying to figure out what to do."

Stemms agreed.

"Yeah. You're probably right."

"I'm always right."

Traffic thinned as they headed downtown. This made it easier to keep the Nissan in sight, but forced Stemms to drop farther back.

They cruised across the top of DTLA, crossed the Los Angeles River, and followed Rickey north toward the mountains through rolling dark hills. The distance between them grew.

Harvey leaned forward again.

"He's speeding up, dude."

Stemms drove faster.

The gap closed, then opened again.

"C'mon, Stemms. He's running."

They chased the little black car through a tunnel of light surrounded by darkness. The city became a background, as if they were racing to the end of the world. Stemms liked it. The traffic was behind them. They flashed past leviathan trucks, as if the trucks were sleeping behemoths.

Alec Rickey raced past a truck on the inside lane, vanished ahead of the truck, then dove crazy-fast across the freeway toward an exit.

Stemms braked hard, but didn't think they would make it. The ramp dropped off the freeway hard, and the big Chrysler shouldered into the curve. The curve grew tighter, and Stemms braced for a crash, but the Chrysler shouldered lower, hung on, and slowed. Then Stemms saw the Nissan, and Stemms let the Chrysler roll to a stop.

The Nissan lay on its roof in a cloud of swirling dust on the far side of the guardrail. Alec Rickey had lost control, spun, and pinwheeled over the rail.

Harvey threw open the door.

"Get off the ramp. Go."

Harvey vaulted the rail, and ran to Rickey's car.

Stemms drifted to the bottom of the ramp and parked on the shoulder. He turned off his lights and studied their surroundings. Deserted.

Stemms got out, and walked up the embankment. Alec Rickey was alive, but hurt. Harvey had dragged him from the upside-down car, and gone back to search the interior. Harvey's legs stuck out from the driver's-side window like a couple of twitching pipe cleaners. The smell of gasoline was strong.

Stemms said, "Find anything?"

"He's all messed up, damnit. He can't talk."

"Get the keys."

Stemms walked over to Rickey. The kid's chest appeared crushed, and his left arm was shattered. His face was bloody and swelling. He tried to say something, but only managed a bubble.

Stemms said, "Thank God for air bags, right?"

Rickey tried to speak again, but his jaw made a weird sideways move like a bug's mandible.

Stemms pulled on vinyl gloves and felt the kid's neck. Rickey's pulse was thready and fast, which wasn't so great, but his pupils were the same size, and dilated normally. The sclera were bright red. If the kid died, the red would turn black, and his eyes would look like a couple of eight balls.

"Alec? What's up, Alec, you hear me?"

The kid made eye contact, and moaned. The pain was burning through the adrenaline.

"Who are your friends, Alec? Tell me, and I'll call the paramedics."

The boy's jaw twisted. He moaned even louder.

Stemms searched him, and found a slim wallet holding a California DL, issued to Alexander Dean Rickey. Stemms noted the address, and slipped the wallet into his pocket.

Stemms called toward Harvey.

"Key?"

"Here."

Harvey's hand emerged with the key.

Stemms popped the trunk, but found nothing useful. He returned to the boy, and squatted beside him.

"Work with me, Alec. If you want to live, you have to help me."

Red bubbles. Red tears leaked from red eyes.

Harvey backed from the car, and came over, brushing his pants. He had the boy's cell phone.

"This is effed up. We finally get one, and he can't talk."

"You got his phone."

"It's locked."

Stemms frowned at the boy. The phone would give them the girl and the other boy, and everything the boy couldn't say.

"What's the code?"

Moan.

"I'm not playing, boy. If you can't talk, hold up some fingers. First digit. C'mon, make a number."

Stemms grabbed Rickey's hand, but the kid only screamed.

Harvey said, "His hands don't work, Stemms. Stop."

"So now what?"

"Whatever. They'll crack it."

Harvey slipped the phone into his pocket, then snapped his fingers. Loud. Rickey looked.

"You see that? His eyes track."

"Yeah. He sees us."

"Think he'll make it?"

Stemms stood, and they stared at the kid.

"I dunno. Maybe."

Harvey said, "This kid is pissing me off."

Harvey and Stemms walked back to their car. Harvey dug out a fingerprint kit, and walked back up the embankment.

Stemms waited by the Chrysler, watching the street in case someone approached. It was one of those streets that came from nothing and went nowhere. Empty.

He watched Harvey press the kid's fingertips onto clear plastic slides. When he saw Harvey box the slides, Stemms headed up the embankment.

"Got'm?"

"All ten. We're golden."

Stemms drew his pistol. He shot Alec Rickey in the head. He fired a second shot, and holstered the gun.

Harvey said, "We should burn him."

"Yeah."

They walked down the slope to their car. The night was young. They were men, doing work.

PART II

CRIMINALS

9

ELVIS COLE

Dawn came early after a fitful sleep. I ran in the darkness, following the silent streets from my home to Mulholland, then along the Mulholland snake to the Hollywood Bowl, and back. Dawn came early, but I was home before the sun touched the sky. Sweating out beer was a bitch.

Breakfast was leftover veal with a side of eggplant. I showered, dressed, and put on a pot of coffee. The coffee was dripping when someone knocked at the door. Four quick, hard raps.

A man and a woman were making the noise. The woman stood front and center, with the man to the side and behind. They were the couple in the brown sedan who cruised past the Slausons' house.

When they knocked again, I opened the door.

"It's early. I hope you brought donuts."

The woman ignored my crack, and held up a badge.

"I'm Cassett. He's Rivera. Remember us?"

"Should I?"

Rivera grunted.

"It's too early for jokes. You remember."

Cassett put away her badge.

"He remembers. That's why he's letting us in."

They stepped in past me, and moved apart like street cops clearing a disturbance call. The A-frame's ceiling peaked like a glass cathedral above us, and bathed us in morning light. Rivera did a slow three-sixty, eyeing the room like I lived in a dump.

I said, "Do you people know what time it is?"

"Sure. Are we alone?"

"My cat's in the kitchen. Want to meet him?"

Cassett went to the sliders, and studied the canyon.

"Nice view."

Rivera noticed the stairs to the loft.

"What's up the stairs?"

"Whatever's up there, it isn't for sale. I was about to feed my cat, Cassett. His food's getting cold."

Rivera said, "Tough."

He circled toward the kitchen, trying to see.

Cassett said, "Sorry about the hour, Mr. Cole. We'll try not to keep you."

I motioned to the couch.

"Whatever. You guys want some coffee?"

"Like I said, we'll try not to keep you. Why were you at the Slausons?"

Her eyes were as flat as paper plates, but her manner was conversational.

"I wanted to see them about the burglary. Is there a problem?"

Rivera said, "How's the burglary your business?"

"I'm looking into it."

Cassett turned from the view.

"Why would you be looking into it?"

The cat padded out of the kitchen. He stopped when he saw them, folded his ears, and growled.

I said, "Watch yourself, Rivera. He bites."

Rivera squinted at the cat.

"How come his head's crooked?"

"Someone shot him."

The cat turned sideways, and arched his back. Rivera sidled away.

Cassett said, "Let's get back to the Slausons and why you were there."

"I heard the Slausons got ripped, and decided to nose around. Insurance companies pay recovery fees. That's it."

Rivera scowled.

"Which SIU you with?"

Insurance companies had Special Investigations Units to verify claims and sniff out insurance fraud. Staff investigators handled most SIU cases, but during periods of high work load or with specialized cases, outside contract investigators were hired. I had worked for most of the big companies.

I said, "None. I'm working for me. Freelance."

"You're not on with a company?"

"Freelance."

Rivera glanced at Cassett, and cocked his head.

"He's kidding, right? We don't have enough, and now we've got some freelance cheesing around for a payoff?"

"Take it easy, Mike."

Rivera's face was puffy, like he had spent the night drinking.

"Okay, Mr. Freelance, who told you about the Slausons?"

"A friend in the business. What's the big deal?"

The cat edged closer, and growled again.

"What's wrong with you people? You've got eighteen high-end burglaries. It's all the insurance people are talking about."

Rivera came closer again, and stopped just short of my nose.

"Maybe you were up there trying to sell their stuff back. Thieves do that, you know? They rip a house, and hire a stooge to sell the stuff back to the victims."

"Step away from me, Rivera."

The cat's growl spiraled louder, and his fur bristled.

Cassett snapped at her partner.

"Take it easy, Mike. Stop."

Rivera stepped back, but didn't go easy. He was sucking air like a whale, and close to a stroke.

"We have too many assholes riding our backs now, Cole. We sure as hell don't need a cheeser like you making it worse. Keep away from the Slausons."

"Bite me, Rivera. Get out of my house before I call the cops."

Cassett said, *"Mike!"*

She tipped her head toward the door.

"I'll be out in a second."

Rivera stalked out. I expected the door to slam, but it closed soft as a whisper.

Cassett looked at my cat.

"Is your cat always like this?"

"I could ask the same about Rivera."

She smiled, and looked tired.

"We've had a rough few weeks."

The cat sniffed once, and returned to the kitchen. His claws snicked the floor when he walked. Snick-snick-snick.

I said, "Start again, Sergeant. Why are you here?"

She went to the glass door and studied the canyon. The mist below was lifting.

"We get the high-profile stuff, all the glitzy headline cases, but, man, rich people are a pain in the ass."

She turned from the view.

"Half of these vics golf with the mayor. The others have a councilman on speed dial. Two of our vics donate hundreds of thousands of dollars to the Department, and one even more. You know what all these connections and donations mean?"

"Pressure."

She made a little nod.

"People looking over our shoulders. Insurance reps. Investigators the rich people hire. My boss even has to brief these clowns. You believe this shit? My boss does *not* like to give briefings."

She took a breath, and shrugged.

"So if Mike was testy, it's because we're tired of being nice."

"Why did you come here?"

"I asked around. People said you're pretty good, so I thought, never know, maybe this guy has something useful."

I felt like a dog.

"Sure."

"Do you?"

"I didn't know about the Slausons until yesterday."

She gave me her card, and went to the door.

"If you hear anything, call me."

"Sure."

Rivera was behind the wheel of their D-ride. He stared straight ahead, and wouldn't look at me.

Cassett stepped out, but turned back.

"Your friend. What's his name?"

"Which friend?"

"Your insurance friend. The one who told you about the Slausons. Maybe I know him."

Her eyes were flat like plates again.

"Les Peyton. Scadlock Mutual."

She gave a polite smile.

"Have a good day, Mr. Cole."

Cassett got into the brown sedan, and I closed the door.

I didn't like withholding information. I felt small and shifty, and told myself Cassett's case would close as soon as Tyson surrendered. The rich people would be off her back, Dr. Slauson's watch would be returned, and everyone would move on with their lives. I told myself the case was almost over, but I was wrong.

I was pouring a cup of coffee when Devon called.

"He's missing. Tyson ran away, and didn't come home. I need you!"

I dumped the coffee, and drove to the Valley.

10

TYSON: Sorry I didn't answer you. We drank some beer and this rum drink. I shouldn't drive. I'll spend the night at my friend's. Nite.

MOM: Where are you? I'll come get you.

MOM: I'm calling. Answer.

MOM: You said you would be right back. Where are you?

MOM: I'll keep calling until you answer.

MOM: I'm worried.

MOM: I'M WORRIED. WHERE ARE YOU?

MOM: Who are you with?

MOM: Who's with you, Tyson? What are you doing?

MOM: PLEASE answer.

MOM: You are in trouble. I know what you're doing.

MOM: I cannot believe you won't answer. ARE YOU ALIVE?

MOM: I'm calling the police.

TYSON: Fell asleep. Sorry. I'll go to school in the morning. Home after. Turning off phone coz u keep waking me. Don't worry. Luv u. Nite.

11

ELVIS COLE

THE MORNING AFTER Tyson Connor disappeared, Devon's house didn't smell like pancakes. Her eyes were sunken gray caves locked in purple shadows, and her halting, jerking movements were angry.

"School my butt. He didn't go to school. I called first thing, and he hasn't shown up. He's with them."

Amber and Alec.

Devon stalked to the window, turned, and stalked to the hall.

"I'll kill him. The police could show up any second, and he disappears. What does he think, he'll be a fugitive for the rest of his life?"

"I guess he didn't like the idea of turning himself in."

Her sunken eyes flashed like roadside flares.

"You should have heard him. Aghast. Incredulous. The police had him confused with someone else. Jesus, *really?*"

She stalked to the window, and the flares dimmed.

"Once we got past his outrage, he calmed down. I told him about the lawyer. I laid everything out. Dr. Rossi helped. Tyson relaxed, and asked questions, and stopped denying it. He even thanked me."

"He agreed to surrender."

"Yes. We kept talking after Dr. Rossi left. We really talked. We haven't talked like this since the summer. He seemed fine. I wouldn't have let him leave if I thought he would do this."

At nine thirty-two that night, after three hours of talking, Tyson asked if he could go to the minimart for a frozen yogurt, and bring one home for her. Devon hesitated, but he seemed fine, and the minimart was only four blocks away. She told him she'd like a nonfat chocolate with peanut sprinkles.

Tyson said, "Okay, I'll be right back."

Tyson did not return, and did not respond to her texts or calls, so she went to the minimart. The owner, Mr. Shabazz, reported that Tyson had not been to his store that evening.

I said, "Tyson called them. They panicked, and got together to figure out what to do. They don't have many options."

She studied me for a moment, and went to the aquarium.

"We used to have more fish. He would sit here on the couch, and watch them the way other kids watch TV. He was a little guy, five or six."

I wanted to begin searching for him, but she wanted to tell me about the fish. It seemed important.

"One day, and I have no idea where this came from, he wanted to know their scientific names. He couldn't read, so I looked them up and read the names for him. *Poecilia reticulata, Pterophyllum altum, Paracheirodon innesi.* Big words, but I only had to read them once. He remembered. He knew the binomial name of every fish in this tank."

She stared at the remaining fish as if they were fading memories, then faced me.

"I don't have many options, either. Just you."

"Miracles are my business."

"I hope you're running a special."

"Alec and Amber. When you and Tyson were talking, did he tell you about them?"

"I didn't ask. He was so upset, I didn't want to make it worse. We talked about him."

"What about Rossi?"

"Tyson never mentioned them to Rossi. He had no idea what Tyson was doing."

"Would Tyson call him for help?"

"It's possible. I let him know Tyson left. If Tyson reaches out, he'll call. I also called the attorney. She thinks we should move forward, and approach the D.A.'s office. I agree."

I didn't like it.

"Moving forward is risky. You can't promise something you can't deliver, and we can't deliver Tyson."

"Leslie knows and she'll tell them. Her client is a parent who believes her minor child has committed a string of burglaries. This child has not yet agreed to cooperate, but the parent believes he will, and believes she can arrange a voluntary surrender. This establishes our intent and good faith, and buys us two or three days before we have to produce him."

"Two or three days isn't a lot of time."

"Miracles are your business. Right?"

Smart people irked me.

I tried to imagine paths that could lead to Tyson. People who lived in their rooms playing video games didn't leave wide trails, but he probably called Alec or Amber or both when he left the house.

"Are you and Tyson on the same phone plan, or does he have a separate account?"

"A family plan. It's my account. Why?"

"Get his billing records for the past two months. We need the incoming and outgoing numbers. You can get his call log online through your account."

She nodded vaguely and frowned.

"The charges for this billing period might not be available. They don't post until the end of the month."

"If they're not online, call your provider. Talk to a human. Get the most recent information you can."

"Okay."

"How does he buy gas?"

"He has a gas card. Should I cancel it?"

"No. The charge log can tell us where he buys gas. If this thing strings out, we might need to know."

I thought harder, and remembered the pictures I'd seen on their fridge. Tyson at Disneyland. Tyson with friends. Life before Alec and Amber.

"Does Tyson have friends here in the neighborhood, or from his old schools?"

"Not really. Making friends was difficult."

"C'mon, Devon. He's with other kids in pictures on your refrigerator. Give me something."

She pursed her lips as she thought.

"Donnie and Bret, but they were in elementary school. There was Kevin, but they weren't really close. Kevin liked zombies."

"What about gaming friends?"

A flash of surprise brightened her eyes.

"There was Carl. Carl built his own games. Tyson and Carl would play all night, and have terrible fights."

"Carl sounds good. I'll start with Carl."

"Carl can be odd. They haven't played together in almost a year."

"I'll take my chances."

She led me into the kitchen, and went to a phone on the counter. She flipped through a tattered day book, and came up with a number.

"I'll call his mother. Carl probably still lives at home, but he could be anywhere."

"How old is this kid?"

"A year younger than Tyson."

"And he could be anywhere?"

"Carl's smart. I mean *really* bright, but hyper and loud. And odd. He quit school."

Devon was punching the number into her landline when her cell buzzed with an incoming text. Her face seemed to collapse as she read the message.

I moved closer, and touched her arm.

"Tyson?"

She gave me the phone.

> **TYSON:** I am sorry I'm so much trouble. Don't text or call coz I am
> tossing this phone. I will send U a new number when I can. I luv U.
> U are the best Mom. I will figure this out. Bye.

I didn't know she was crying until she trembled.

I said, "You okay?"

"I'm going to kill him."

I put my arms around her, and held her until the trembling stopped.

Devon phoned Carl's mother. She learned Carl was still living at home, and asked if I could speak with him. Carl's mother said that was up to Carl.

Devon copied Carl's address, and tore off the page.

"Good luck."

12

HARVEY AND STEMMS

STEMMS AND HARVEY searched for house numbers as they eased along the street, Stemms privately clocking the dismal surroundings. Old people walking mongrel dogs, housekeepers trudging to work. The occasional Jet Ski tarped to a trailer, an unwanted RV plopped in a yard like an oversized turd. FOR SALE. The Valley.

Harvey said, "You should've stopped me, is all I'm saying. I ate too much."

"You shoveled it in fast enough."

"I was hungry."

They dropped off the phone and the prints just before two that morning, and had to kill time while the geniuses cracked the phone. The Chrysler sucked as a bed, so they tossed and turned for a couple of hours, then threw in the towel and decided to eat. Being downtown, they went to The Original Pantry, which had been open 24/7/365 since 1924. Stemms and Harvey had eaten there dozens of times.

Stemms ordered tuna on white with a side of coleslaw. Harvey got the country fried steak with gravy, hash browns, two eggs over easy, sourdough toast, and a double side of salsa. All Stemms could do was shake his head. Harvey had enough food on his plate to feed a family of four, but he fell to like a blood-crazy wolf and didn't look up until the plate was clean. Dessert was black coffee, vanilla ice cream, and Adderall.

The eastern sky was turning gold when the genius called. Stemms copied the names and addresses, and grinned at his partner.

"Yippee-ki-yi-yay. Cash in the bank."

Harvey loosened his belt.

"I gotta poop."

One poop later, they rolled up to the Valley, and looked for the first address. One block, two blocks, three blocks. Stemms slowed the car.

Harvey said, "This one."

A neat little ranch house. The garage door was up, revealing an Audi sedan. Blue.

Stemms craned his head.

"You see the Volvo?"

"Uh-uh."

"Brown. A four-door sedan."

"Take it easy."

They drove another two blocks, turned around, and stopped a half block shy of the house. Stemms shut the engine.

"I don't see the Volvo."

"Maybe he's out getting coffee. Maybe he shacked with the girl. Relax."

"I wonder who drives the Audi."

"Who gives a shit? Run the plate, you care so much."

"You don't have to snap at me."

Harvey sighed.

"My bowels. Sorry."

The front door opened, and a man stepped out. Stemms called him at six feet, one ninety. Looked fit. A brightly colored, unbuttoned short-sleeve shirt hung loose over his Walking Dead T-shirt. Stemms liked the shirt.

Harvey sat up and leaned forward.

"That's him."

"That's a grown-ass man, Harvey. He isn't the kid."

Harvey squinted. Focus problems.

A woman appeared behind the man. They spoke for a few minutes, then the man turned away and walked down the drive. The woman went back into the house and closed the door.

Harvey said, "What, she's the mother, he's the father?"

"No idea. Could be anyone."

"Looks the right age."

When Harvey got a notion, he worked it like a bulldog worked a bone. Harvey could wear you out.

"This kid steals so much money, she's probably the goddamned maid. Let it go."

"The mother. The guy? Her boyfriend. Dropped by for a hummer."

"Quit."

"Sniff, sniff. What's that, tuna?"

"You're such an asshole."

Their information was limited. The kid was tied to this address through the DMV, but they had no way of knowing whether the address was current, and who else, if anyone, resided at the address. The kid could have moved. He might use the house for a crash pad, and they'd find it crawling with burned-out tweakers, Aryan bikers, or Russian whores. Limited information was frustrating.

The man in the shirt crossed the street, and climbed into a dirty Corvette convertible.

Harvey brightened when he saw the car.

"Hey. What's that, a '65, '66?"

"It's a maintenance hog."

"Shut up, Stemms. It's a Chevrolet Corvette Stingray *classic*. All it needs is a wash."

The Stingray pulled out, and drove toward them. Stemms hunkered low, trying to hide, but Harvey peeked over the dash.

"'66."

Stemms wondered if Tyson Connor and Amber Reed were inside the house. They could be shacked up right here, right now, snorting blow and sucking bongs, lying around all day so they'd be rested and ready to rob more houses that night. Stemms wanted to make entry. He wanted to crash in so bad his rectum cramped, but the woman and God knew who else was inside. Stemms didn't want to run up the body count. If the Volvo was here, he would have pressed it, but the Volvo was missing. Pressing it now and piling up more bodies could blow their shot at the score. Stemms wasn't going to blow it.

He fired up the Chrysler.

Harvey said, "We're leaving?"

"For now."

"The barfer might be home."

"Maybe."

"Alec isn't home. It's too late for Alec."

Stemms glanced at Harvey.

Harvey was waiting for the glance. He made a sad face.

"Poor Alec. Boo-hoo."

"Jesus."

"Boo-hoo-hoo."

"You're really an asshole."

Harvey grinned.

"Yeah. But I'm *your* asshole."

Stemms turned toward the freeway. They had Alec's address. That's where they went. Just to spite Harvey.

Boo-hoo-hoo.

13

ELVIS COLE

CARL RIGGENS AND HIS FAMILY lived a few minutes north of the Connors, not far from the Ronald Reagan Freeway. Orange groves once covered their part of the Valley. The groves were bulldozed to make way for houses, but a few of the original trees still dotted the yards. The old trees were gnarled and dark, with twisted trunks, but still proud with brilliant green leaves and bright orange fruit. They made me think of aging veterans dressed for a VFW parade. I guess they were veterans of their own special war.

A young woman wearing a tank top and tights answered the door, and stifled a yawn.

I said, "Elvis Cole. I'm here to see Carl."

She closed the door a few inches.

"Are you here to arrest him?"

"I'm here about one of his friends. Your mother said I could talk to him."

"He's in back. He doesn't open until ten."

"Open?"

"Are you a federal agent?"

"No."

"In back. Down the drive."

The door closed, and she threw the dead bolt.

I walked down the drive and through a gate onto a concrete deck surrounding a kidney-shaped pool. The garage had been converted into a pool house. The side facing the pool had been replaced by a sliding glass door so people inside could admire the pool, but paper now covered the glass on the inside, blocking the view. Two kids in shorts and T-shirts were seated on the concrete with a couple of skateboards. They looked to be thirteen or fourteen, and should have been in school, but weren't.

I said, "Carl?"

They pointed at the slider.

I went to the slider, and knocked. Explosions and gunfire came from the pool house, so I knocked again.

"Carl?"

The gunfire stopped, a hatch in the paper lifted, and eyes peered out.

"Elvis Cole. I spoke to your mother."

The slider opened. The kids with the skateboards scrambled to their feet, but Carl froze them with an imperious glare.

"Scrubs must wait."

They slumped, and resumed their positions.

Carl Riggens was fleshy and soft, with a bulbous nose and small eyes. A minefield of scarlet eruptions cratered his chin. Despite the pool house and skateboards, he wore a black business suit, a white dress shirt, and a bright red bow tie. The suit whiffed of body odor.

Carl locked the slider behind us.

"May I see some identification, please?"

He made a little hand-it-over gesture with his fingers. Carl was sixteen, looked like an overgrown twelve, and acted like he was forty-six.

"Sure."

I gave him my license.

The pool house that was once a garage had been converted into a video game man cave. An oversized monitor hung on the wall, bracketed by studio speakers. A computer-generated soldier firing a next-gen assault rifle was frozen on the monitor, surrounded by metal shelves stacked with video games, gaming consoles, and boxes of controllers. A table and swivel chairs sat beneath the monitor. A towel covered the table, rising with the peaks and valleys of a mountain range from the hidden things beneath.

Carl finished inspecting my license, and handed it back with a sneer.

"You're interrupting my work, but my idiot mother demanded I see you."

Idiot mother. Man.

"Thanks for making the time. What kind of work do you do?"

Carl ignored my question.

"Something about Tyson? Tyson's a dick."

So much for them being friends.

"He's missing. His mother asked me to find him."

Carl's face pinched with annoyance.

"I don't know where he is. Why would I know?"

"His mom said you guys were tight."

The pinch grew deeper.

"Were, as in *hasta la vista, dickhead*. His level of play depressed me. I dismissed him. The Carl moved on."

He burst into a loud, honking laugh. Hyuk-hyuk-hyuk.

"Maybe he went to Dickland."

Devon was right. Carl was odd. And annoying.

"This was last year, before he left for the new school?"

"They expelled him. I quit. He wanted to quit, but his mommy wouldn't let him. He calls his mother *mommy*."

The Carl made a condescending sneer.

Hyuk-hyuk-hyuk.

"Got it. Have you heard from him since?"

"Uh-uh."

"Know who he hangs out with now?"

"Who would hang out with a loser like Tyson? Another dickhead, maybe."

He tried to sneer, but the sneer collapsed. He dropped into a swivel chair, and studied the frozen soldier.

"Why is Tyson the dickhead missing?"

"He's in trouble. Tyson and a couple of friends."

Carl stared at the soldier. Powerful, armed, yet trapped by forces beyond his control.

I said, "Carl? Do you know something?"

Carl didn't answer.

"If you know who he's with, or anything about this, you can help."

The kids outside knocked on the glass. I shouted.

"SCRUBS MUST WAIT."

Carl fingered the edge of the towel, and kept his eyes on the soldier.

"I don't want to get into trouble."

I lifted the towel, and folded it away. Game consoles with exposed circuit boards were hardwired to laptop computers and featureless black boxes bearing labels printed in Chinese and Russian. Incomprehensible software code scrolled endlessly on the laptops, coming from a place I didn't understand, on its way to a place I couldn't imagine. Carl was a hacker, but he didn't hack email accounts or database systems. He hacked video games. Game hackers hacked into software kernels, where they uncovered hidden secrets, modified games, or programmed home-brewed games of their own design to run on existing hardware. All of which was illegal, and frowned upon by the manufacturer.

"Are you going to arrest me?"

"I don't care about your work."

"Not my work, Tyson. I didn't believe him. If I didn't believe him, I'm not an accomplice, am I?"

"What did he tell you?"

"He showed up one day. He didn't text first, or call. He just showed up, and flashed this deck of cash, and said who's the loser now, loser, you're just a loser jerking a joystick."

"Must've hurt."

"I wasn't hurt."

I nodded.

"I said fuck you, dickhead, I'm The Carl, and you're not, game over, so he starts making up bullshit about his hot new girlfriend, and these cool clubs he goes to with his cool new friends, and them sneaking into houses like ninjas, and stealing all this stuff, and I'm like, really, dude, *new* girlfriend, you never had an *old* girlfriend, so do *not* expect me to believe you took a badass ninja pill."

Carl was lost in the moment, and made the laugh. Hyuk-hyuk-hyuk.

I said, "I wouldn't have believed him, either."

Carl glanced up, and seemed sad.

"But now you're here. He told the truth?"

"Not the part about being a ninja, but, more or less, yeah."

Carl shook his head.

"Damn."

"Did he tell you their names?"

"Amber. I mean, really, *Amber*?"

"What about the boy?"

His face pinched. Thinking.

"Alex, maybe. I think it was Alex."

"Alec?"

"Yeah."

"What about their last names, or where they work, or go to school?"

Carl seemed even more miserable.

"He said she's a model. A smokin'-hot sex freak. Did she really make pornos?"

"He probably lied about that part, too."

Carl seemed relieved.

"I knew it. I said, you're lying, dickhead. Bring over your smokin'-hot Amber porn freak, and prove she's real. Prove it, and I'll give you my Atari 2600, new in the box, never been opened."

"That Atari was something."

"Right???"

"Did he?"

Carl smirked.

"No. He sent a picture."

My heart beat faster.

"You still have it?"

"Sure."

Carl found the pic on his phone, and showed me. It was a selfie of Tyson with a young woman and man in a bar. The lighting was poor, but their faces were clear. Tyson was wearing the black sport coat with velvet lapels. The female held a wide fan of cash.

I said, "Amber?"

"So he says."

"This is Alec?"

"Yeah. If this is the friend he was bragging about."

Tyson and Amber were about the same size, and about the same age. Amber was pretty, and dressed to draw eyes. Alec was a good-looking guy with a lean face, dimples, and the darker beard of a man in his early to mid-twenties. It was easy to imagine how an insecure boy like Tyson could be influenced by Alec and Amber. Their relative heights and builds matched pretty well with the three unknown subjects I'd seen in the Slauson video.

"Can I have this, please?"

"Sure."

Carl texted the picture to me, and also printed a hard copy. I tried to think of other questions as the printer hummed.

"Did Tyson say what they did with the stuff they steal?"

"They sell it."

"Through a fence?"

"At the flea market."

"A flea market."

"Dude, you don't know. Flea markets are *money*. When Tyson got his license, we hit this flea market in Venice every Saturday. We scored games, consoles, controllers, analog joysticks, digital joysticks, touch screens, sound cards, graphics cards, memory cards, CPUs, speakers—"

"Carl."

"What?"

"Over my pay grade."

"Okay."

"Which flea market did you guys hit?"

If Tyson knew a particular flea market, he would probably return to it.

Carl didn't know the address, but he gave me directions. When we opened the door, the two kids jumped to their feet. Anxious to spend time with The Carl.

I thanked The Carl, shook his hand, and glanced at the equipment on his workbench. I wondered why he wore the suit, but I didn't ask. I wondered if he had friends, and hoped he did. I thought about his sister, asking if I'd come to arrest him. She hadn't seemed concerned.

I said, "Anyone who can do what you do doesn't need a badass pill. You aren't a loser, Carl. People like you own the world."

The Carl blinked, and suddenly laughed. Hyuk-hyuk-hyuk.

I left him with the scrubs, and followed his directions.

14

THE WEEKDAY DRIVE to Venice went quickly. Traffic on the 405 was light, construction slowdowns were absent, and the usual multi-car pileups were running behind schedule. I phoned Devon's cell as I climbed the Sepulveda Pass.

"Has he called?"

"No. And you were right about the cell company. They haven't posted his calls from this period."

"Call. Speak to a human."

"I will."

"Okay. I'm texting a picture to you."

I explained about Carl and the picture as I sent it. Her phone buzzed when the picture arrived, and her voice was low when she finally spoke.

"This is Amber and Alec?"

"Tyson identified them as Amber and Alec. Carl doesn't know their last names, or how Tyson met them, but Tyson admitted the burglaries."

"And Carl didn't tell?"

"Carl didn't believe him. Carl thought Tyson was making it up to get even."

"She looks cheap."

"Have you seen them before? At his school?"

She hesitated.

"No. Neither."

"Okay. What about his previous school?"

"Last year's school was huge. His class had almost a thousand kids."

"If you have a roster or yearbook, check. We might get lucky."

"What are you doing?"

She recognized the flea market when I told her.

"Tyson and Carl used to buy old games there. You wouldn't believe the junk they brought home."

"The more junk the better. If he liked it as a buyer, maybe he went back as a seller."

Carl's directions led to a large, fenced parking lot on the wrong side of Main Street a few blocks from the beach in Venice. Giant hand-painted signs hung on the fence.

FLEA MARKET SATURDAY!

FARMER'S MARKET SUNDAY!

FOOD TRUCK FRENZY FRIDAY!

SEE MANAGER NEXT DOOR ➡

The arrow pointed to an aging storefront office next to the parking lot. Crenza Investment Properties.

The office was larger than it appeared from the street, with a high ceiling that made the room feel even bigger. A line of tired wooden desks stretched the length of the room, and the yellowed walls were stained. A young woman with braided black hair and nervous eyes sat at the desk near the door. An older woman with fleshy cheeks read a magazine at the second desk. The remaining desks were bare.

The younger woman smiled, but said nothing.

I said, "Hey."

She said, "Hey."

"I'd like to speak with someone about the flea market."

The older woman shouted over her shoulder.

"Martin! Martin, come out here!"

Martin Crenza came through a door at the back of the office. He looked to be in his mid-fifties, with a balding head, a pot belly, and thin arms. His arms were furred with wiry hair.

The older woman pointed at me.

"Flea market."

Crenza smiled like a cruising shark, and came forward.

"A millionaire in the making! You want a table? Only two left. They're going fast."

I unfolded the screen-grab of Tyson and the selfie of Tyson with Amber and Alec.

"No, thanks. One or all three of these people might have rented a table from you. Anyone look familiar?"

He glanced at the pictures, and scowled.

"Is this them, the kids with the stolen goods?"

Crenza's matter-of-fact question surprised me, and left me guessing how he knew.

I said, "The police were asking about them?"

"We've had so many cops, who can keep count? Marge, come look."

The older woman was Martin's wife, Marge. The young woman was their niece, Charlotte. Marge and Charlotte joined us, and Marge took the pictures. Tyson's picture was on top.

"The green boy. Every cop comes here shows us this picture."

She shuffled the pages, and studied the selfie.

"This is the green boy again."

"Yes, ma'am. Have you seen him?"

Crenza said, "For the millionth time, no. How many times do we have to tell you people?"

"I'm not a policeman, Mr. Crenza. I'm private."

"Private what?"

"A private investigator. I'm trying to find these people."

"You and a million cops. We've never seen this kid, and I'm fed up with you people wasting our time."

Marge glared at him.

"Shut up, Martin. You're being a pain."

She adjusted her glasses, and showed the selfie to Charlotte.

"Maybe these two, you think? This tall boy, the good-looking one. And this girl. They're the kids Fiedler described, aren't they?"

Charlotte studied the picture uneasily.

"I dunno. Could be."

"What, could be? You're useless. This is them."

Marge snatched back the picture, and Charlotte stared at the floor. Useless.

Marge turned back to me.

"These two, I've seen. Was it them, sold Dr. Fiedler the camera?"

"I need some help here. Who's Dr. Fiedler?"

Martin Crenza waved a hand. Angry.

"Fiedler's an asshole. It was him, started all this."

Five weeks earlier, a dentist named Warren Fiedler purchased a collectible Leica camera at their flea market. The following week, Dr. Fiedler took the camera to a dealer to have it refurbished, and, as with Richard Slauson's Rolex, was told that the Leica was stolen. Fiedler immediately filed a complaint at the Pacific Division Police Station, and an army of police officers and detectives descended on the Crenzas.

When Crenza finished, Marge gave me the selfie.

"The police didn't have a picture of these two. I can't say it was them sold the camera, but I know they were here. They took a table."

High five, Carl.

"Great. Can you give me their names?"

Crenza jumped in again. He was still angry.

"No, we can't. This was what, five weeks ago? We got sixty-two tables, different people every week, how in hell you expect us to remember?"

"Don't people fill out a form, or sign a release? Don't you have records?"

Crenza glowered at Marge.

"This one sounds like the cops."

He shifted the glower to me.

"It's a flea market. People show up, wanna sell their old crap, what am I supposed to do, take a check might bounce? You want a table, it's cash in advance, good for one Saturday. No credit cards, no checks. Greenbacks."

He tapped his palm like I should fill it with greenbacks.

I thought for a moment, and noticed the plans on the walls. Large, framed layouts for the Flea Market, the Farmer's Market, and Food Truck Frenzy hung on the walls. The layouts were professionally drawn, and designed to maximize the parking lot's available space for each event. I moved to the Flea Market plan. Sixty-two numbered tables were laid out in a rectangular maze.

"Any chance you remember the table they used?"

Crenza came over, and joined me.

"No, but Fiedler remembered. The police brought him. What a prick that guy was."

Margie said, "Condescending. Who died and made him king?"

Crenza tapped a rectangle. The table was labeled with a thirty-seven, and sat at a corner between thirty-six and forty-two.

Crenza said, "Here, not that it did any good. We've been through this with the cops. That lady detective—"

He glanced at Marge for help.

Marge said, "Cassett."

"Yeah, she asked us to scare up people around thirty-seven here, and we busted our humps. We got a couple security guards. We got a guy, sells fruit juice and popsicles. We got regulars."

Margie said, "You have the list, right? Give him the list."

"Charlotte had it."

Charlotte hurried to her desk as Crenza went on.

"We dug up some regulars, but, believe me, they weren't easy to come by."

Marge sniffed. Resentful.

"Like we don't have enough to do, running a business."

Crenza shrugged.

"Whatever. So the other one, what's his name, the one looks like a bowling ball?"

He waved at Marge for the answer.

"Rivera."

Bowling ball. Rivera would love it.

"That's it. So we give them the names, and Rivera comes back. The people we gave them didn't know squat, so he wants us to come up with *more* names, which we did, and you know what happened?"

He arched his eyebrows. Waiting.

"Rivera came back again."

"Nah, not Rivera. Rivera sent a couple of asshats. I guess he couldn't be bothered. All this work we've done, all the names, they tell us we're wasting their time. I told'm, maybe you guys are asking bad questions. Can we help it nobody remembers?"

Marge said, "Terrible people, those two. Rude."

Charlotte found the list, and handed it to her uncle. He frowned.

"There's supposed to be two sheets. This is the first. What'd'ja do with the second?"

Marge glared at Charlotte again.

"I guess I have to do everything."

Marge stalked to the desk, and returned with a second page. I felt bad for Charlotte.

Six names were on the first list, and four names were on the second.

Three of the names had phone numbers and addresses, and a fourth name had only a phone number. The remaining six names had no contact information.

"You don't have phone numbers for these people?"

"What am I, psychic? These people are strangers. If someone said they saw someone here that Saturday, their name went on the list."

I glanced at the first list.

"So Rivera talked to these people, and no one could help?"

"So said the bowling ball."

I glanced at the second list. The first three names were typed. The fourth name was written. Louise August, along with an address.

"He struck out with these people, too?"

Crenza smirked.

"The first three, I guess. The last name here, Ms. August, we dug up for the asshats. We had to drop everything. They threatened to close us."

He glanced at Marge.

"What were their names, those nasty pricks?"

Marge frowned as she tried to remember.

"Neff? Ness? I'm drawing a blank. What were their names, Charlotte?"

Charlotte cringed, and looked miserable.

"I'm sorry."

"Useless."

Martin ignored them, and pointed out Ms. August's name.

"She's a regular. One of my security guys saw her yakking with a couple of young people, but they coulda been anyone. We get three or four thousand people through here, every Saturday. That old lady, she yaks with everyone."

"Could I get a copy of this list, Mr. Crenza?"

Crenza shrugged.

"The cops already talked to them."

"I know. Maybe I'll ask better questions."

Crenza stared for a moment, and laughed.

"Yeah, you might. You're not an asshat."

Marge pushed the lists at Charlotte.

"Make him a copy, or do I have to do that, too?"

Charlotte made the copies quickly, and proved herself useful.

I let myself out, and walked along the fence at the edge of the parking lot. The names without an address or phone number were worthless. Louise August showed an address, but no phone. I mapped her address on my phone, and saw she was only eight blocks away. I left my car by the Crenzas, and walked.

15

LOUISE AUGUST LIVED six blocks from the beach, in an area filled with turn-of-the-century bungalows built as weekend getaway homes for affluent Angelenos fleeing the inland heat. Back then, the drive from the mansions of Bunker Hill or West Adams to the milder clime of the beach was a two-hour trek through orange groves, palm orchards, and stretches of undeveloped land. A hundred years later, we had freeways and electric cars, but little had changed. The drive from downtown L.A. to Venice at rush hour took just as long, but passing through scenic orange groves had been replaced by creeping bumper-to-bumper traffic and vengeful drivers. This was called progress.

I called the people with phone numbers as I searched for Ms. August's address. Nancy Hummell's voice mail answered. I left a message asking her to call back, and dialed Carlos Gomez next. His phone rang, and kept ringing. Strike two. Victor Pitchess answered on the first ring, but Victor was annoyed. He didn't remember a young couple at the flea market, didn't like being harassed by strangers, and threatened to sue if I called him again. No wonder Cassett and Rivera had come up with nothing.

I found her street, turned, and saw a homeless man with a skinny brown dog sitting on the curb across from a blue Craftsman house. The man was watching a workman lower a FOR SALE sign into the house's front yard. A woman in a purple pants suit was directing him. The Craftsman had a peaked roof, a covered porch, and a blue picket fence with a blue picket gate. The address belonged to Louise August.

The dog saw me approaching, and whined. Its eyes were fearful. The man saw me, and his eyes were fearful, too. He struggled to his feet, and ducked his head.

"This poor dog is hungry. Spare a dollar for kibble? I swear to God and Jesus Above I will not buy alcohol."

I gave him five dollars, and crossed the street.

The woman said, "To the left. No, it's leaning to the right, bring it more left."

The workman straightened the post.

The woman said, "Better. That's good. Plant it."

BURGESS REALTY. FOR SALE.

The woman was blocking the gate, and didn't move.

I said, "Excuse me."

She glanced at the homeless man, and arched her eyebrows.

"If you give them money, they won't leave. I'm trying to sell this place."

"Sorry. I'm looking for Louise August. Is she home?"

The woman faced me, and hesitated.

"I'm sorry. She's gone."

"When will she be back?"

"Not that kind of gone. Amy Burgess, Burgess Realty. Are you a friend of the family?"

She gave me a card.

"No, ma'am. I need to see her about something. Business."

Amy Burgess hesitated again, and shrugged.

"Okay, well, I should tell you. Louise is dead. One of these addicts murdered her."

She waved toward the homeless man. He put his arm around the dog, and averted his eyes.

I flexed her card, and studied the house. The front yard was tangled with overgrown rubber trees and banana plants. A concrete walk from the gate to the porch was lined with garden gnomes, terra cotta pots, and quirky, sun-bleached signs. The signs said things like UNICORNS WEL-COME, I BRAKE FOR RAINBOWS, and PLEASE BE KIND. I slipped the card into my pocket.

"I'm sorry. When did it happen?"

"Last week. They wanted drugs. Broke in through a window there, and killed her with a steam iron. Blunt force trauma, the police said. It must have been awful."

The homeless man bellowed.

"FORGIVE ME, FATHER, I DID NOT SIN."

Amy Burgess ignored him.

"I told her daughter, you're going to take a hit on the price. I have to disclose. It's a murder house."

She frowned at the murder house, then considered me.

"Interested? Her daughter wants a fast sale."

The workman interrupted.

"What do you think, straight?"

Amy Burgess studied the sign.

"Perfect. Thanks, Armando."

The workman gathered his tools and let himself through the gate. Amy Burgess smiled, and gave me a second card.

"If you change your mind, you'll get a great buy. Believe me, she's over a barrel."

"Will do. Thanks."

So much for Louise August. All I had left were names with no way to reach them. I turned, and headed back for my car.

The homeless man stared at the ground as I approached, and spoke with a very soft voice.

"The lady was kind."

I knew he meant Louise August.

"She left water for thirsty dogs. The occasional treat. Kind."

He petted the dog. I glanced at the sign in the little front yard. PLEASE BE KIND.

"Good to know. Kindness is in short supply."

He nodded.

"Two men."

He glanced up, met my eyes, and looked away.

"We told the police. Her kindness, avenged."

"What about two men?"

"Well dressed, ties. Young men with authority. One large, one larger. We saw them open the gate."

"The day she was killed?"

He stared at the ground, and stroked the dog.

"We cannot be sure. Forgive us."

The two men he saw could have been detectives, come to see what she knew after leaving the Crenzas.

"Were they policemen, you think? Detectives?"

"Government men. Clandestine agents. Obvious."

Obvious.

"Did you see them leave?"

"We did not. Forgive us. Urgent business required us elsewhere."

He stroked the dog.

"But you told the police?"

"We did, and now you. Her kindness, avenged. Your kindness, repaid. Could you spare a dollar for kibble? This poor dog is hungry."

I gave him ten dollars, and walked back to the Crenzas. Charlotte was at her desk, but I didn't see Martin or Marge. Charlotte lurched to her feet when I opened the door. She probably thought I was Marge.

"Hey."

"Hey."

"Are your aunt and uncle here?"

She touched the base of her neck, and closed her collar.

"They went to lunch."

"Okay. Maybe you can help."

"I'll try."

"The detectives your uncle called asshats. Were you here when they talked to him?"

"Yeah, me and my aunt and uncle. I don't remember their names, though. I told you."

"I understand. What did they look like?"

She thought for a moment, and made a halfhearted shrug.

"I dunno. Like the others, I guess. Nice clothes, shiny shoes. They were kinda big. Good builds, like they work out."

"How old?"

"In their thirties? The one guy, he was about your height, maybe, or a little bigger. Dark. He did most of the talking, and smiled a lot. The other was a lot bigger, and kinda mean. He stood too close. I didn't like him."

One large, one larger. Young men with authority. They were probably the two men the homeless man saw.

"Were they going to see Louise August when they left here?"

She made a face. Uncertain.

"I dunno. I don't think they said. They just left."

"Did they leave a card?"

"I dunno. I'm sorry."

"You don't have to be sorry, Charlotte. You've been a big help. Thank you."

"You're welcome."

I smiled. She smiled back, but she looked uncomfortable. I turned to leave when she stopped me.

"Can I ask you a question?"

"Sure. What's on your mind?"

She looked even more nervous, and checked the door. Worried that Martin and Marge would catch us.

"You work with the police?"

"Sometimes. I usually work for a client, or myself. Like now."

"But you know the police who were here?"

"I know Cassett and Rivera. Not the asshats."

She touched her neck again, and seemed even more nervous.

"Are they nice?"

I didn't know how to answer, but I knew she was worried.

"Depends, I guess. How can I help?"

She opened her collar and lifted her chin. A simple pendant necklace hung around her neck.

"He gave it to me."

The gold chain was delicate. The pendant was classic, and beautifully simple. A facet-cut ruby was ringed by smaller diamonds. The ruby was a deep blood red with a glint of blue, and the diamonds sparkled with color-less light.

"I kept it, and now I don't know what to do. I don't want to get into trouble."

"Who gave it to you?"

"The boy in the picture. Alec."

She took a breath, and straightened herself.

"I know who he is. I know how to find him."

I locked the door, and asked her.

16

CHARLOTTE PRESSED a folded pink Post-It slip into my hand.

"He was having a party. He kinda came on to me, and said I should come. I never called."

"What's his last name?"

She gestured at the Post-It.

"It's here. Rickey. Alec Rickey. He's an actor."

I unfolded the note. Alec Rickey's name, a Burbank address, and a phone number were on the slip.

"You can tell the police, if you want, but please keep me out of it. I don't want anyone mad."

She checked the street again. Watching for Martin and Marge.

"What about the girl?"

"They're just friends. He was helping her."

"Not that. What's her name?"

"Amber. She barely spoke to me. I don't know her last name."

I tucked the slip into my pocket.

"Did you tell Alec the police were looking for him?"

"Uh-uh. I haven't talked to him since they were here with that camera. He scared me."

She fingered the necklace again. Nervous.

"He told you the necklace was stolen?"

"He never came out and said, but he had this gun in a bag. He showed me."

"Alec has a gun."

"This silver gun, with a white handle. The first time they were here, he was totally cool. He told me about his acting class, and all these actors he knew. But the next time, when he gave me the necklace, he acted all weird, like he wanted me to think he was shady. I was like, really? He thinks I'll be impressed if he's a criminal?"

I pictured a silver pistol in a paper bag. The paper was crumpled. I pictured him opening the bag, just enough to let her see.

"Did he tell you how he used the gun?"

"He just showed me. I kinda didn't believe he was like that, but then the police came, and I got scared."

She reached behind her neck and took off the necklace.

"I kinda wanted to keep it, but now I don't. Someone probably misses it."

She held it out.

"Would you give it back?"

The necklace glittered in the light coming in from the street. I took it, and slipped the necklace into my pocket with the Post-it note.

"I'll make sure the owner gets it."

"And keep me out of it? I don't want anyone mad at me."

She checked the street again, looking for Martin and Marge. She already had enough people mad at her.

"I won't tell."

She closed her eyes. Relieved.

"Thank you. Thank you so much."

"One more thing. You said Alec mentioned his acting class. Did he tell you where he studies?"

She remembered, and named a workshop class in North Hollywood.

I thanked her, and swapped my card for her cell number. I thought about Tyson, Alec, and Amber as I walked to my car. They had changed.

Tyson and his friends were no longer immature teenagers playing make-believe burglars. Alec had a gun, and the gun made them dangerous.

I climbed into my car, and dialed Rickey's number. His voice mail answered before the first ring.

"I'm Alec. Say it."

I hung up, and Googled Alec's acting school. The school was highly regarded by veteran actors from several network series, and run by an acting coach named Deena Ross. The website claimed she was legendary. If Alec told Charlotte the truth, I had something to work with. I bought a used playbook from Small World Books, grabbed a burger to go from the Sidewalk Café, and ate as I made the long drive to Burbank.

Alec's address led to a narrow, three-story building north of the Ventura Freeway, not far from Warners and Disney. Concrete steps climbed to a ground-floor entrance, and a do-it-yourself moving van was double-parked outside the door. Two guys were trying to wrestle a mattress out of the building, but the mattress was winning. I parked by a fire hydrant across the street, and pondered the building. I wondered if Alec was home, and whether Tyson and Amber were with him.

A Dan Wesson revolver in a gray suede holster was resting under my seat. The Dan Wesson woke, and found its way under my arm. I pulled on a pale linen jacket to cover the pistol. The jacket clashed with my shirt, but one often made sacrifices. I slipped the pick gun into a pocket, picked up my prop, and crossed the street.

I squeezed past the movers, climbed to the second floor, and found his apartment. I listened, and heard nothing. I pressed the buzzer, and heard someone move.

A female voice called from behind the peephole.

"Yes? Can I help you?"

I backed up to give her a better view, and smiled.

"Hey. I have something for Alec. From Deena Ross, his acting teacher. She asked me to drop it off."

I held up the playbook. If Alec was with her, he would either tell her to blow me off, or tell her to open the door.

The lock turned, and my hand reached under the jacket.

A young woman with short red hair and dark skin opened the door. She wasn't the woman in the selfie.

I lowered my hand, and smiled even wider.

"Sorry to just show up, but Deena wants him to have this."

Her eyes were pink, and uncertain.

"You're in his workshop?"

"Different workshop, but I study with Deena. Alec and I haven't met."

I held up the playbook, and the pink turned red.

"Alec is dead. He was murdered last night."

I tried to see past her. I listened, but heard no one else in the apartment. Her eyes were flat, and held the empty confusion of someone trying to cope with a terrible shock.

I said, "Is this for real?"

"*Yes*, it's for real. The police just told me, and I'm freaking out!"

"Were you and Alec—?"

"Roommates. We were just roommates. Claudia Lawrence."

She offered her hand, and we shook.

"Phil. I'm sorry. I don't know what to say."

She went back inside, and left the door open.

"I don't know what to say *either*. I don't know if I should tell anyone. I think I should call his parents, but they don't know me. They live in Kansas."

I stepped inside, and closed the door.

The living room was separated from a dining area and a kitchen by a hall that led to a bathroom. Two doors bracketed the bathroom, and probably opened to bedrooms. I wanted Tyson and Amber to be in the bedrooms. I wanted them safe, and alive, but I was scared they had been with Alec.

"Did the police tell you what happened?"

"Someone shot him. Can you believe it? He was driving, and someone just shot him. He crashed over this wall, and they said it was awful. He burned. In Pacoima."

She grimaced at the thought of the fire, and turned away.

"Was anyone with him?"

"I don't know. They didn't say."

"Do they know who did it?"

"From the way they got in my face, they acted like I shot him."

She dropped onto a corduroy couch, and pulled up her legs.

"I don't even know where Pacoima is. How can I tell his parents?"

I felt bad for her.

"It's in the Valley. North of Burbank."

"They scared the shit out of me. Assholes."

She was talking about the police.

"I walked in, and here they were, these two men. Mylie screamed."

"Who's Mylie?"

"Mylie and Kramer live up on three. We went for coffee."

"The police were here when you got home?"

"Looking for evidence. The stupid manager let them in. On account of the murder."

She suddenly sat up, and looked at me.

"Alec really messed me up. My fucking roommate turns out to be a thief, and now he's *dead*. I can't afford this place by myself."

A coldness spread from my belly into my chest.

"The police told you Alec was a thief."

"*Yes!* He was stealing laptops. They searched. They took stuff! They even took some of *my* stuff."

"What did they take?"

"Our laptops! I hope they give it back. Kramer said I should've asked for a receipt."

"They specifically asked about laptops?"

"They asked what he did with the laptops, and I'm like, *what* laptops? They're accusing me, right? And Kramer was like, don't say anything, call a lawyer, and I'm like, I didn't know he was stealing, I don't know anything about this. It was *crazy*."

She took a breath, and closed her eyes again.

"They threw Kramer out. Literally, the one guy, the bigger one, he grabbed Kramer and walked him right out the door. I was kinda glad. Kramer was making it worse."

The chill spread from my chest into my head. I watched her, and wet my lips. The police had tied Alec to the burglaries. If they knew Alec was Unknown Male Subject Number Two, they probably knew Tyson was Unknown Male Number One, which meant Tyson had lost his chance to negotiate a voluntary surrender. On the other hand, if Tyson and Amber were riding with Alec when he was murdered, they were probably dead, too. Unless they were the shooters.

I said, "Did the police ask about Amber or Tyson?"

Her eyes widened.

"How did you know?"

Bad.

"From the workshop. I've heard things."

"You should tell the police."

I nodded, and wondered what Cassett knew. I took out my pad.

"I will. Did you get their names, or a card? I'll call."

She thought for a moment, and screwed up her face.

"Neff, maybe. Neff and Hensman? They didn't give me a card. Mr. Yeun would know. He let them in."

Neff was one of the asshats.

"What did the officers look like, in case I have to describe them?"

She screwed her face again.

"In their thirties. Kinda hot, except they were scary. Big guys, fit, like they work out a lot, short hair. You know. Cops."

One big, one bigger. Asshats.

"I'll ask Mr. Yeun. Is he here in the building?"

"First floor, by the entrance. One-oh-one."

I stood. Claudia stood with me, and walked me to the door.

I said, "It's a nice apartment. I hope you find a new roommate."

She brightened.

"You interested?"

"Thanks, but I like where I am."

She reached for the knob, and hesitated.

"Kramer says the police will tell Alec's parents."

"Kramer's right. Someone has to claim the body."

She thought for a moment, and nodded.

"I should call. These guys weren't very nice."

I liked her for wanting to spare Alec's parents.

"You're a good person, Claudia. They'll appreciate it."

She opened the door.

"If you know anyone who needs a roommate, I'm easy to live with."

"I'll ask."

I left, and double-timed down to the first floor. The movers were gone, and the entry was closed. I found 101, knocked, and Mr. Yeun answered.

I said, "Hi. I just saw Claudia, up in two-oh-four. I need to speak with the detectives you let into her apartment. Did you get their names, or a card?"

Mr. Yeun squinted. Suspicious.

"I let no one into her apartment."

"Two-oh-four. Policemen. One big, one bigger. They told her you let them in."

Mr. Yeun glanced over my shoulder, trying to see behind me.

"Is this a trick? Yeun lets in no one."

I hurried back to my car, wondering why they lied.

17

TYSON HAD ALMOST CERTAINLY called Alec and Amber when he left home the night before, and the odds were good they had gotten together. If Tyson and Amber were with Alec when Alec was murdered, they might have been murdered, too. If they hadn't been with Alec, the police would consider them suspects.

I called a criminalist I knew named John Chen. John worked as a field investigator for the LAPD's Scientific Investigations Division. He was an excellent criminalist. He was also paranoid, needy, and burdened by less self-esteem than the average grapefruit.

John answered on the third ring. A whisper.

"I'm at work."

John always whispered when I called him at work. The other criminalists might be listening.

"This is important. I need information on a murder vic, and I need it now."

"What's in this for me?"

Along with paranoia, greed and fame were high on John's list of emotional needs. He loved seeing himself on television, especially when he was interviewed by attractive female reporters.

"Maybe nothing, John. I can't make any promises."

"Maybe is not persuasive."

"You know the string of rez-burgs in Beverly Hills and Bel Air?"

"Sure. Eighteen scores, three unknown subjects, rich people. Four of those cases are mine."

"Last night, an Anglo male named Alec Rickey was shot and killed on the freeway in Pacoima. Rickey was driving."

"This is connected?"

"Rickey is one of the burglars. I need to know if Rickey was alone in the car. If there were other victims, I need their names."

"Wait. This guy is one of the unsubs?"

"Yes."

"For real?"

"Yes, John, for real. He's one of the burglars."

John said, "Henh."

This was Chen, smiling. His hand would cover his mouth to hide his glee from the other criminalists, but John was seeing his name in the headlines, and headlines made him smile. *CHEN CRACKS BURGLARY RING. GRATEFUL RICH PEOPLE LAVISH PRAISE.* I hated to burst his bubble.

"The police already know he's one of the burglars."

"Oh."

Deflated. Feeling bad for himself.

"I need this, John. C'mon, man."

He finally sighed. The weight of the world.

"Okay."

"One more thing. Find out if a pistol was recovered. Rickey had a pistol."

"No problem. It's not like I have to clear my schedule for an interview."

Sullen.

I hung up and wondered how the police put Alec with the burglaries. The two dicks who questioned Claudia sounded like the asshats who leaned on the Crenzas. The Crenzas had sent the asshats to Louise August, who probably gave them Alec's and Amber's names. This made sense, but if such was the case, Cassett had known the identities of her unknown subjects for over a week. I wondered why she hadn't picked them up for questioning, or obtained warrants for their arrests, and no good reason occurred to me. This usually meant a lack of evidence, but Tyson and his friends had left fingerprints and DNA at their crime scenes like dandruff. I found Cassett's card, and dialed.

"Elvis Cole. Got a minute?"

"Not really. I'm busy."

"You asked me to call if I found something."

She brightened.

"What do you have?"

"Congratulations. I heard you ID'd the burglars."

Cassett snorted, which wasn't the reaction I expected.

"You heard wrong, Cole. Now what do you have?"

Her response felt natural, spontaneous, and real. So did my question.

"Really? I heard you had names."

"C'mon, Cole, I'm up to my eyes. You have something or not? I gotta go."

Everything about her tone and energy level felt real, but cops lied better than normal people. Working undercover sharpened their skills.

I decided she was keeping it quiet while they developed their case. With eighteen rich people breathing down her neck, she couldn't afford to screw up. Rich people wanted convictions.

"Hey, Cassett, can I ask a favor?"

"Is this why you called?"

"How about giving me a victim list? The more I know, the more I can help."

"So far, you haven't. Goodbye, Cole. I'm hanging up."

"Kids are selling stolen property at a flea market in Venice. I got a witness might know who they are."

Cassett's voice turned cold and held a threatening edge.

"Who told you about the flea market?"

"I have sources. I'm a detective."

"If one of my guys told you, I'll have his ass. Pass the word, Cole. His ass is mine."

"Relax, Sergeant. I wouldn't know your guys if I tripped over them."

She was upset.

"Whatever, but make sure you keep your mouth shut. Don't go blabbing about the flea market."

"What's the big deal?"

"The deal is we sat on it. Nobody knows these kids move their take at a flea market. I've had undercovers on that market since we found out, and if those kids sniff cop, they'll never go back."

The truth in her voice was as real and unmistakable as a solid steel door. Cassett did not know Tyson and Amber and Alec were the three unknown subjects. Neff and Hensman knew, but Cassett knew nothing.

I said, "Neff and Hensman told me."

"Told you what?"

"About the flea market."

"So who are Neff and Hensman, and why do I give a shit?"

Keeping secrets about an investigation was typical. Pretending you didn't know the detectives who worked on your task force made no sense.

"They told me about Louise August."

"I don't know what you're talking about, Cole."

I drew a slow breath, and didn't like what I was thinking.

"Cole? Are you there?"

"Louise August. Someone saw her talking to a couple of kids."

"Okay. And?"

"That's it. I didn't talk to her. Haven't found her."

"So you called with a tip that isn't really a tip because you don't know anything except for the name of someone you haven't been able to find. Do I have this right?"

"Uh-huh."

Cassett hung up.

I lowered the phone, and stared out the window. Two girls and a boy zinged past on skateboards. I watched them. A man carried a tiny Chihuahua out of a building. He put the dog down on the sidewalk. The little dog sniffed the air, looked at the man, and trembled. The man took a step toward a small patch of grass, and coaxed the dog toward the grass. The dog didn't move. The man lifted the dog, set it in the grass, and waited. The tiny dog shivered. The man picked up his dog, and carried it into the building.

I called Charlotte Crenza.

"It's Elvis. Can you talk?"

"Hang on. I'll go in the bathroom."

More whispering. Everyone I spoke with whispered. Maybe it was me.

The phone buzzed with an incoming call as I waited. Chen. I sent him to voice mail. Charlotte came back on the line a few seconds later.

"She's such a bitch."

"When the asshats came to your office, how did they identify themselves?"

"They said hello and showed me their badges."

"Were their names Neff and Hensman?"

"I'm sure they said, but I'm such a dummy. I don't remember."

"Okay. So they flashed their badges and said hello. They must've said something else, right?"

"The shorter one, he's the one who did the talking, he said Detective Cassett sent them to see my uncle."

"They told you Detective Cassett sent them."

"The shorter one. He was still pretty big, but the other man was bigger."

"Did they say why Cassett sent them?"

"Something about Mr. Fiedler's camera, but I didn't listen. It was Food Truck Friday, so Martin was next door, and Marge said—"

I interrupted.

"Did they ask if Alec and Amber were selling laptop computers?"

"OhmiGod, they *did*. The shorter one, he actually asked us to describe them. I mean, *really*?"

I heard a muffled sound, and Charlotte whispered again.

"I have to go. Marge is calling."

"One last thing. Did they have a picture of the green boy?"

"Of course, and they made us look at it like every other cop who's been here."

I hung up again, only now my head hurt and something large throbbed behind my eye. The phone buzzed. It was Chen, calling a second time. His whisper was frantic and fast.

"How do you know his name?"

"Was Rickey alone?"

"*Yes*, but he wasn't shot while he was driving. He crashed over a guardrail. Somebody pulled him out of the car. They shot him on the embankment."

The throb behind my eye beat harder.

"Suspects?"

"Did you kill him? Did you and Pike kill him? I'm not gonna help you cover up a murder."

The throb pounded so hard it was difficult to think.

"We didn't kill him."

"Then how do you know his name? You told me his name, but he hasn't been identified. They don't know who he is."

"The police know."

"They don't know. Nobody knows but you. He was torched, bruh. Soaked him with high-test, and fired him up. They haven't been able to identify him."

Neff and Hensman knew.

"Suspects and evidence?"

"Pulled shoe prints off the embankment. Men's shoes."

I said, "Two pair."

"It was you and Pike, wasn't it? You murdered him."

I hung up, and remembered the little sign in Louise August's yard.

Please be kind.

I didn't feel kind. I felt angry, and scared.

Two men opened Louise August's gate, and then she was dead. Alec Rickey was murdered, and two men who might or might not be police officers searched his apartment, asking about laptops and Tyson and Amber. Maybe the same two men who left shoe prints on the embankment.

Two men wanted a stolen laptop, and they were killing people to find it. They knew Tyson's name, and if they had his name they could find his address, and Tyson lived with his mother.

I scooped up my phone, but I didn't call Devon. Devon was my second call.

18

DEVON CONNOR

DEVON DROVE HOME from her meeting with Leslie Sanger as if she were trapped within a cloud. She glanced at herself in the rearview, and regretted it. Deep lines, crepey skin, and smudgy caves instead of eyes. She looked a million years old. She felt even older. Life with Tyson was draining.

Devon told herself his Volvo would be waiting, but the driveway was empty. She prayed the Volvo would be in the garage, but her hopes crashed again as the garage door opened. Devon pulled into the empty garage, gathered her purse, and noticed the laundry door.

The door from the garage to the laundry was ajar.

Devon tried to recall whether she locked it earlier. She thought she had, she always did, but with so much on her mind, it was possible she didn't.

Devon slid out of her Audi and entered her house. She passed through the laundry into the kitchen, just as she'd done ten thousand times, and pulled up short.

The cabinets were open, as if someone had looked inside, and not bothered to close them.

Tyson.

Devon frowned toward the hall.

"Tyson! Are you here?"

Leaving the cabinets open would be just like him.

"Tyson!"

The sadness she'd felt for her son only seconds ago blossomed to anger.

"Tyson, you answer me!"

Devon stalked into the dining room, and stopped short again. The sliding glass door to the backyard was full-on wide open. A lazy black fly buzzed past her head. She swatted at it, and missed.

I'm gonna kill him.

"Tyson!"

Devon moved down the hall to his bedroom.

His door was closed, and she certainly didn't bother to knock. Devon flung open the door, and the sight of his room made her gasp.

Tyson's bed was upended. His desk and chest of drawers had been pulled from the walls. Their contents were dumped on the floor. His monitors and games had been swept from the desk, and lay in the jumble, scattered about the room.

Devon tried to swallow, but her mouth was dry. His room looked as if it had been ransacked by vandals.

Tyson would not have done this. Devon did not want to believe Tyson would do this, but the girl or Alec might have put him up to it. They might have encouraged him, and goaded him on.

Terrible, criminal, teenage *assholes*!

Did they vandalize her entire home? Was this an expression of anger?

His bathroom was gutted. Towels and toilet tissue lay on the floor, scraped from the linen closet and cabinets.

Assholes!

She stormed into her bedroom.

"You little shits!"

Her dresser and chest were emptied like Tyson's. Boxes, handbags, and a suitcase were pulled from her closet. The jewelry box Tyson gave her when he was twelve was gone. She didn't bother to look in her closet.

Devon went to her office at the end of the hall. The last room in the house.

Drawers and file cabinets had been emptied, and storage bins pulled from the closet. She felt a breeze, and noticed the open window.

The window was wrong.

Tyson had a key. He wouldn't have to open the window.

She stared at the window, and wondered why it was open. She wanted to close it, but couldn't bring herself to enter the room. The house was quiet. Deathly still.

Stop being silly. Close the damn window, and clean up this mess.

The neighbor's dog burst into frenzied barking.

Devon jumped so hard, she clutched the door. Toby was a big dog with a loud bark. He sounded right outside the window, crazy loud snarling barks like he wanted to tear something apart.

The barking stopped.

Devon heard a car, and a faraway truck, and birds.

Then a creak from the front of the house.

Her heart slammed.

Devon couldn't tell if the sound came from inside the house, or out. It could have been the wind. It might be Toby.

Thump.

Devon peeked up the hall. The hall was empty, but her heart beat a vicious patter, and she wanted to run.

Thump. Creak.

She ducked into the office, but stayed at the door. Listening. Straining to hear.

Inside or out, she still couldn't tell.

Stop! You're imagining things!

Maybe from the dining room, a noise from outside coming through the open slider.

Her phone buzzed, startling her as much as the barking. Devon had forgotten her phone. She saw Cole's name, and covered her mouth.

"Someone's in my house."

"You're home?"

"Yes! Someone searched my house, and I think they're still here."

"Where are you?"

"I heard something."

"Devon, listen. I need you to listen."

"I'm scared."

"I know. Where are you?"

"In the office. In back."

"Can you see the front door?"

"Yes."

"Leave. Go straight to the front door, and open it."

Devon's throat felt swollen, and her eyes burned. She peered up the hall.

"I heard something. I think someone's in the dining room."

"Go to the front door, Devon. Go now. Get out of the house."

"I can't. I'll pass the dining room."

"Do it. Leave now. Go."

Devon's heart thundered. She closed her eyes, and told herself to stop being a baby.

She crept from the office, and stared down the length of the hall and across the living room to the front door. She listened, but a high-pitched hum filled her ears.

Elvis said, "Are you moving?"

She took a step.

"Yes."

"Go to the door. Straight to the door."

She stepped again, and then again. She watched the entrance to the dining room, and readied herself, steeled herself to fight and scream if someone lunged from the room.

She walked faster, and then she ran, flying past the dining room.

"I'm there! I'm there!"

"Open it. I sent a friend."

She threw open the door, and shrieked. A tall, rough man loomed large at the door. He gripped her arm so quickly she shrieked again. Sunglasses hid his eyes, and a sleeveless gray sweatshirt revealed battle-scarred arms roped with muscle. Red arrow tattoos on his deltoids seemed to point at her.

The man pulled her close, and whispered.

"I'm Pike. I've got you. You're safe."

He folded his arm around her, and rushed Devon away from the house.

19

JOE PIKE

THE WOMAN HUDDLED against the door in his red Jeep Cherokee, staying as far from him as possible. Pike thought she looked small, pressed to the door, and more fearful of him than of what she'd found in her home. Pike understood.

Pike held out his phone.

"Elvis."

She glanced at the phone, but didn't take it. Afraid to reach out.

"Talk."

She took the phone and held it to her ear.

"Hello?"

Her eyes never left him. She listened, but said almost nothing. After a minute, she handed back the phone. Wary, but not so afraid.

"He wants you."

Pike watched her house as they spoke. He had shoved her into the Jeep, fired the engine, and roared away all of fifty feet. No one pursued them, so now they sat idling, talking to Cole.

Pike said, "Yes?"

"She's okay?"

"Scared."

"Did you see anyone?"

"No."

"One or two men dressed like police detectives. Sport coats and ties."

"No."

"Did she?"

"Didn't ask."

"I wouldn't ask so many questions if you told me what happened."

"She's safe."

Pike cut the line and lowered his phone. He stared at Devon Connor. Ms. Connor stared back. Pike offered his hand.

"Joe Pike. You doing okay?"

She worked up her nerve, and took his hand. Her hand was damp. His was dry.

"Devon Connor. Thank you. I guess."

Pike took that to mean she was okay. He went back to watching the house.

"Did you see who did this?"

"I thought Tyson was home until I saw his room. His room looks like it exploded. My office is upside down. All my clothes, the things in my drawers, everything's on the floor."

Pike took this to be a no. He studied the neighboring houses, and the street in both directions. This wasn't a neighborhood where people had security cameras.

She said, "Mr. Cole says you work together."

He nodded.

"Are you a detective?"

"No."

Pike let the Jeep idle forward. When they reached her driveway, he stopped, and studied the sides of her house, and the windows, and roof. He stared into her garage.

She said, "What are we doing?"

"Looking."

Pike took a Colt Python .357 Magnum in a clip holster from under his seat. The woman's eyes got big when she saw the gun.

"What's that?"

"A gun."

"Why do you have a gun?"

"The men who came here have guns. I'm going to see if they're gone."

"What men? Who did this?"

The answers would only upset her, so Pike didn't answer. He clipped the Python to his waist, and covered the butt with his sweatshirt.

"We're going to change seats. You're going to drive around the block. When you get back, you'll see me. If you hear shots, keep driving. Call Elvis."

"Shots? I don't want to hear shots."

"If something happens, call Elvis."

"I don't want to drive around the block. I don't want you to   "

Pike got out and rounded to the passenger door. She wasn't moving, so he opened the door.

"Get behind the wheel. C'mon."

She stumbled out of the Jeep, and climbed in behind the wheel. She wasted time adjusting the seat, so he slapped the fender.

"Go now. Drive."

She screeched away, barely missing an oncoming car.

Pike ran directly to the front door and drew the Python as he entered. He went in fast, gun first, and stepped to the side. One sweep to clear the space, then Pike locked the door so no one could enter behind him. Or leave.

Pike had cleared homes and buildings as a combat Marine, a police officer, and a military contractor in the deadliest, most dangerous regions of the world. He had cleared so many hostile structures he moved by muscle memory. Living room, kitchen, laundry room, garage, back through the kitchen into the dining room, moving without effort or pause like water flowing around rocks in a stream. Stepped through the open dining room sliders, scanned the backyard, turned away and into the hall. Bathroom, linen closet, the boy's room, his closet. Her room, her closet, her bath, and out. Office, checked the closet and under the desk, glanced out the open window, one side, the other, and back through the house.

Clear.

Pike waited in the garage by her Audi, watching the street. He phoned Cole while he waited.

"It's clear. What do you want me to do?"

"Where is she?"

"Sent her around the block."

"He had a laptop on his desk and cash taped behind the drawers. See if they're missing. Don't tell her about the cash. I don't think she knew."

"Okay."

"Have her call the police. If these people are cops, they'll watch for a police report. An innocent person finds her home trashed, she'll call the police. A person who knows her son is a wanted thief, and maybe knows where to find him, might not."

"I understand."

The Cherokee finally appeared, creeping down the street at five miles an hour.

"She's back."

Pike pocketed the phone. Ms. Connor turned into the drive, parked, and got out. She didn't look frightened now. The drive had given her time to get angry.

"You scared me."

"We had to move fast. Sorry."

"I didn't know who you were. Mr. Cole didn't tell me he has a partner."

Pike turned away and went into the house. She hurried after him and caught up in the kitchen.

"See if anything's missing and we'll call the police. You'll want a police report for your insurance."

She crossed her arms and grew nervous again.

"The police?"

"Don't mention your son or the investigation. You came home, saw the mess, and called the police. Calling the police is what people do."

She held her arms tighter, and stared at the mess. The open cupboards. The dining room sliders. The mess.

She suddenly looked at him.

"You know who did this."

"Not yet."

"You said the men who did this had guns. What men? How do you know they had guns?"

"Call the police. Tell them someone broke into your house, and you're scared. They'll ask if the bad guy is in the house. Say you don't know. Ask them to send a car right away."

Pike stood with Devon while she spoke with the emergency operator. The operator wanted her to stay on the line, but Pike took the phone and hung up.

"See if anything's missing. I want to look around before they get here."

Pike had a license to carry his pistol, but he didn't want drama. He stowed the Python in his Jeep, and pulled on a blue denim shirt to cover his tattoos. Then he went back to the dining room and checked the sliding glass door. He examined the aluminum jamb and the frame and the latch, then moved to the office and examined the open window. The window jamb showed exterior pry marks, but the slider jamb showed nothing. Pike decided they had entered the house through the window, but left through the dining room. Pike wondered why. The dining room put them in the backyard, which forced them to walk around the house to reach the street. Leaving through the window or even walking out the front door would have been faster.

Pike was still thinking about it when Devon appeared behind him.

"They took my jewelry box. They took Tyson's pills and six hundred dollars I had in a drawer."

"That's it?"

"He gave me that box when he was twelve. It was special."

Her eyes were red, and Pike realized she was upset.

"They want a laptop."

"I don't have a laptop."

"Elvis saw a laptop on your boy's desk."

"Have you seen that mess, all his stuff wired together, and now it's on the floor. I don't know if they took anything."

Pike didn't know what to say.

"I'm sorry they took your jewelry box."

"He gave it to me for Mother's Day."

Cole should be here. Cole would know what to say.

"They want a laptop. They took other things to cover the break-in."

She stalked away.

Pike checked the window again, then went out through the dining room, and circled the back of the house. He approached the window along a chain-link fence threaded with ivy and climbing roses.

The office window was chest-high above a bed of rosemary and scraggly azaleas. The soil was dry and cracked from the recent drought. Pike crouched, and examined the ground. Cole told him shoe prints had been found where Alec Rickey was murdered. Pike pushed aside the rosemary and lowered himself into a push-up position. Overlapping shoe prints cut the dust.

Pike stepped away, and was thinking about this when a black Labrador retriever slammed into the fence, barking like it wanted to rip out his throat.

A man called from next door.

"What's going on over there?"

The dog barked even louder, and Pike understood why the men left through the dining room.

A man in his seventies appeared in the neighboring yard. His skin was dark and deeply lined, and he needed a shave.

"Who's that? What's going on over there?"

"Someone broke into Ms. Connor's house. We called the police."

The man told his dog to shush.

"Toby's been barking his head off. When did it happen?"

"The past couple of hours. You see anyone?"

"I didn't, but Toby's been raising hell."

"They got in through this window."

The man came closer and peered over the fence.

"I heard ol' Toby, but I was in the garage. By the time I got out here, he was quiet."

"The police might want to talk to you."

"That's fine. I'll be in the garage."

Pike remembered seeing the man's garage door open. Pike hadn't seen the man, but the door was up, and the garage was dark with boxes.

"You see anyone out front? Someone you didn't recognize."

"Don't think so. I was working."

"Couple of men in sport coats and ties. Maybe one man."

"Wish I had. Wasn't paying attention."

Pike heard the siren, far away but coming fast. He started back the way he had come when the man suddenly spoke.

"Saw a car I hadn't seen."

Pike stopped.

"A big ol' black Chrysler, looked like a limo. Had those dark windows. Gone now, but it was across the street."

"See the driver?"

"Didn't see anyone. It was parked out front of the Wymans. Didn't think anything of it, but they don't own a big ol' Chrysler."

"When was this?"

"After Toby raised hell. I went back into the garage and saw it. A big ol' black Chrysler with black windows."

The siren was so loud it sounded beside them, then abruptly stopped, and the patrol car roared to a stop on the far side of the house.

Pike said, "Thanks."

The old man said, "Send'm on over. I'm happy to help."

20

HARVEY AND STEMMS

SIX MINUTES AFTER trashing the Connor residence, Harvey and Stemms tossed the jewelry box into a Dumpster behind a *taqueria*, and picked up drive-thru from Tommy's World Famous Hamburgers. They'd found a laptop computer and forty-six thousand dollars in the boy's room. The laptop would be delivered to their client for analysis. The cash, they would keep. Tommy's was a reward.

Stemms ordered two hamburgers, pickles and onions only, with extra pickles. Harvey bitched about his intestines, but wolfed down a chili tamale topped by an egg and a hot dog with extra mustard and onions. Dude was a beast. They parked behind Tommy's and ate in the car while they worked.

A grocery bag with the papers, files, and materials they'd taken sat on the console between them. They went through the bag, searching for clues to the kid.

Forty minutes earlier, when they returned and found the garage closed, Stemms felt hopeful they'd find the Volvo behind the door and the kid in the house, passed out on filthy pillows in last night's clothes, hoses from one of those ornate, monster-tall hookahs tangled around him, old pizza boxes everywhere, maybe the girl tangled up with him, your typical low-life, a-hole, criminal teenagers, but no one was home and the house was surprisingly normal.

With their limited DMV information, they had known almost nothing about James Tyson Connor. Now, they knew he lived at home with his mother, and the two of them lived alone. They knew which school he attended, and the name of his doctor. A federal tax return filed by Devon Connor gave them her place of employment. Stemms circled the address and noted she filed as the head of household and claimed one dependent. This meant dad was out of the picture and the boy was an only. A tax return was a gold mine.

Harvey dug in the bag and came out with a brown prescription bottle. He studied the label, and rattled the pills. Stemms took a bite of his burger, and noticed the bottle.

"What's that?"

"Had the kid's name on it so I took it."

"Medicine?"

Harvey read from the label.

"You heard of sertraline?"

Stemms took another bite, and spoke with his mouth full.

"Generic. A reuptake inhibitor."

Stemms knew things.

"What's it do?"

"They use it to treat panic attacks, social anxiety, things like that."

"Mm."

Harvey fished out a second bottle, and flashed an evil grin.

"Ritalin! Yes, thank you, don't mind if I do!"

Harvey made a show of pocketing the pills.

Stemms said, "I can't believe you took someone's medicine."

"It's *Ritalin*, and he ain't gonna need it much longer. Relax, Stemms. You scared I won't share?"

Harvey raised another bottle.

"Lorazepam?"

"A benzo. Anti-anxiety stuff."

Harvey grunted, and turned to his phone. Stemms put the tax return aside, and chomped a bite of his burger.

Harvey said, "You think this kid's retarded?"

Stemms stopped chewing. He stopped breathing, and felt a stillness settle within him. A Tommy burger, pickles and onions only, extra pickles, was one of his most treasured pleasures, but now his mouth seemed to be filled with cold grease and paper.

Stemms forced himself to swallow and looked at Harvey.

"What did you say?"

Harvey glanced up from his phone.

"This high school. It's one of those special schools. You know. For kids who can't hack it in real schools."

"I meant the word."

Harvey shook his head. Confused.

"What?"

"That word. What did you say?"

"I don't know what you're talking about."

"You don't call someone retarded. What's wrong with you?"

Harvey showed his phone.

"I'm reading about the school."

"That word. Don't use it."

Harvey raised his hands.

"I apologize."

"It's hurtful."

"I said I was sorry."

Stemms stared at his hamburger. His appetite was gone, but he tried another bite. Ruined. He bagged the remains, and checked the time. It was close to the end of the school day, but they might be able to make it.

"The school's not a bad idea. Let's check it out."

He started the Chrysler.

Harvey looked surprised.

"Are you serious? He isn't at school."

"It's a weekday. It isn't a holiday. Why wouldn't he be at school?"

"Because he's a degenerate criminal with the cops on his case? Because his friend Alec told him we chased his ass all over town, and Alec was shot?"

Stemms felt tired.

"They have no idea what happened, Harvey."

"They were yakking when we ran him off the road."

Stemms made his voice patient.

"Alec didn't know what was happening. So, okay, they all got on the phone, and Alec told them a big black car was chasing him. So what?"

Stemms spread his hands, like, wasn't it obvious?

"No black-and-whites. No flashing lights. He didn't know why we were on his butt. Dude could've cut us off and we were pissed. A road rage thing. You see what I'm saying?"

Harvey shrugged. Glum.

"I guess."

"Then the moron hit the rail, and the play-by-play stopped. What can they know? They might not even know the poor fucker's dead, but if they do, even better. You know why?"

Harvey rolled his eyes.

"Please tell me."

"The news won't say Alec was a burglary suspect. It won't say he died running from the police. Am I right?"

"If Alec wasn't a suspect, they aren't suspects."

Harvey made a big sigh. He always got mopey when Stemms showed him up.

"Correct. And you don't have to be such a drama queen."

"You made your point. I agree. They cut a hellacious relief fart, and life goes on. School."

"Worth checking. This kid could be sitting in class right now, pretending he gives a shit."

"You think?"

Stemms guided the Chrysler out of the parking lot without answering. Checking the school was a waste of their time, but it was a box they had to check. He was thinking about the boy's mother, and what they had learned in her home, when Harvey spoke.

"I meant it."

Stemms didn't know what he was talking about.

"What?"

"What I said. That word."

The stillness returned. Small, but growing. Harvey never knew when to quit.

"Forget it."

"I can be thoughtless, and you're sensitive about certain things. I get it."

"Shut up."

"I meant it, is all, my apology. I feel like a bad friend."

"Stop. Talking."

Harvey. Finally. Stopped.

They drove in silence. The quiet was good. Necessary.

Stemms concentrated on the boy and his mother.

The boy was emotionally young and uncomfortable with others. Pictures of the boy and his mother covered their fridge and dotted her dresser. Stemms sensed the mother was key. The boy might run, but he would not leave. He might hide, but he would always go home.

Home was his mom.

Stemms knew things.

If they couldn't find Tyson Connor, they knew where to find his mother. Mom would give them the boy.

21

ELVIS COLE

PIKE CALLED as I hit the Cahuenga Pass and headed for home.

"The laptop you saw in the boy's room is missing. So is the cash."

"Could Tyson have taken them while Devon was gone?"

"Not enough time. A neighbor saw a black four-door Chrysler. Dark windows, he said. New. He didn't see people."

"Get a plate?"

"No. It was parked across the street, so I asked the neighbors. No one else saw it. Work day, people were gone."

"I don't suppose one of the neighbors has a security camera with a view of the street."

"No. The dead kid?"

"Can she hear you?"

"She's with the officers."

"Alec Rickey. What about him?"

"You mentioned shoe prints."

"Yeah. The police found shoe prints at the scene. Two sets of men's shoes."

"Shoe prints here, too. Outside her office window. They're faint, but maybe enough to compare."

I thought about it, and knew they would match.

"I'll call Chen."

"One more thing. If these guys are hunting, they might come back. I should stay. She shouldn't."

Pike was right.

"Is she okay to drive?"

"She's fine."

"Send her up. Have her bring enough for a couple of days."

"Rog."

I hung up and called John Chen. His voice was soft and suspicious.

"I'm working a murder. Can't talk."

"Fake it. You'll be glad you did."

"Is this about the other thing?"

The other thing.

"Yes. Copy this address."

Chen interrupted, a whispery hiss.

"He's been identified."

"Alec Rickey?"

"His parents called. They heard he was murdered and called to see if it was true. That gave us dental, and now it's confirmed."

Claudia had told his parents.

"Have the police put him with the burglaries?"

"No prints to match. As of now, he's only a vic."

I gave him Devon's address and told him what happened.

"Officers are at the residence now. They'll roll it to detectives, and the dicks will ask for a criminalist. Can you be the guy?"

"No way, man. I'm up to my elbows in blood. You should see this mess."

He lowered his voice even more.

"Dude killed his family with a hatchet, then chopped off his own feet. Six vics and a bleeder with no feet. I love this job."

I said, "Listen, John. If another criminalist works the site, they'll get credit for the connection."

Chen was immediately suspicious.

"Which connection are we talking about?"

"Rickey's murder and the Sunset burglaries. Maybe additional murders. Maybe, eventually, to the person or persons who hired the men who killed Alec Rickey."

I was laying it on thick, but I needed John's help.

John said, "Who do they work for?"

"They're looking for something the Sunset crew stole, so, my guess, it's someone the Sunset crew robbed."

"One of the victims?"

"Yes."

"They're important people."

"They are."

"Rich people."

I heard the wheels turning, even over the phone. Chen was seeing the headlines. Seeing himself interviewed by smokin' hot TV babes.

"Pike found shoe prints under a window where entry was made. They'll likely match the prints from the Rickey killing, but only if someone compares the impressions. Another criminalist might not find the link."

"But I would, if I compared them."

"Yes. Unless the second-rater who comes out ruins the prints, and leaves you with nothing."

I laid it on so thick I was using a bulldozer.

Chen said, "I like having my ass kissed, but you're giving me butt-burn."

Maybe too thick.

Chen said, "It's a simple break-in, right? No one was hurt."

"Right."

"They won't send anyone for a couple of days. I'll go tomorrow morning. Early. Is anyone at the house?"

"Pike. I'll tell him you're coming."

I pulled into the carport, let myself into the house, and opened a beer. The only thing I knew was that two Anglo males, one big, one bigger, were searching for a laptop computer stolen by Tyson and his idiot friends.

If Neff and Hensman were working for one of the eighteen homeowner victims, I needed to know who they were.

I found Cassett's card, and gave her a call. I was surprised when she answered, and took this as a good sign.

"Elvis Cole again, Sergeant. Sorry to bother you."

"You gotta be kidding."

"Can I get a list of the eighteen homes these kids hit? It'd be a big help."

The line went dead. Guess the answer was no.

The cat wasn't home. I set out a clean dish anyway, and traded the beer for a water. The veal chop I'd made for Hess was still in the fridge. I ate it leaning against the counter, holding it like a lollipop. Cold.

I washed my hands, tossed the water, and took up where I left off with the beer.

I had worked as a contract investigator for most of the major insurance companies and more than a few of the regional firms. I took out a list of company contacts and began making calls.

Many of my contacts were unavailable, and more were unable to help, but one company wrote policies on three of the homes, and another held policies on two. This gave me names for five of the eighteen burglary victims, six if I included the Slausons. Step aside Batman, make way for BatCole.

I spent almost two hours on the phone without learning more, and was about to call it a Batday when Matt Simms came through. Matt was the V.P.-Director of Operations for a regional company called Landale General Insurance. None of the eighteen victims were insured by Landale, but his company maintained a database of all burglaries occurring in L.A. County. Their data was sourced from police reports and customer claims, and included the eighteen burglaries committed by Tyson and his idiot friends.

Actuaries were awesome.

Matt promised to email the files as quickly as possible. I cracked another beer to celebrate and found an email from Devon. She had forwarded Tyson's billing statement earlier that day. I printed the statement and swung into action. If I kept making this kind of progress, the case would be solved before Devon arrived.

Tyson had called and received calls from only three numbers on the night he left for the minimart. One was Devon's. Another I knew to be Alec's. It didn't take a cape and a cowl to identify the third. I blocked my Caller ID and dialed.

A cheery female voice answered before the ring. Voice mail.

"It's Amber. If you're lucky, I'll get back."

If you're lucky.

I hung up and called a friend named Carla Ellis. Carla worked for a major cell service provider and loved Dodger baseball. I gave her Amber's number, and told her I needed the billing information. Cassett and Rivera would need a court order, but I had something better. A former client paid me with seats in the Dodgers Dugout Club. In the City of Angels, even angels bleed Dodger Blue. Unless they played for Anaheim.

Carla got straight to business.

"Dugout Club, two on an aisle, Bobblehead Night?"

"No problemo."

"Great. Lemme check."

The wait was longer than usual.

"Sorry, man. Different provider. I can get it, but I'll have to trade favors and I may not hear back until tomorrow."

I was more concerned about waiting than favors.

"What do you need?"

"Two on an aisle, any game. Two on an aisle, behind the net, Giants or Cards."

The any-game tickets would be for the trade. The Giants or Cards she'd keep for herself and her husband.

"I need this yesterday, Carla."

"If this was our account, you'd have it now. I'll push for you, Elvis. Hard."

"ASAP."

"First thing tomorrow or sooner."

As soon as possible. Tomorrow or sooner. Neff and Hensman probably weren't waiting for tomorrow. They seemed more like 'sooner' people. They knew more than me, and I was stuck with 'as soon as possible' and 'tomorrow or sooner.'

The cat door clacked in the kitchen. The hard food crunched. I was glad he was home and went to the door and watched him.

"Hey cat."

He didn't look up. He ate.

I finished the beer and stared at the hills across the canyon. They flattened into a band of gray haze in the distance. Hollywood lay beyond the haze, but the haze covered the city like a shawl. I couldn't see it.

I didn't know what to tell Devon, but I had to tell her what I could, and she would have to make a decision she wouldn't like. I didn't know whether Tyson was alive. Neff and Hensman had murdered Alec, and searched his apartment the following day. Maybe they'd found Tyson, and Tyson told them the laptop was at his home, so they murdered him just like they murdered Alec and tore apart his house to find it. Maybe his body would never be found and Devon would never see him again or know what happened, and Neff and Hensman or whoever they were would vanish and no one would know what they had done except them and the person who sent them to do it.

Something bumped my leg. I looked down, and the cat looked up.

I said, "We can't let it happen, can we?"

He did not look away.

22

THE FIRST KISS OF PURPLE had deepened the sky when Devon arrived. I heard her park, and opened the door to greet her. An overnight bag with bright yellow daisies hung from her shoulder.

She said, "Do I really have to stay here?"

First words out of her mouth as I showed her inside.

"No, not at all. Stay with a friend, or at a hotel, or wherever you want. Just not at home. The men who broke in could come back."

She stopped at the edge of the living room, and frowned at the view.

"Your friend, Joe? You didn't tell me you have a partner."

"It didn't come up. Sorry."

"He doesn't say much."

"Words aren't his strong point. Can I take your bag?"

I touched the strap, but she held tight to the bag.

"If he's staying at my house, I don't see why I couldn't stay."

"He's staying in case they come back. If they come back, you shouldn't be there."

The cat came out of the kitchen. He stopped when he saw her, and made a low growl.

Devon said, "You have a kitty."

He spit, jumped sideways, and scrambled into the kitchen. The cat door rattled.

I said, "He's never been right."

She held the bag even more tightly, and blinked as if I were a stranger. Her eyes were too bright, and finally showing the strain.

"Two men. Men with guns. Now there's a man with a gun spending the night in my house. What does this have to do with my son? Where's Tyson?"

I touched the bag again, and this time she slipped the strap off her shoulder. I guided her to the couch.

"I've learned a lot since this morning, and we have to discuss it. I found Alec."

"What about Tyson?"

"I don't know, but he wasn't with Alec. Something happened to Alec, but Tyson wasn't with him. I don't know where he is, but he wasn't with Alec, okay?"

"He wasn't with Alec. I heard you. Stop saying it."

"Alec is dead. He was murdered last night, but Tyson and Amber weren't with him. Alec was alone when the police found his body."

She wet her lips and started to say something. She stopped herself.

"I understand."

"The police found shoe prints left by two men. The men who killed Alec are probably the same men who ransacked your house."

"What does this have to do with Tyson?"

"Tyson and his friends stole a laptop computer. Whoever they stole it from wants it back."

I started with Carl and the flea market, and walked her through everything. I told her about the two detectives who pressed the Crenzas about a laptop, and how Charlotte knew Alec, and that Claudia described two similar detectives who knew Tyson and Amber by name. I was telling her about Louise August when she interrupted.

"I thought the police didn't know about Tyson."

"They didn't, and I'm not sure they do. The head of the task force claims Tyson and his friends haven't been identified."

She squinted and shook her head.

"Then how did they know his name?"

"I don't know if these men are police officers. They say they are, and they know things only cops inside the investigation should know, but badges are easy to come by. Whatever they are, they're running their own investigation. They're two steps ahead of the task force, and they're killing people. We need to decide what to do."

"What about the voluntary surrender?"

"Finding Tyson before a warrant drops isn't important now. We have to find him before the men who found Alec."

"Yes. Of course we do."

"The police can help. Not the task force cops, but ranked officers who aren't part of the task force. If we share what we know, they'll help us."

Devon said, "No."

"Think about it. They can help."

"I'm not going to risk it."

"Devon—"

"You explained. They know everything the police know. They might be real policemen. Maybe they're working for one of these rich people to get this computer back, and taking money on the side. Have you thought of *that*, Mr. Detective?"

"Devon—"

"We're talking about my son. I want you to find him. *You.*"

"I might be able to find him faster if we bring in the cops."

"Don't quit. I'm begging you."

"I'm not quitting."

"Then it's settled. If I have to stay here, I'll stay, but it's settled."

It was settled.

Devon wanted to freshen up, so I showed her to the guest room and put out fresh towels. Having a client browbeat me into settling an issue called for a reward. I helped myself to another beer, and scrounged through the fridge.

Dinner was coming. Bacon, a wedge of romano, a link of andouille a friend sent from Louisiana. I turned up a package of frozen peas, two stalks of asparagus, and a lemon. Inspired. I filled a pot with water, threw in some salt, and kicked up the heat. I took out a skillet and started a sauce. Devon returned a few minutes later wearing jeans, a loose sweatshirt, and pink sneakers. She stood in the door with her hands in her pockets.

"Penne or spaghetti?"

"Whatever you like."

I went with the penne.

She said, "If I was rude before, I'm sorry."

"He's your son. I get it."

She pulled her hands from her pockets and crossed her arms.

"This is awkward, me being here at your house."

"Clients have stayed before. Would you like a beer?"

"No, thank you."

I pointed at the fridge with an elbow.

"Water? I have Diet Coke and tangerine juice. Dinner in five."

She opened the fridge, and studied the contents.

"A beer sounds good."

I drained the pasta, dumped it back in the pot, and added the sauce. We plated the food in the kitchen, and ate in the dining room. The conversation was pleasant, and superficial, as if we needed a break from the reasons we were together.

She said, "How old is your son?"

Her question caught me off guard and surprised me.

"I don't have a son."

She looked just as surprised.

"I'm sorry. I saw the pictures of you and the little boy. I thought he was your son."

I ate more pasta. I sipped the beer.

"A friend's son. Ben. When he visits, he stays in the guest room."

"That's nice."

"Very."

"He looks like a sweet boy. You must be close."

I sipped more beer. This was the part of the evening where she wanted to share.

"We were. Ben and his mom moved here from Louisiana. They lived here for a while, but they didn't stay. They went home."

"Oh, that's too bad. Were you married?"

"I thought we might, but no. She wanted something else."

She nodded and drank some beer.

"Tyson's father wanted something else."

I didn't know what to say, so I changed the subject.

"I'm getting a list of the people who were robbed. Maybe something will suggest who's behind this. We're getting Amber's cell account information, too. If we find Amber, we'll probably find Tyson."

She studied the pasta on her plate.

"Do you think he's dead?"

I glanced up, and found her watching.

"No."

"Maybe they found him. Like Alec. Maybe that's why he doesn't answer."

"He's alive."

She stared, and her eyes glistened, and she blinked hard, but she couldn't stop the tears that dripped down her face. I reached across the table and rested my hand on her arm.

"Keep texting. Warn him. Tell him about Alec and what happened to your house and about the men who are looking for him. He might not know."

"He changed phones. He doesn't answer. I don't know if he gets my messages."

I squeezed her arm. Harder.

"Don't stop, and don't give up. Warn him."

She lifted her phone and held it and the tears fell.

I left her with the phone and took the plates into the kitchen. I put away the leftover pasta, loaded the dishwasher, and opened another beer. I drank it, and put away the bottle, and went back to the living room wondering if I was a drunkard. Devon was by the bookcase. The shelves were unfinished redwood planks, and lined with books I've read many times, and pictures, and personal things.

She said, "I warned him. Would you like to see what I sent?"

"I'm sure it's fine. Text again later. Text early and often."

She smiled, but it was sad. She drank a little beer and tipped the bottle at a picture.

"She was stupid."

"Who are we talking about?"

"Your girlfriend. The girl who wanted something else."

I moved closer, and saw the picture. I had rented a cabin in Lake Arrowhead and taken Lucy and Ben. The three of us had walked to the lake to feed ducks, and Ben and I jumped in the water. When we surfaced, I lifted him over my head. In the picture, I stood waist deep in the lake, holding Ben Chenier over my head like a barbell, our faces silly with laughter. Lucy had taken the picture.

The bottle tipped to the picture again.

"Look at your face. You loved him. Look at his. He adored you. You would have been a wonderful father."

She tapped her bottle against the shelf.

"Stupid. What more could she want?"

She stared at the picture a few moments longer, then glanced at me. Embarrassed.

"I shouldn't have said that. I'm not used to drinking."

"Don't worry about it."

"I'm drunk."

"It's okay."

She apologized some more, and then she went to her room. I climbed the steps to the loft, showered, and put on fresh clothes. When I went down, the guest room door was closed, but light beneath told me Devon was awake. Texting. Sending her son an endless stream of texts, one after another fired into an empty void, only to be unanswered.

I shut off all the lights but one, opened another beer, and called Joe Pike. First ring, he answered.

I said, "Need anything?"

"Uh-uh. How's she doing?"

His voice was low, a whisper from a hidden place.

"Hanging in. Scared. Chen's coming out first thing."

"Tell her I fed the fish."

Took me a beat, but I remembered.

"The aquarium."

"She asked me to feed her fish."

"I'll tell her."

I put the phone aside and studied the calls Tyson had made and received on the night he disappeared.

Tyson had phoned Amber three times and Alec four times on the night Alec died, the longest call being his first, to Amber, which had lasted almost twenty minutes. Alec had phoned Tyson once. Most of their calls lasted between five and eight minutes, with significant gaps between calls. These gaps were probably when Alec and Amber were speaking. I wondered if Alec knew the men who were chasing him, and why he was being chased. I wondered where the chase began, and why it ended as it had, his car flipping over a guardrail, alone in the middle of nowhere. Alec could have delivered himself to police stations, Sheriff's substations, fire stations, LAX with its army of airport police, or a thousand other brightly lit, crowded places. He could have phoned the police instead of Amber, and told them someone was chasing him and that he feared for his life. He didn't. Alec was a wannabe actor with a gun in a bag he showed to girls to impress them. Alec was young, childish, and stupid. Like Tyson and Amber.

The beer and I went outside, and considered the canyon. The night was clear. Homes on the far ridge and along the slopes glittered with golden lights. Families ate dinner and watched television and read books. I wondered what Ben was doing. And Lucy.

I went inside to check on Devon. Her door was still closed, with light beneath, but now I heard crying.

I got my phone and Tyson's number, and took them out onto the deck. I didn't want Devon to hear.

I dialed, and the inevitable beep was my permission.

"My name is Elvis Cole. I'm helping your mother, which means I'm helping you. She's worried. Let her know you're okay. Do it, boy. If you don't, I'll kick your ass when I find you."

I hung up, thought for a moment, then texted the same message.

Father of the Year.

I had more to say, but those things I would tell him in person.

If I found Tyson Connor before the men in the shiny black car.

If I could keep him alive.

23

TYSON CONNOR

TYSON FLOPPED BACKWARD on the living room floor, spread his arms and legs, and made snow angels in the deep blue shag rug. Amber was amazing. Jazzi's apartment with the incredible shag rug and hot tub on the roof was amazing. Jazzi was Amber's sister. She was a flight attendant on private jets, and flew all over the world with rock stars and celebrity DJs and basketball players. Amber and Jazzi hated their mother, so Amber lived with Jazzi. Jazzi was gone a lot.

Amber was taking a shower, so Tyson went into the kitchen, and scrounged a PowerBar, a bag of pickle and sea salt flavored potato chips, and a Diet Coke. Amber and Jazzi didn't keep much food. Tyson was always starving, and couldn't get over how little Amber ate.

Tyson carried the snacks into the living room, and watched red and white streamers on the Ventura Freeway. Tyson had seen freeway traffic at night a million times, but seeing the red and white ribbons from Jazzi's window in her awesome apartment changed them into a scene from a movie, super clear, hyper real, and perfect the way life should be perfect. The view was even better from the roof.

Jazzi's apartment was on the second floor of a two-story, six-unit building in Woodland Hills. The building was right out of a design magazine, with hip black tile and gleaming steel and rough earth-colored stone. Nothing like Tyson's house. Amber had taken him to the roof one night to see the hot tub. They hadn't been in it yet, but she promised they would. The night he saw it with Amber, the hot tub glowed like a magical pool, filled with shimmering green light. Tyson had wanted to slide into the water, and stay in the glow forever.

Tyson was angry at his mother for messing it up. Alec and Amber had freaked when he told them his mother knew about the burglaries and wanted him to turn himself in. Now Alec was missing, and probably wouldn't speak to him again. Amber thought they didn't have anything to worry about, but Tyson wasn't so sure. He managed to sneak eleven thousand dollars from his room the night he left home, and he'd kept all his new clothes at Amber's since his mother made such a stink about the Barneys jacket. If he decided to run, he had money and clothes, but he wasn't sure he wanted to run.

The running water stopped, and the hair dryer came on, high-pitched and loud, even behind the door.

Tyson wondered if his mother had called the police. He hadn't checked his old phone since they got the burners. His old phone was on his mom's account, so Amber was scared the phone company could figure out their location if his phone was on. Tyson was pretty sure this wasn't possible, but Amber didn't believe him.

The hair dryer was blasting. Amber jumped in and out of a shower, but took forever with her hair.

Tyson hopped off the couch, and hurried to Jazzi's bedroom. Jazzi's apartment had two bedrooms. The larger bedroom belonged to Jazzi, and Amber used the smaller. Amber's stuff was in her usual room, so Tyson was bunking in Jazzi's room.

He knelt on the floor beside the bed, took his old phone from his backpack, and pressed the power button. His mother had sent a million texts, and they began loading the instant his phone went live. Zzt, zzt, zzt. All these texts, one after another, ordering him to come home, demanding he respond, pleading. She was livid, but he knew she was worried about him.

Tyson felt pretty bad, and kinda guilty, and then he came to a text much longer than the others.

It stopped him.

> **MOM:** I left this same message on your voice mail. Your friend Alec
> is dead. You must know, don't you? He was murdered, and the men
> who murdered him are looking for you and Amber. You are in
> terrible danger, baby. You took something these men want. A
> laptop, I think. They killed Alec, and other people. They are trying to
> find you and that girl. They will hurt you. Baby, do NOT go home.
> They searched the house, and might be watching. Please call.
> I hired a man. He's helping us. These people killed Alec. Please,
> baby. I don't know if you are alive or dead. I don't know if they
> found you. Please don't be dead. I love you. I want to take care
> of you.

Tyson was reading the text when Amber giggled.

"Dude. She's really good."

Tyson startled, and felt like a dork. Amber was right behind him, and had read the text over his shoulder. Her crooked grin was kind, and made her beautiful face even more amazing.

Tyson said, "You think it's true?"

Amber rolled her eyes, and pushed to her feet.

"It's a story. She wants you to call."

"I'm worried about Alec. How come he hasn't called?"

"Alec is probably under his bed. He totally freaked when you dropped the mom bomb. I told him she was only being dramatic, but Alec, I know Alec, I'm sure he saw policemen everywhere. He's a drama queen."

She swayed to the mirror, and checked herself out. Tyson felt mesmerized. She was the most beautiful, funny, sexiest woman he had ever seen, and she was wonderful.

She spread her hands, and posed. She wore tight black pants, and a shimmery silver top.

"Look okay?"

Tyson said, "Hot."

Her smile was blinding.

"Thank you, sir. You're sweet."

Amber changed the fall of hair across an eye, and considered herself again. She pancaked a hand in a kind of 'en' move, then came back and knelt in front of him. She gazed into his eyes, and her face was thoughtful.

"I hope your mom doesn't tell, but if she does, we'll figure it out."

"I know."

"I'm worried about Alec, too. He gets involved with sketchy people, and doesn't think. Alec isn't a thinker. I hated that gun."

Alec had started carrying a gun, and talked about buying a Porsche, and showed up at clubs wearing these hundred-thousand-dollar watches they stole. This was how people got caught and ended up in jail, so Amber made Alec give her the gun, and straightened him out. Amber wasn't just pretty and nice. Amber was smart.

Tyson said, "Alec's really nice, but I didn't get the gun. I'm glad you took it away from him."

Amber was quiet for a moment, and seemed thoughtful.

"That car. The one he said was following him. I know he's all about the drama, but that was so weird, wasn't it?"

"Yeah."

"Do you think he was followed? For real?"

"I don't think he made it up. He sounded scared."

"Maybe he cut off some dude, and the guy got mad. You know how Alec is."

Amber smelled of cherries, soap, and clean mountain air. Her bottomless eyes were concerned, and searched his for answers.

She touched his cheek.

"I hope he's okay."

"Yeah. Me, too."

Her beautiful eyes saw him, and Tyson fell into her eyes. Amber talked to him, and had since the day they met. She spoke, and heard his answers. She asked his opinion and laughed at his jokes, and when his jokes weren't funny she never made fun of him. They talked for hours, about everything, and she never made him feel stupid, or ashamed, or treated him like a weird little geek. Here was this amazing, beautiful woman, and she didn't see the Tyson other kids saw. She treated him like he mattered. She opened her world to him, and her world was magical. Amber was magic.

She suddenly sat back, and grinned.

"I don't want to sit here all night. Let's go out."

Tyson felt a queasy stab of anxiety.

"I dunno. What if the cops are looking for us?"

She stood, and grabbed his arm to pull him up.

"I look too good to stay home. Are you ashamed to be seen with me?"

Tyson said, "Ha ha."

"Get dressed. Maybe someone at the club heard from Alec."

She went to the door.

"Wear the blue jacket. You'll look really hot. And you're hungry. You're always hungry. We'll eat."

Tyson smiled as she left the room. Amber made him feel like the person he had always been on the inside, and no one had seen, until now.

She called from the living room.

"Hurry up. We'll take my car. It's nicer."

Tyson was changing when his old phone buzzed. He had forgotten to turn it off, and another message had loaded.

He scooped up the phone, hoping Alec had texted, but the message came from an unknown number. He opened the window and stared.

My name is Elvis Cole. I'm helping your mother, which means I'm helping you. She's worried. Let her know you're okay. Do it, boy. If you don't, I'll kick your ass when I find you.

Tyson glanced to see if Amber was coming, and quickly deleted the message. His mother had mentioned a guy who found out the watch was stolen, and this was probably him. Tyson was furious. She was making up stories to scare him, and paying this dude to harass him. His mother was totally out of control.

Amber was right. He should have turned off the phone, and left it off.

He touched the power button to shut down the phone when it buzzed with another incoming message. This time he knew the number. Another message from Cole.

Tyson opened the window.

I mean it.

A-hole!

Tyson turned off the phone as Amber shouted.

"Did you fall asleep?"

"Coming!"

Tyson stuffed the phone in his backpack, pulled on his jacket, and left.

24

JOE PIKE

As TWILIGHT DEEPENED TO NIGHT, Pike sat in shadows between a hedge and Devon's house. The air grew chill in a way he liked. Overhead, stars struggled to be seen through the glow cast by millions of Valley lights. During those hours, Pike watched for black cars and movement. A black Trans Am with a missing grille rumbled past, wheezing blue smoke. A black Chevy coupe with acne corrosion passed in the opposite direction, and two aging black pickups. No gleaming four-door sedans. No police detectives decked with jackets and ties.

As the hour grew later, fewer cars passed, and Pike considered the dirty RV parked in a driveway three houses away. Earlier, after Devon left and before the sun set, Pike walked past the RV for a closer look. It faced the street with a FOR SALE sign taped inside its windshield. Three of its tires were flat, and weathered grime streaked its gray hide with stripes like a bloated zebra. The RV was parked facing the street so people could see the sign, but no one had taken the bait. The ink was faded from undisturbed months in the sun.

At five minutes after midnight, Pike left the shadows beside Devon's home, and circled the sleeping behemoth. He cleaned thumb-sized spots high on the side windows and at the top corners of the windshield, both sides, left and right. When Pike finished this work, he parked his Jeep across from the RV and returned to the darkness beside Devon's house.

Few cars and no people passed.

At one forty-five, a raccoon shambled down a drive, crossed the street, and disappeared behind a shrub. An hour later, a coyote trotted out of the gloom and up the middle of the street. The hill dog was thin, with lean shanks and long, sinewy legs, but its coat was rich, and it moved with determined purpose. Pike slowed his breathing, and watched.

The coyote passed him, but as it reached Devon's drive, the coyote stopped.

Pike's breath was so shallow and slow his chest barely moved, but the coyote's snout came up, and swung toward him. Pike didn't think the coyote saw him, but sensed a presence, or smelled him, and searched for Pike in the darkness. The coyote looked directly at him, but did not run. Pike wondered where the coyote had come from and where it was going, and if it would reach that place before dawn stole its safety. They were miles from hills and canyons, surrounded by humans in a human world. The coyote watched him, but did not run.

Pike spoke, a quiet word.

"Go."

The coyote broke hard away from his voice, and vanished between shadowed houses.

Pike whispered.

"Be safe."

At four a.m., Pike shouldered his pack and returned to the RV. The side of Devon's house was fine at night, but he would need a hide during the day. Pike picked the lock on the flimsy door, and climbed aboard. He cupped a small flashlight with a red lens, and turned it quickly on and off to reveal the tattered interior. He put the light away, moved to the windshield, and peered through the peepholes he'd made in the dirty glass. The passenger's side window gave him a view of the Connor house. The driver's window let him see the street in the opposite direction. Pike lowered his pack, and settled in. Like the coyote, he would stare at the darkness.

At four-thirty, the first sleeping house woke. At four-forty, the second. A white station wagon appeared just before dawn. Small black letters spelled SCIENTIFIC INVESTIGATION DIVISION on its side. Chen, looking for Devon's address.

Chen passed Devon's house, stopped, backed up, and parked in her drive. Pike took out his phone, dialed, and Chen answered.

"Elvis said you'd be here. Where are you?"

Chen climbed out of the wagon and stared at the house.

Pike said, "Don't turn."

"I'm not turning. Where are you?"

"Three houses to your left and across the street. In an RV."

Chen turned, and squinted at the RV.

"John."

Chen turned away

"Sorry. Where's the window?"

"Gate to the right of the garage. The last window on that side of the house. It's her office."

Chen went to the gate and peered down the side of the house.

"Shit, it's really dark. I'll have to light it up."

"Dog next door. He'll bark. The neighbor is Mr. Watkins."

"You coming, or you're stuck in the van?"

"The van. But if you need me, I'll come."

"I've got it. Lemme get to work."

Chen pocketed his phone and went to the wagon. He pulled on a blue Windbreaker with SID printed on the back in large white letters. He shouldered a large bag, turned on a flashlight, and let himself through the gate. Pike heard Toby. Barking. But after a while the barking stopped. Mr. Watkins must've come out.

By the time Chen finished and drove away, the sky was a bright blue dome.

Neighbors left for work or school in a building migration, but the migration finally slowed, and the street settled into a lethargic calm. Breakfast was an apple, a banana, a hard roll, and a bag of trail mix.

The day was only beginning, but Pike was prepared to wait.

He didn't wait long.

The black sedan was only a few hours away.

PART III

THE GIRL WHO WANTED
SOMETHING ELSE

25

ELVIS COLE

MY LOFT WAS BRIGHT with lavender light when I woke. The cat was curled by my head, snoring so softly he might have been purring. He smelled of damp earth and rosemary. Once, I woke to a squirrel's head. Another time, a gopher. He meant well, but he's a cat.

I was enjoying the lavender light when my phone buzzed. Chen.

"Get anything?"

"A couple of partial casts and some pictures. Thin, really shallow impressions, barely three-D, but I got some clean edges. Thank the drought. Dirt was hard as a table."

"Same shoes in Pacoima?"

"Gotta run the pix through the computer, and get my hands on the Pacoima impressions, since, you know, Pacoima isn't my case."

"Thanks, John. Let me know."

"One thing I can tell you. Dude was big, for sure. Size fourteens."

One big, one bigger.

"One pair of shoes, or two?"

"On the face, one. One guy entered through the window and let in the other through a door. These guys know what they're doing."

"Because one guy let in the other?"

Chen laughed.

"New shoes. As in, fresh out-the-box new. And the dude was gloved. I found finger smudges on the window, but no characteristics within the smudges, like his fingertips were blank. You see this with vinyl gloves."

"I don't get the new shoe business."

"You walk around, step on stuff, the heel gets nicked, the sole picks up dings and cuts. A pattern develops, right? It's called a Schallamach pattern. And since no two people walk exactly alike, the Schallamach on your shoe is unique to you."

"Like a fingerprint."

"Yeah. Brand-new shoes, fresh out the box, are like fingerprints with only a couple of swirls. New shoes don't give you much to compare."

One big, one bigger, and now they were smart.

I hung up, feeling glum, but a message from Matt Simms made me feel better. Files on the eighteen known burglary victims were attached. Then an email from Carla Ellis arrived with the billing information for Amber's number. I felt like I was on a roll until I saw that the name on the account wasn't Amber. Carla had sent the email an hour ago, so I decided to call.

Carla was breathing hard when she answered. Music blared and people shouted behind her. Spin class.

Carla said, "Hang on. I can't hear."

When she spoke again the music was muffled.

"Did you get it?"

"I was expecting a different name. You sure this is right?"

"If I wasn't sure I wouldn't have sent it. Stupid."

You see how she is?

"Nora Gurwick?"

"Correct. The account is paid on a Visa card bearing the same name, with the Palisades address as the current billing."

Nora Gurwick. Not Amber.

"Any other names on the account?"

"Uh-uh. Five other numbers for a total of six, but only the one name. It's a commercial account. Accounts like this, the phones are used by employees or family members."

Nora was probably Amber's mother.

"Looks good, Carla. Thanks."

"Giants or Cards, behind the net. Aisle."

"Got a hot dog with your name on it."

Carla said, "Ho ho. I've heard about your little weenie."

Carla was something.

I pulled on a T-shirt and shorts, and crept down to the kitchen. Devon was still in the guest room. I put on a pot of coffee, opened the sliders, and stepped out onto the deck. The air was chill, and a thin mist softened the canyon. I did the Twelve Sun Salutations from the hatha yoga, rolled the last Sun Salute into a slow tae kwon do pattern, then a faster pattern mixed with Tiger and Crane poses, and a third, even faster, sprinkled with Wing Chun forms. I drove from one end of the deck to the other and back again, lunging and spinning until my muscles burned and the deck was sprinkled with sweat. I finished the workout sprawled on my back, my T-shirt wet and growing cold.

Devon said, "Do you do this every morning?"

I craned my head, and saw her upside down. Devon stood in the door.

"Only if the neighbors are watching. How'd you sleep?"

"I'm fine."

She didn't look fine. Her face was pasty and shadows circled her eyes.

"Like some coffee?"

"Yes, please. It smells wonderful."

She followed me into the kitchen. I didn't tell her the coffee came from the stupid woman in Louisiana.

I poured two cups, offered sweetener and milk, then grabbed a towel from the washer. She tasted the coffee.

"It's good."

"Glad you like it."

She sipped again. She didn't lower the cup, but held it close. Maybe the warmth and rich aroma were comforting.

She said, "Was that karate, what you were doing?"

"Some tae kwon do, a little kung fu. I like a mix."

"Tyson loves those movies, all the kicking and everyone flying around. He wanted to do it, so I found one of those places."

"A dojo."

"He was twelve. He didn't like it."

"Seeing is different from doing."

"He said the other kids made fun of him. I never saw anyone make fun, but Tyson believed they did."

Devon fell silent and stared at something beyond the cup. Maybe seeing a younger Tyson kicking and flying.

She said, "He isn't getting my texts. He wouldn't ignore me. He just wouldn't."

I finished my coffee and rinsed the cup.

"Amber's cell account bills to an address in the Palisades. I'll check it out, and maybe Amber and Tyson will be there. If they aren't, maybe someone knows where she is."

Her face sparked to life, as if the chance at finding her son had brought her new hope.

"I'll get dressed."

I stopped her.

"I don't know what I'll find or where it might lead. I'd rather you didn't come."

"You can't be serious. This is my son. I want to help."

I thought for a moment and realized how she could help.

"You will. Come see—"

She followed me to the little desk where I keep my computer. I opened Matt's email, and downloaded the files.

"These are police reports and insurance claims from the eighteen burglaries. Can you open the documents and print copies for me?"

She nodded, and the excitement returned.

"Of course. I know what to do."

"The files will give us names and addresses, but we need background on these people. What they do for a living, whether they've been arrested, things like that. You'll have to dig. Can you do the research while I check out Amber?"

She nudged me out of the way and sat at the computer.

"I'm on it."

"Print whatever you think looks important."

"I'm on it. Find Tyson."

I double-timed up to the loft, showered, and dressed. I was tying my sneakers when the phone rang. Cindy. Cindy ran a beauty supply business from the office next to mine. We dated a few times, but I could count on both hands the times she had called me at home. I scooped up the phone.

"What's up?"

"Not that I ever see you anymore, but if you're coming to your office, you might want to wait until your visitors leave."

"Clients?"

"Police. They asked when you'd be in. I told'm you don't come in anymore, not since you got me pregnant."

"Detectives?"

"That's what it said on their badges."

"Two men? One big, one bigger?"

"Two men, but they weren't all that big. I wasn't like, wow, I'm wet."

"Did you really have to say that?"

"You love it when I talk dirty. Anyway, I asked if they wanted to leave a message. They didn't."

"Did they enter my office?"

"I don't think so. I heard them try the knob. They walked down to the end of the hall, then they came back and stood around by the elevator. I think they left, but I can't be positive."

"Thanks, buddy. I'll stay clear."

"Smart. Smart makes me more wet than big."

I finished tying the shoes, and considered my wardrobe. Faded stone-washed jeans, blue mesh sneakers, and a blue-and-white rayon Hawaiian shirt sporting a stylish tropical design. Detective couture, but lacking certain accessories. I added a brushed leather Bianchi shoulder holster, a Dan Wesson .38-caliber revolver, and a lightweight, dark blue sport coat to cover the gun. Devon was still at the computer. The printer was already printing.

She said, "My. Don't you look nice."

One night at my house, we were Ozzie and Harriet.

"I don't know how long I'll be, but you aren't a prisoner. If you want to go out, fine, but let me know."

"I'm staying here to print these things. I'll call work and tell them I won't be in."

"If you hear from Tyson, call me. If anything happens, call me. If you need anything, call."

"I will. Thank you. Now please let me work."

Ozzie leaves for the office. Harriet tends to the house. I felt like I should give her a peck on the cheek, but I left to find Amber.

I worked my way down through Laurel Canyon to the flats, turned west on Sunset Boulevard, and aimed for the ocean. Pacific Palisades waited at the end of the line, where Sunset met the sea, but I didn't make it out of my neighborhood. A dark sedan swerved around a taco truck, and powered up behind me, so close they could kiss my bumper, so close I saw the men in the car clearly.

Two men.

Big men.

26

I DIDN'T STOMP on the gas or scream across oncoming lanes or fishtail away in a cloud of burning rubber. I pretended I didn't see them. I stayed in the right lane, and drove as if having a car ride my butt two inches away happened every day. Normal. I slipped the Dan Wesson from its hiding place, and put it between my legs.

Devon's neighbor described a black car, but cars were easy to change. The neighbor was older, so maybe the dark gray car looked black.

I drove another two blocks until I came alongside a cement truck in the left lane. I eased a few feet ahead of the truck, put on my blinker, and changed lanes. The gray car didn't give ground. They cut in front of the truck, swerved only enough to avoid a collision, and stayed on my tail. The truck driver locked his brakes and leaned on his horn. I put on my blinker again, and eased into the left turn lane at La Cienega. The left turn signal was red. I wanted to stop. I wanted to see what the men in the car would do.

I gripped the Dan Wesson, touched the brake, and eased to a stop. The gray car stopped with me. The two men were close in the mirror. Their faces were ruddy, grim, and flat as piss on a plate. Their sport coats, ties, and sunglasses were straight out of Central Casting. POLICE DETEC-TIVES. I wanted them to be Neff and Hensman. I wanted them to get out of their car. They didn't.

The cement truck pulled up beside them. The truck's horn bellowed and the driver shouted curses and threats. Neither man reacted or responded. They stared ahead. At me.

When the signal changed from red to green, I turned south on La Cienega. The dark gray car turned with me, and stayed on my butt like a barnacle. They didn't try to stop me or interfere with me or run me off the road or shoot me. They sure as hell didn't hide. They followed, and stayed on my tail.

I was trying to figure out why they were riding my tail and what I could do about it when my phone rang. The Caller ID surprised me. The incoming number read ELVIS COLE. Someone was calling from my office.

I answered.

"Who is this?"

A female voice responded.

"Cole? It's Sergeant Cassett. How are you doing this morning?"

Cheery.

"What are you doing in my office?"

"Waiting for you. We need to talk."

I drove south, keeping an eye on the men behind me.

"I'm busy, Cassett, and I don't appreciate you breaking into my office. Make an appointment."

"See the car in your mirror?"

I glanced at the men.

"Of course I see them, Cassett. They're on me like rust."

"My guys. A couple of SIS units are on you, too, but I'm guessing you haven't seen them. Is the gray car still behind you?"

I glanced at the men again.

"Yes."

"Wave bye-bye."

The dark gray car fell off my tail like a tumbling rock, and was gone.

"What do you want?"

"What I said. I'm here at your office, and I'd like us to talk. I'd appreciate it if you made the time."

She was being nice, but only after she flexed her muscles.

"The dicks in the gray car, what are their names?"

"Quirkmeyer and Baines."

"You send them up to my office earlier?"

"I did. Did you really make the woman in the next office pregnant?"

Maybe she thought she was being funny. Maybe she thought she was
being friendly. I didn't laugh.

"Make the time, Mr. Cole. It's important. I'll explain when you get
here."

"I'll be there in five."

Eight minutes later I parked in the parking garage, climbed the four
flights to my floor, and walked down the hall. The building has an elevator, but tough guys climbed stairs. Picture me bristling with manliness.
Also, impatience. Cindy's door was closed. The door to the little insurance
agency across from my office was closed. My door was open.

I walked in and found Cassett.

My office suite included two rooms, and came with a little balcony off
the main room. The main room was my office. The back room belonged
to Pike, but Pike didn't want an office, and left the room empty. Maybe the
emptiness added to his mystique. I had a desk, a couple of director's chairs
for meetings with clients, and a couch. A little fridge sat opposite the
couch beneath a Pinocchio clock. Pinocchio's eyes swept the room as it
tocked.

Cassett was alone on the couch, watching the eyes.

I said, "Where's Rivera?"

She stood, but offered neither her hand nor a smile.

"I wanted to speak privately. I thought your office would be the best
place."

I checked Pike's office. Empty. I checked the balcony. Empty. Maybe
Rivera was under the desk.

"You couldn't call, say how about we get together? You had to make a big show?"

She studied me like she was having second thoughts, then took the same seat, crossed her legs, and glanced at the fridge.

"You wouldn't have a bottle of water, would you?"

"I would, but the water is for people who don't break into my office."

She smiled.

"You're going to make this hard, aren't you?"

"What did you want to talk about, Cassett? I'm busy. I've got a mani-pedi on deck."

She uncrossed her legs, shifted, and crossed the other leg.

"You lied."

"True. I'm not getting a mani-pedi."

"You're not sniffing around after claim money. Doesn't line up with the Elvis Cole people describe."

"Those people haven't seen my credit card bills."

"I don't think so, Cole. Whatever you're doing, you're on the job. You're in this for a client."

She was edging closer to something, but I didn't like the direction.

"Yeah, Cassett, I am. Me. Like I said."

"The people I talked to, even the dicks who hate you, say you're for real about the confidentiality thing. The more I thought about it, the more it made sense. You're lying to cover a client."

"Get out of my office, Cassett. Please."

She raised her palms.

"I'm not accusing you. I'm not saying you're breaking the law or involved in anything crooked."

"Then what?"

"I'm saying I understand why you've been shading the truth. I get it. I really do. But the shit's getting deep, and you seem to know a lot more than me, so we're here—"

She spread her arms.

"—in your office, just us, alone with Pinocchio—"

She raised her hands to the clock and made a weird face.

"—because I need more than you've been giving. I need some honesty here. I need help, even if you have to violate a confidence."

I took two bottles of water from the fridge, gave a bottle to Cassett, and sat at my desk with the other. We unscrewed the caps at the same time, and drank at the same time.

I said, "Talk to me."

"Louise August."

"And?"

"I followed up. Funny, how you dropped her name."

"Told you I had something, didn't I?"

"She was murdered, which I'm sure you knew. Her skull was crushed, supposedly during a robbery."

"Supposedly."

"You believe she was murdered for a different reason?"

"She may have had information about one or more of the burglars. If so, I don't know what, but she may have been murdered by a person or persons who is trying to find them."

She leaned toward me, frowning.

"Trying to find the kids committing the burglaries?"

"Yes."

"For what reason?"

"Don't know."

"You dropped two other names. Neff and Hensman. Did they kill her?"

"Don't know."

"They told you Ms. August had information?"

"I lied about that part. I haven't met them."

"Then why did you say they had?"

"I wanted to see if you knew them."

"How would I know them?"

"They told the Crenzas they worked for you."

"Martin and Marge?"

"Flashed badges, identified themselves as police, and said they worked on your task force. Ask the Crenzas. Ask them about Louise August."

She stared at me for a very long time. I wondered what she was thinking, but her face was empty. She finally sat back.

"Anything else?"

"Nada."

"I still don't know how you're involved."

"I didn't tell you."

She stared a few seconds longer.

"I can live with it. For now."

She stood, and tipped her water at the Pinocchio clock.

"How do you expect people to take you seriously with this thing on the wall?"

"He's up there for me, Cassett. I don't give a damn what people think."

She looked at me and smiled.

"Yeah. I heard that about you."

She tossed the water bottle to me and left. I listened to her footsteps fade, then closed the door, locked it, and went through my desk. Nothing seemed disturbed, and nothing was missing.

27

PACIFIC PALISADES LAY at the edge of the world where Los Angeles kissed the sea. Safe and secure between Santa Monica on the south, Malibu on the north, and Brentwood on the east, the Palisades offered a desirable location for affluent Angelenos. The Riviera Country Club made the location even more desirable. Rich people liked golf.

The address for Nora Gurwick led along gentle streets lined by gracious homes into hills overlooking the ocean. Most of the homes were immaculate Spanish or Mediterranean villas, reminiscent of an earlier time and rich with genteel elegance. More Ross Macdonald than Raymond Chandler.

Nora Gurwick lived on a cul-de-sac. The buy-in price was steep, but Nora's home was neither elegant nor genteel. It was newly built, ugly, and faced with marble, granite, and steel, as out of place on the lovely street as a fly in a glass of juice.

I cruised to the end of the cul-de-sac, looking for Tyson's car, but no aging brown Volvos were present.

An older woman wearing breeches and riding boots pushed a stroller out of a driveway and into the street. I stopped to let her cross. She smiled, thanking me. I smiled, saying take your time. A tiny hand reached from the stroller and waved at the sky.

When the woman and baby were out of the street, I idled back to the house.

Black concrete steps the size of small patios climbed to a courtyard entry with an oversized steel door. Bright green bamboo inside the courtyard towered above the door and the house. Black camera domes watched the street and the courtyard from white marble walls. A keypad entry topped by another dome waited beside the door. I walked up the steps, pushed the ringer, and waited. I felt like I was back at the Slausons. A lot of ringing, but no one answered.

"She's gone."

The woman with the stroller was across the street.

"Nora?"

"I think she's in Banff. Or maybe it's Aspen. She travels."

She made a little smirk when she said it. I liked the smirk. The smirk told me she had more to say and might be willing to say it if I gave her the chance.

I made my way down the oversized slabs and joined her. The baby arched her back, and smiled.

"Your baby's a doll."

The woman adjusted the baby's blanket.

"My granddaughter. Number three, and a fourth on the way."

"Wonderful news. Congratulations."

I wiggled my fingers and made a face. The baby laughed and kicked, and her grandmother and I laughed along. We were all so happy, I asked about Amber.

"Actually, I'm not here to see Nora. I'm looking for Amber. Has Amber been around?"

The laugh and the smile faded.

"Is that poor girl in trouble again?"

Trouble.

"A friend of hers. A boy. I'm hoping Amber can help."

"Like mother, like daughter. What a mess."

I introduced myself and gave her a card.

Rae Bracken's grip was firm, and her manner was relaxed and casual, like a person who was comfortable with herself.

She studied the card and handed it back.

"I've never met a private detective before."

I tried to give modest.

"The others are kind of a letdown."

She blinked, and then she laughed.

"You're funny. I like funny."

"Good. A girl's first should be special."

The laugh became a grin.

"And a flirt. I'm liking you even more."

Mr. Likable.

"Has Amber been around? I need to ask her a few questions."

She made a 'who knows?' face.

"I haven't seen poor Amber in months. They fight."

"Amber and her mother?"

"All three. It's like a reality show over here, the trashy mother with all the ex-husbands, duck lips out to here—"

Rae held a hand a foot from her mouth to show me.

"—one drama after another, all the fighting and nagging and craziness. No wonder those girls are a mess."

Girls.

"Does Amber have a sister?"

"Jazzi. Jazzi's older. She got out of Dodge as soon as she could. And who could blame her, all the fighting."

"Is Jazzi's last name Gurwick?"

"Reed. Same as Amber. Reed was the first husband."

She arched her eyebrows and tipped her head at the house.

"Dick's the fifth."

"Dick is Nora's husband?"

"Was. Past tense. Probably got sick of those lips."

The baby began to fuss. Rae picked her up, and bounced her.

"Amber could be with Jazzi. When the fighting got *really* bad, Amber would stay with her sister. She should've moved out sooner, you ask me. Maybe she wouldn't've been such a mess."

Amber being a mess reminded me of something she mentioned earlier.

"You said Amber's been in trouble."

She frowned at the house, but whatever caused the frown was hidden by marble and granite.

"One thing after another, to hear Nora tell it. Drugs, boys, all the acting out and wild behavior."

"Was she ever arrested?"

"I don't think so, but I don't know. They've only lived here the three years."

Rae stroked her granddaughter's head. She snuggled the baby close as she looked at me.

"She tried to kill herself. Twice that I know of."

"Amber?"

She nodded.

"The ambulance woke us. I thought she'd done it again when I saw the police."

She glanced at the house when she said it, and I glanced with her.

"The police were here?"

"Yesterday. Someone broke in."

"Yesterday during the day?"

"I guess. I was at the barn. When I got home, the street was blocked, and I thought, oh my God, Amber has finally done it. I couldn't get past the police cars."

"Scary. Did the officers tell you what happened?"

"Just that someone broke in and I shouldn't worry. I guess the alarm went off. They didn't say very much."

"Have you seen a black sedan recently, here in the cul-de-sac?"

"Like a limo?"

"Could be, I guess. A four-door sedan with dark windows. Black."

She made a half-hearted shrug.

"A car is a car."

"Would you have a phone number or an address for Jazzi?"

"No, but Nora left her cell. She says to me, if Dick shows up with a truck, call me right away. Can you imagine, like I want to get involved in their divorce?"

"Drama."

The baby kicked and fussed, and Rae bounced her again, but this time the bouncing didn't help.

"Let me give her to the housekeeper and I'll be back with Nora's number."

Rae Bracken bounced her granddaughter into her house, and I returned to Nora's. With all the cameras dotting her home, Nora Gurwick almost certainly subscribed to a security service. I found their sign by the garage. WHITE SHIELD HOME PROTECTION. Twenty-four-hour surveillance. Armed response. I studied the camera domes on Nora's house, and liked what I saw. The Slausons' surveillance cameras had snagged a picture of Tyson, so maybe Nora's cameras returned the favor. Maybe they recorded the person or persons who broke into Amber's house, and White Shield was willing to share.

Rae Bracken returned with Nora's number a few minutes later. I called, and got the inevitable voice mail.

"Hi, this is Nora. Please leave a message, and I'll return your call."

Nora's voice message surprised me. She sounded normal.

I left my name, number, and a message I hoped she couldn't resist.

"Rae Bracken gave me your number. I have information about Dick you'll find helpful."

I put down the phone, and thought about White Shield. They probably wouldn't share with a private investigator they didn't know, but Dave Deitman might have better luck. I called him.

"I need some info about a White Shield account. You have an in over there?"

"One or two, maybe. Whatcha need?"

I gave him Nora's address and explained.

"The house is covered with cameras, so they'll have video. I need a shot of the people who entered. Two cameras in front look like they cover the street. If they caught a black sedan roll past, I want it."

"This tied in with the Slausons?"

"If it's who I think it is, yes. If a bunch of teenage girls broke in to party, then no."

Dave told me to give him a few minutes, but I waited for almost twenty before he called.

"Wasn't a bunch of girls."

"Two men? Big guys?"

"No video. They got nothing, bud."

"Waitaminute. I'm outside the house. I'm looking at cameras."

"Somebody put'm to sleep. Near as White Shield can tell, somebody hacked the homeowners' system through the Wi-Fi, which isn't easy to do."

"What about the alarm? The police rolled out."

"Pool boy called'm. You know who did this?"

"No."

"You telling the truth?"

"When I know who did it I'll tell you."

"Must've been something real nice inside."

"Why?"

"It takes custom equipment and rare skills to do what they did. People like these, they're for real. Not just anyone can do this."

I hung up and stared at the house.

One big, one bigger, smart, with rare skills.

The two men found Nora's home a full day before me. They found the Crenzas before me, Louise August before me, and Alec before me. If they found Jazzi before me, their winning trend would continue. Maybe they already had, and Tyson and Amber were dead, but I did not believe it.

Since I wasn't smart and didn't have rare skills, the answer was obvious. The only way I could find Tyson was with Tyson's help.

I figured out what I wanted to say, and tapped out a message.

> The men who killed Alec want a laptop you stole. They killed a woman named Louise August to find you. Google her. They know who you and Amber are, and where you live. They've searched your homes. If your mother had been there, she would be dead. You can't run or hide from these people. Remember the Terminator? They are the Terminator. They will find you and Amber, and it won't matter whether you have their computer. You understand this, right? They do not leave witnesses. You're smart. Think. Talk to me.

I sent the text, and waited.

The phone didn't buzz.

Tyson didn't respond.

After a while I felt stupid and angry, and put the phone aside.

Not just anyone can do this.

I started my car and got on with the hunt.

28

TYSON CONNOR

THEY WERE SEATED on the patio of a popular vegan café in West Holly-wood. The patrons around them were young, hip, and stylishly posed, sip-ping herbal tea from Peru or Spanish soy lattes. Tyson felt like a kid at the zoo, spying on exotic beasts who could not see him. When Tyson and Amber arrived, the sidewalk had been crowded with people waiting to be seated, but Amber grabbed his hand and pulled him through the crowd to a girl with a clipboard. Two minutes later, they were shown to a table.

Amber said, "I love this place. Isn't it great?"

Tyson said, "Yeah."

Tyson covered his phone when the waitress delivered their food. A wild mushroom tofu scramble for Amber, avocado toast with black bean cho-rizo and cashew crema for him. Everything was organic, plant-based, and contained no animal products. Tyson didn't think he would like it.

The waitress spoke to Amber.

"Can I bring you anything else?"

Amber made this amazing smile.

"This looks fantastic. Thank you so much."

The waitress glanced briefly at Tyson.

"You okay?"

"Fine. Thanks."

Amber said, "I love your earrings."

The waitress rolled her eyes.

"Boyfriend medicine."

"Girl, don't I know!"

They laughed together like besties forever. Tyson had seen Amber's magic too many times to count, but it still left him awed. People fell in love with her.

When the waitress left, Tyson uncovered his phone, and turned it so Amber could see.

"Do you know this lady?"

Amber glanced at the picture.

"She kinda looks familiar."

"She lived in Venice, close to the flea market. It says she was a regular. Maybe you and Alec met her."

Amber studied the picture, and slowly nodded, like she remembered, but wasn't positive.

"Maybe, yeah. Who is she?"

"Her name was Louise August."

Tyson glanced at the picture and article he'd found online.

"She was murdered. Like Alec."

Amber frowned and pushed his phone away.

"Please stop reading this stuff. It makes me sad. It makes me sad and upset, and I don't want to be upset."

Posts about Alec had been appearing on Facebook, and then Cole mentioned Louise August. Tyson Googled her, and learned she was a seventy-six-year-old woman who sold handmade pillows, dolls, and stuffed animals at the flea market. Beloved by neighbors and known for her kindness, she had been bludgeoned to death.

Tyson lowered his voice so the people nearby wouldn't hear.

"My mom was right about Alec. What if they're connected?"

"She isn't right. Not how you mean."

"Alec was shot!"

A dude at a nearby table looked, and Tyson felt himself flush.

Amber said, "Yes, and I'm really upset, but Sophia said it was road rage. You know what Alec was like. He probably flipped off some crazy gang-banger."

Sophia knew Alec from his job waiting tables. Tyson had seen her post on Alec's Facebook page the night before, and searched for more. None of the posts mentioned the burglaries, but Tyson was worried. The facts he found fit with the claims his mother and Cole had made. He even thought about sneaking home to see if their house had been searched, but decided against it. The police might have set a trap. Or Cole.

Tyson said, "The road rage thing is just a theory. The police don't know what happened. They said so on the news. They're investigating."

Amber leaned across her tofu. She opened her eyes really wide, as if her eyes were saying this should be obvious.

"Nobody. Knows. Who. We. Are."

Cole knew. And according to Cole, the men who killed Alec knew.

"I hope you're right."

"I'm right. If they knew, we'd be in jail."

"Not knowing works both ways."

She shook her head and spread her hands.

"Confused. I have no idea what you just said."

Tyson lowered his voice even more.

"We don't know who we robbed. We walked into houses. We don't know who lived there. What if we robbed the Godfather? The Godfather doesn't call the police. He sends Luca Brasi. Hitmen."

Amber straightened. She pursed her lips, and her pretty face grew hard.

"You're really becoming a pain."

"I'm not trying to be a pain."

She picked at the mushrooms.

"You started all this. You and your stupid mother."

Tyson felt himself flush again, and stared at his food. He didn't want

Amber to be mad. Amber was the greatest thing that ever happened to him.

They sat in silence, and Tyson stared at his food until Amber finally spoke.

"These mushrooms are really good."

Tyson tasted the black bean chorizo. The texture was weird and the cashew crema left a film in his mouth.

"This chorizo is really good, too."

"The Godfather didn't kill Alec, all right? That's a story your mother made up to fit your confession. You wrote the script for her."

Tyson felt embarrassed, but kinda angry.

He said, "Yeah. You're probably right."

"Don't freak, okay? That's how people get caught."

"I'm not freaking."

"Talking about hitmen sounds like you're freaking. *Hitmen.*"

She rolled her eyes.

"All I'm saying is we should find out what happened to Alec, and whether my mom is right about anything else."

Amber put down her fork.

"No, you're saying you want to go home to Mommy and turn yourself in."

Tyson hated the word 'mommy.' A man had a mother. A child had a mommy. Amber called her mother Nora. Like they weren't even related.

"I don't want to go home."

"Well, duh. How else can you find out what's happening? Was your house really searched? Go home and see. Did the Godfather kill Alec? Go home. You and your mommy can ask the police."

"I'm not going home."

"Then stop going on about it."

Amber picked up her fork, hesitated, then put it down.

"You broke my heart."

Her statement dropped out of nowhere and rocked him.

"What are you talking about? I didn't do anything."

"I trusted you, and you betrayed me. You betrayed all of us. When you confessed."

Tyson's face and neck burned with shame.

"I didn't tell about you. Or Alec."

"We had a secret, and you told. We promised we wouldn't tell anyone, and you told."

"I didn't tell her about you. I *didn't*."

"You did. You told her even without saying my name. Don't you get it? We are *blessed*. We have all this money and cool friends and we go to great clubs and we're having so much fun, and nobody knew. Everything was fine. Perfect. Then you told and now we're hiding at my sister's and you're peeing your pants about *hitmen*."

The dude at the next table looked again, and this time he stared.

Amber noticed, and stared back. She slowly stood, never looking away, and leaned toward him so far she seemed boneless.

"Did I get loud? So sorry. Please enjoy your oolong and stay the fuck out of our business."

The dude turned his chair.

Amber sat, made an 'eek' face only Tyson could see, and took a bite of her tofu.

Tyson said, "I'm sorry."

"I know. I don't blame you, baby. She caught you off guard. She jammed you up with that guy she hired."

Tyson said, "Yes."

He didn't know what else to say.

"We're having a blast, aren't we? Please don't screw it up."

"I won't."

"You haven't eaten your breakfast."

"I'll grab a couple of tacos."

She smiled.

"Then pay up, cowboy. I want to go shopping. There's a great taco place on the way. You'll love it."

She was on her feet in an instant.

"Meet you at the valet. Gotta pee."

Tyson studied the people on the patio as Amber left. Heads turned. Girls checked her out. The dude at the next table stared at her ass.

Tyson signaled the waitress for their check, and reread the texts from Cole. He had wanted to show Amber the texts, but Amber was so weird about it he didn't. Tyson hadn't told her about Cole, or the texts and messages his mother left. Amber didn't want them using their old phones, so he kept his hidden or turned off unless he was alone, which was usually in the bathroom. Sometimes, when he listened to the voice mails his mother left, he covered his face with a towel. He didn't want Amber to hear him cry.

Amber wouldn't talk about Alec or how he died, and totally weirded out when he mentioned the hitmen, but Amber had recognized Louise August, and the old lady was murdered three days before Alec was killed.

They killed a woman named Louise August to find you.

The more Tyson read about Alec and the old lady, the more he believed Cole and his mother. Alec had been killed by a couple of guys who wanted one of the laptops they stole, and now they were looking for him and Amber.

They've searched your homes. If your mother had been there, she would be dead.

The waitress placed a dish with the check by his arm, and walked away. Thirty-four dollars.

Tyson reread Cole's message again. He had read it so many times he knew it by heart, but reading it made him feel stronger.

> They will find you and Amber, and it won't matter whether you
> have their computer. You're smart. Think.

Tyson had thought about it a lot, and was still thinking. If these guys were killing people to find a laptop, something pretty damned valuable or really bad dangerous was on it. Either way, the person who owned it was scared shitless someone would find whatever was on it.

Tyson tucked the old phone into his pocket, and stood to pay the bill.

The dude at the next table glanced over. The dude had this face, and Tyson knew what he was thinking. Loser. Geek. Must be her brother.

Tyson took out a roll of cash, peeled off a hundred, and tucked it under the bill.

The smirker watched. His eyes followed the money.

Geek.

Tyson peeled off a second hundred, then a third, and dropped them onto the first. He glanced at the smirker, and walked away.

Keep the change.

Loser.

29

HARVEY AND STEMMS

STEMMS CALLED YESTERDAY. Harvey called earlier that morning, twenty minutes after the law office opened for business. Both times, a receptionist told them Devon Connor was unavailable.

The Law Offices of Klinger & Klinger occupied a small, three-story building on Ventura Boulevard in Encino. Six partners, four associates, and staff. A parking level beneath the building was accessible from the street and elevators in the lobby. Security cameras covered the lobby and the parking level, but Stemms sauntered into the lobby the day before and checked the garage. Harvey checked again ten minutes ago. Devon Connor's Audi had not been present on either occasion. Her son's brown Volvo had not been present at school.

Harvey and Stemms were parked outside the Klinger & Klinger building. Stemms dialed, with Harvey watching from the passenger side.

Female. Not young, but not old.

"Klinger and Klinger. How may I direct your call?"

Stemms said, "Ah, we're delivering a gift of tropical fish today. I'd like to confirm your address and hours, please."

The woman said, "Tropical fish?"

"Yes, ma'am. That's right. Three tetras, a cherry barb, and two angelfish."

Harvey shook his head.

The woman said, "They're alive?"

"Yes, ma'am. That's why I have to confirm. Wouldn't do if no one's home, would it?"

Stemms made a friendly chuckle.

"Who's the gift for?"

"Ah, they were ordered for delivery to, ah, a Ms. Devon Connor. Is Devon a lady's name? I might be wrong about the Ms."

"Ms. Connor isn't in."

"Well, okay. Will someone be there to accept delivery for her?"

"They're alive?"

"In a little bowl. Live delivery is guaranteed."

"I'm sorry. We can't accept delivery."

"I understand. What time tomorrow would be good?"

"We can't accept delivery."

"I understand, but the gift is for a Ms. Connor, the gift of living crea-tures. So if she isn't available today, what time tomorrow may we deliver?"

"She won't be in tomorrow."

"Okay. That's fine. If tomorrow won't work, when should we bring her fish? They're alive, you know."

"Ms. Connor will be out for several days. We can't be responsible."

"Alrighty then. I hope they don't die."

Stemms winked at Harvey and ended the call. Harvey burst out laughing.

"The gift of living creatures? You asshole! I hope they don't die? And you call *me* an asshole!"

Harvey laughed like a hyena.

Stemms didn't like it.

"Something's up. She's out for a few days."

"She's helping her kid. Watch, she's probably getting him out of the country."

"They're here. No one's tried to arrest the kid. No one's dropped a warrant. Why leave the country?"

"Let's swing by the house, and see what's what. Maybe they're watching TV. Sound better?"

"Don't be patronizing."

"I'm serious. If they didn't split for Manchuria, they should be home, right? If not, we can plant a gizmo."

Stemms nodded. Grudging.

"Makes sense."

"Of course it makes sense. I am the Master and Commander of sense. Then we can drop the box downtown, and get to work on the honeys."

The box being a laptop they pulled from the Gurwick home, the honeys being Amber and her sister, Jasmine. Jasmine was a new discovery, and likely to prove fruitful.

After checking Tyson Connor's school the previous day, they had driven to a house in the Palisades where they hoped to find Amber. Instead, they found a tasteless, five-bedroom home, and learned Amber had a sister named Jasmine.

Amber and Jasmine had separate bedrooms and baths in the Palisades house, but the absence of soiled clothes and linens, near-empty closets and drawers, and undisturbed dust in their bathtubs made it clear the sisters lived elsewhere. Harvey and Stemms had searched for their current addresses, but found nothing.

Unlike the Connor boy's mother, Nora Gurwick kept almost no financial or billing records, which meant an accountant probably paid her bills. What she kept were huge, poster-sized photographs of herself plastered all over the house. In some, she wore bikinis, in others, yoga pants, and in others, skin-tight silvery dresses cut so high they rode her butt cheeks. Fake tits, a spray tan, and duck lips gave her the look of a third-rate showgirl.

Harvey considered one of the posters and shook his head.

"Is this the picture of low self-esteem or what?"

They scored two vials of coke from her nightstand, a third vial in an enormous walk-in closet, a couple bottles of Adderall, and two tabs of what Harvey believed was MDMA, not to mention the medical marijuana they found in a yoga room filled with candles and crystals and prisms.

They took a laptop from the mother's bedroom, which was the only computer device in the house. It wasn't the laptop they were sent to recover, but it might give them a lead to the girl.

The real leads came from Amber's room, and Jasmine's. A couple of photographs left in a drawer, a couple of names, and matchbooks from bars and dance clubs a barfer would frequent.

Stemms found some old snapshots of Jasmine. She appeared to be three or four years older than Amber. Nice-looking girl. Ponytail. Played soccer in high school. One in particular, he liked.

Now, outside the law office, Stemms was thinking about Jasmine when Harvey interrupted his thoughts.

"I agree."

Stemms fired up the Chrysler.

"Agree with what?"

"I can read your mind, Stemms. Like a swami. I agree."

Stemms pulled away from the curb.

"Second time. What?"

Harvey settled back and crossed his arms.

"Jasmine. You're thinking Jasmine's our go-to lead."

Stemms nodded. Impressed.

"Damn, Harvey. You're right."

"So let's get this other stuff out of the way, and go find us some Jasmine."

Stemms glanced at Harvey, and grinned.

"Outstanding idea, Harvey. Outstanding."

Stemms turned north toward the Connor house, thinking about Devon's absence from work and the boy's absence from school. She would want to know if a warrant had been issued for her son's arrest. They had likely gone into hiding, and would remain in hiding until she knew.

Stemms believed their home would be empty, but Stemms was wrong.

The Connor home was not empty.

Someone was waiting.

30

JOE PIKE

THE BLACK SEDAN APPEARED at ten fifty-five. A shiny four-door Chrysler with tinted windows.

The car approached from behind him, so Pike didn't see it until the car passed the RV, heading toward Devon's home. Brake lights flared. No plate. The license frame held a dealer's cardboard filler, too far to read.

The car picked up speed as it passed the house and turned at the next corner. Gone.

The RV was warm and growing warmer. Heavy dust on the windshield and windows cast the interior with ocher light. Pike wiped sweat from his face. If these were the men who searched Devon's home, they would have returned for more than a drive-by. Pike decided the slow pass was a first pass. He moved to the opposite peephole, and sipped from a bottle of water.

Two minutes later, the black car reappeared. Man driving, man in the shotgun seat. Pike couldn't make out their faces, but they wore jackets and ties. No plate in front, same as the rear. A white rectangle showed in the windshield's lower left corner. This would be the car's registration, which any police officer would expect on a new car without plates.

Pike moved fast to the opposite peephole.

This pass, the black car slowed to a crawl. Devon's garage door opened, stopped halfway up, and closed. Pike was impressed by the forethought.

They had paired a remote to the garage door opener. Now they knew her garage was empty.

The car reached the corner, and once again turned.

Pike considered returning to his Jeep, but an empty garage meant little. Pike decided to wait.

Four minutes later, the black car surprised him. He expected it to approach from behind, same as it had the first two passes, but this time it reappeared at the corner where it had turned. The car stopped, and a man wearing a sport coat, tie, and slacks got out of the passenger side. The car continued across the intersection, and the man walked up the street toward Devon's house.

Pike readied his camera.

The man was tall, bigger than Pike, but not so big he would draw attention. Fit. Dark hair, trimmed close. Lean cheeks and broad shoulders. Pike snapped three pictures with a telephoto lens, checked the focus, snapped two more, and stowed the camera.

When the man reached Devon's drive, he pulled on vinyl gloves. The garage door lifted. The man ducked under the rising door, and the door trundled down. Pike phoned Cole.

"They're here. One in the house, one in the car."

"What's the tag?"

"No tag. Looks new. Four-door, black, the dark tint."

"Think they're cops?"

"Does it matter?"

Cole hesitated.

Pike said, "It isn't a D-ride."

"Get pictures. Let's see where they go."

Pike stowed his phone.

The garage door opened a little over three minutes later. The man ducked out, and went to the side of the garage. He checked to see if anyone was watching, took something from his pocket, and placed it high on the garage by a sidelight. He made an adjustment to whatever he put by the light, then walked to the street as the black car appeared at the corner.

Pike slung his pack, bailed out of the RV, and saw the tall man get into the sedan. He waited until the car turned, then ran for his Jeep. He pulled a tight U and powered hard to the corner, and saw the black sedan three blocks ahead. Pike closed the gap, and they made it easy.

They were men in no particular hurry. They drove within the speed limit, stopped for yellows, and were careful to use their turn signals. Pike moved close only once, to take a telephoto shot of the dealer card in the license plate frame.

The two men rolled south into Hollywood, and stopped for Thai food in a strip mall on Hollywood Boulevard. Pike parked across the street outside a convenience store. Forty minutes later, the two men came out, and Pike saw the driver. He was smaller than the passenger, but still big. Square jaw, hard eyes, strong neck. The bigger man laughed, but the driver didn't laugh with him. His face was empty, like a man who kept himself hidden. Pike snapped his picture, but the angle was bad. When the driver turned to get into their car, his jacket opened. Something gold shone on his belt. It looked like a badge, but Pike wasn't sure.

They drove east on Hollywood to Sunset, and down through Silver Lake and Echo Park past Chavez Ravine. Their drive across the city seemed casual, but when they entered the maze of one-way streets in downtown L.A., Pike knew they were nearing their destination. He edged closer. Overcrowded streets and swarms of pedestrians blocking traffic at badly timed crosswalks made following difficult.

The black sedan finally stopped in a red zone outside a tall, imposing office building, not far from Pershing Square. Pike pulled into a loading area across the street, and readied his camera.

The black car sat motionless for almost ten minutes, then the passenger door opened and the taller man climbed out. When he closed the door, Pike saw he carried a laptop computer. A man in a gray business suit broke through the streams of people entering and leaving the building, and approached. The big man flashed a big smile. The businessman took the laptop and tucked it under his arm. Pike snapped a picture.

The two men were talking when a DOT cop rolled up behind the black car and beeped. The big man and the businessman glanced at the cop, and the big man made a little wave at the car. The black car pulled away, and the big man and the businessman continued talking. Pike figured the Chrysler would circle the block.

The big man and the businessman spoke for another few minutes, then went into the building.

Pike got a bad feeling, and sensed something was wrong. The two men wouldn't have talked on the sidewalk for so long if they had planned to enter the building. Going inside was a change in their plans.

Pike worked across lanes, turned, and circled behind the building. Streams of people entered and left a second entrance identical to the first. The office building was so big it had entrances on both streets. The taller man could have walked through the lobby, and found his friend idling on this side of the building.

The black sedan was gone.

The two men were gone.

Pike thought, he should have killed them when he had the chance.

31

ELVIS COLE

PALISADES VILLAGE was a pleasant collection of low-key shops and unassuming restaurants along Sunset Boulevard at the bottom of the hill. Maybe because the beach was so near and the city was far, the Village had a relaxed, small-town vibe I liked. The meandering drive down from the Gurwick house felt longer than the climb, but the topaz blue sky and brilliant sun were encouraging.

I parked across from an elementary school, bought coffee and a scoop of gelato at an ice cream shop, and sat in a little park. The Information operator found no listings for Amber Reed or Jazzi Reed anywhere in Los Angeles County. A friend at the DMV found an Amber Reed on the DMV rolls, but Amber's address of record was the Gurwick address.

The search for Jazzi Reed produced even fewer results. The DMV had no record of anyone by that name, which meant Jazzi had never been issued a California driver's license, which was unlikely, or she was licensed under a different name.

I said, "How many Reeds do you show in the county?"

"A little over two hundred."

So much for calling the Reeds.

I finished the gelato, sipped the coffee, and decided Nora Gurwick probably wouldn't return my call. People usually didn't, so I phoned her again, and struck out again. I left a second message, and wondered if telepathy was a rare skill. Neff and Hensman probably used mental telepathy instead of a phone, and didn't have to wait for callbacks. A definite advantage.

I was wondering if I should give up detecting to open a gelato shop when Joe Pike called.

He said, "Say location."

No hello. No howzitgoin. All Pike all the time.

"The Palisades. I'm thinking about opening a gelato shop. Why?"

"Stay away from the Connor house. The man who entered planted something outside the garage when he left."

"What kind of something?"

"A motion detector, most likely, so they'll know if someone comes home. I'll pick up some gear and head back to check."

This was good news. They wouldn't bug Tyson's house if they had him.

"Where'd they go?"

"Downtown. They delivered something to a man outside an office building. I got the address. I wasn't close enough to be sure, but it looked like a laptop."

"Pictures?"

My phone chimed with incoming mail as he answered.

"Sending now. Can you copy?"

"Go."

He recited an address for one of the newer office buildings near the financial district, then described the two men and told me what happened from the point they arrived at Devon's house.

I said, "Think they were cops?"

"They match the descriptions you had. Both big, one bigger. Everything else is optics."

Pike.

The pictures he sent were of the two men, the businessman they met, and their car. The clearest image was of the man who entered Devon's home. The picture of his partner was hazy with glare and the focus was soft, but if Alec's roommate or the Crenzas identified either man as Neff or Hensman, Cassett could distribute their pictures and have every cop in the city looking for them. The picture of the businessman also gave me something to work with.

The fourth picture showed the Chrysler sedan and the fifth was a close-up of the dealership card. Ezekian Motor Craft. A quick Internet search produced no results. Ezekian Motor Craft did not exist. This should have surprised me, but didn't. Their attention to detail was impressive. The two men were thorough.

I was studying their pictures when my phone buzzed with an incoming text. The message was short, and even more exciting than the pictures.

James Tyson Connor had replied.

TYSON: What's on their laptop?

I set the coffee on the bench by my leg and held the phone with both hands. Tyson had been off the grid, out of touch, and could vanish again just as easily. Demands, questions, and warnings might drive him away, so I typed a simple response.

ELVIS: I don't know.

Seconds ticked past, and each passing second was a war with restraint. Tyson would text again, or he wouldn't. I stared at my phone, and finally the phone buzzed.

TYSON: What kind of laptop is it?

I answered quickly, but still carefully. We were having a conversation.

ELVIS: I don't know. I don't know what kind of laptop they want or why they want it. All I know is they want a laptop.

TYSON: OK.

The time stretched again, and nothing arrived. A question could be threatening, but a statement might encourage a response. I didn't want him to withdraw. I didn't want to scare him away, or make him regret reaching out to me, but I needed to warn him. I sent the pictures of the two men without explanation. He responded almost at once.

TYSON: Is this them?

ELVIS: Yes.

I let the time drag. He had read my earlier text, and thought about what I wrote. He had probably found out as much as he could about Alec's death, and Louise August, and the other things, but his information would be limited. He was trying to figure out what was happening, and what he could do about it, and had reached out for help.

ELVIS: Everything I told you is true. Show Amber. If you see them, run. Stay in open places with other people. Keep yourself safe.

TYSON: Who are they?

ELVIS: Don't know.

TYSON: Whose laptop is it?

ELVIS: Don't know.

TYSON: Know any real detectives?

Smart-ass, but his being a smart-ass was good. We were developing a relationship. He might pull back if I pushed too hard, but I wanted to keep him alive.

ELVIS: If you have their computer, it could tell us who these people are.

He didn't respond. These kids had been selling the things they stole, so this particular laptop was almost certainly gone.

ELVIS: If you sold it or gave it away, I might be able to get it back.

Nothing.

ELVIS: If it's gone, it's gone. I get it. I can still help you.

More time passed. He was probably trying to remember what he had done with the laptops they had stolen. I wondered where he was and what he was doing and whether he was alone. He could be driving north on the 5 or boarding an airplane or watching TV. He could be hiding in an Airstream or on his way to Vegas or in Vegas. I wondered if he was frightened. I wondered if he was smart enough to be frightened.

My phone buzzed again.

TYSON: Tell my mom I'm okay.

ELVIS: Your job.

TYSON: Gotta go.

ELVIS: Tell her.

My hands felt clammy.

ELVIS: She needs to hear it from you. Tell her.

Nothing came back.

ELVIS: Are you safe?

ELVIS: Are you safe?

His next text was angry.

TYSON: YES

I thought hard about what to say, and chose my words carefully.

ELVIS: I'm here if you need me, son.

I sat on the bench with the phone in my hands for another ten minutes, but Tyson was gone. I tossed the coffee and gelato cup in a trash bin, and used the bathroom in the ice cream shop. Devon would be relieved, and thankful, and had every right to know her son was alive, but I did not tell her. Tyson could have texted his mother, but he reached out to me. I wasn't sure what this meant, but we could build on it if he reached out again.

When I left the ice cream shop I walked past a realty office, and noticed their sign. The realtor was a local outfit specializing in Palisades properties. Pictures of houses in their window were labeled with little signs. FORECLOSURE. BANKRUPTCY. DIVORCE FORCES SALE.

I broke out my phone. Maybe I didn't need Nora. Maybe someone else could help me find Jazzi and Amber.

A quick property search of Nora Gurwick's address showed the title was held by Richard L. and Nora A. Gurwick. Hundreds of Reeds lived in the county, but only three Gurwicks. Richard L. owned a patio furniture showroom in Santa Monica. I didn't call. I plugged the address into my phone, and followed the coast to Santa Monica.

32

GURWICK PATIO LIFESTYLE OCCUPIED an entire block on a side street south of Broadway. Arrangements of outdoor furniture and full-sized patio umbrellas filled an enormous showroom stretching from one corner to the next. Outdoor kitchens more elaborate than the kitchens most people had in their homes had been built between the umbrellas so browsing customers could imagine themselves entertaining family and friends. I'd seen Cadillac dealers with smaller showrooms.

I walked up to the nearest salesman.

"Hi. Is Dick Gurwick available?"

"Sure. Can I tell him who's calling?"

I gave him a card.

"It's about Nora."

The salesman glanced at the card, arched his eyebrows, and walked away. Divorce was serious business.

A few minutes later the salesman reappeared with another man, pointed me out, and Dick Gurwick came over.

Gurwick was tall, thin, and a regular at the local tanning salon. His hair was unnaturally dark, and pulled into a tiny man-bun. It looked silly on a man his age. He didn't offer his hand.

"Dick Gurwick. You another process server?"

"I don't work for Nora, and I'm not involved in your divorce. I'm trying to find Amber and Jazzi."

Gurwick scowled, his face folding up like a stack of plates.

"They aren't my kids. You know that, right?"

"I understand. I tried to reach Nora, but she's away. Banff. Or Aspen. I called her cell, but—"

Gurwick interrupted.

"Fuckin' bitch, with the traveling. That woman spends money like a monkey shits soup."

I made a noncommittal shrug.

"Can you help me find Amber or Jazzi?"

He scowled even deeper and turned away.

"I dunno. Maybe Jasmine. C'mon in back."

I followed him along a hall past shelves stacked with product brochures to a cluttered, windowless office. The office was spare, cheaply appointed, and didn't look like the office of someone who made a great deal of money, but this might've been why he was successful. His office was a place to do work.

Gurwick took a seat behind the desk, put on a pair of reading glasses, and swiveled to a battered metal file cabinet. He opened and closed drawers with something specific in mind, but had no idea where to find it.

He glanced over the top of his glasses.

"What kind of trouble is she in?"

"Her sister, Amber. I was told Amber used to stay with Jazzi when things at home got rough."

He grunted, and opened and closed more drawers.

"That's true. Couldn't blame her, a nutcase like Nora for a mother. I don't know what I was thinking."

I nodded, letting him rant.

"The worst three years of my life, *only* three years, and you wouldn't believe how much money the bitch is trying to squeeze out of me."

He opened the next drawer, fingered through files, and fell silent. He adjusted the glasses, read for a moment, then swiveled back to his desk and wrote on a pad.

"I don't know if this is still good. Been a couple of years."

He tore off the slip, but didn't give it to me. His dark face was scowling, but the scowl seemed softer.

"Nora wanted a house, so I bought a damn house, not her, *me*, and the next thing I know I'm in this toxic maelstrom, the three of them, every day, all the bullshit. I felt bad for those kids. Living with those three was hell, but I felt bad."

He paused, and the scowl deepened.

"I tried to fix it. That's a mistake we make, us guys, thinking we can fix this dysfunctional bullshit. Amber was a mess. Sad, but a mess. Jasmine, she was older. Maybe tougher, and smart. Smart enough to know living with her mother was toxic."

He called her Jasmine, not Jazzi.

"Are you and Jasmine close?"

He waved the slip.

"Nah. I helped her find a place. Told her, I'll pay the first six months. You don't have to pay me back, but after that you're on your own."

I nodded, watching the slip.

"Generous."

"It was like throwing a life preserver. Someone's drowning, how can you not?"

He held the slip closer, and let me take it.

"Jasmine's a flight attendant now. I don't know if she still lives here. Flies all over the world on charter jets."

A Woodland Hills address was written on the slip.

"Thanks, Mr. Gurwick. Do you have a phone number for Jasmine, too?"

He leaned back and shrugged.

"I don't have anything to do with them. They aren't my kids."

Gurwick was behind his desk, staring at nothing, when I left.

I hurried to my car, and drove hard for the Valley. The Sepulveda Pass was a blur. I hit the Ventura, raced across Encino and Tarzana, and followed the map to a small, modern apartment building three blocks north of the freeway.

I parked by a fire hydrant, eased out of my car, and saw Tyson's Volvo parked three cars ahead. I moved closer to check. The plates matched. The interior was a trash bin. Tyson.

I studied the building, crossed the street, and took a closer look.

Mailboxes and a call box were set into the wall beneath a covered entry by a wrought-iron gate. Six mailboxes for six units. Unit five was Reed. The buttons by the call box were numbered. I pressed the button for unit five. When no one answered I pressed again. A young female voice answered. Amber.

"Hello?"

"UPS. Package for Jasmine Reed."

"You can leave it, thanks."

A package for Jasmine, Jasmine would come. The voice was Amber.

"On the sidewalk?"

"Yeah. That's fine."

"I need a signature. It's a pretty big box. It's from Neiman Marcus."

Amber hesitated.

"Okay. Hang on."

I trotted across the street and hid in my car.

Tyson Connor opened the gate. He stepped out onto the sidewalk, expecting to find the UPS driver. He checked around the gate for the package, maybe thinking the driver had left it, then checked the street in both directions, looking for the truck.

Tyson appeared calm, relaxed, and unharmed. His manner suggested neither he nor Amber were being held at gunpoint by killers in Jasmine's apartment. Tyson stood on the curb for almost two minutes, waiting for a

UPS truck that did not exist. He finally got tired of waiting, went inside, and closed the gate.

I sat in my car, enjoying the moment.

Hello, Tyson. I found you.

I called Devon Connor, and told her what I had wanted to tell her since the night her son vanished.

"He's safe. Tyson is safe. I found him."

33

DEVON SOBBED ONCE, the gasp of a heart returning to life, and then she drew a breath.

"Put him on the phone. I want to talk to him."

"I haven't approached him. I wanted to let you know he's okay."

"He'd better enjoy it while it lasts. When I get that boy home I'm going to kill him."

I watched the street for the black sedan. Maybe I beat the two men to Jasmine, but they wouldn't be far behind. They could show up at any moment, and might have already arrived. They might even be watching me. I tried to look tough.

"We can't take him home, Devon. The men who searched your house went back. They're still trying to find him."

She was quiet for several heartbeats. Devon had thought it would end when we found him. She probably believed their lives could go on. I got out of my car and leaned against the door. Better to watch the street. Tyson was inside the building one hundred feet away. I wondered what he was thinking.

Devon said, "I understand. Where is he?"

"Woodland Hills. They're with Amber's sister."

"He's with that girl?"

"I haven't seen her, but Amber lives with her sister, so Amber would be here. The sister, I don't know. She travels."

"All right. I'll leave right away. Where are you?"

"Not yet. I'm going to move them."

"Move them where? Why are you moving them?"

"The men. They're coming."

"You're scaring me."

"I'll take him to a safe house. Someplace not connected to Jasmine or Amber or you, where they can't find us."

"I want to see him."

"You'll see him at the safe house. Joe's going to call. He'll tell you where. Did you finish printing the documents?"

"Yes. And the research you wanted. It's a lot."

"Bring it."

I gave her the downtown address, and explained what I wanted.

"It's an office building. Find out about the developers and the leasing agency. Check for a tenant list. Print what you find."

"Okay. I'll do it."

"Pack your things and be ready to roll. The safe house might be spare, so bag up towels, sheets, cleaning stuff, things like that. You'll find garbage bags under the sink and next to the washer."

"Got it. I know what to bring."

I forced myself to slow down, and tried not to miss anything.

"One more thing."

"What?"

"Don't warn him. Don't call or text. We don't want him to know he's been found."

"I'll see you soon."

I called Pike next, and told him about Tyson and Amber.

"Have you reached Devon's house?"

"Close."

"Come here instead. We need to move them."

A friend of Joe's in the real estate business had helped us with safe houses before.

"It's short notice, but you think she can help?"

"A safe house is always short notice. I'll call."

"Give Devon the address. I'll stand by here and watch for our friends."

I gave him Jasmine's address, and hurried across the street.

Anyone entering her building through the gate or the parking garage would be obvious, but I couldn't see much past the front wall, and didn't know whether someone could gain access from the rear. I went to the wrought-iron gate, but the view was limited. Lady palms, yuccas, and bright orange ginger lilies stood tall in decorative planting beds along the length of the building, hiding the ground-floor apartments and the rear of the property. A quick spin around the block would answer my questions, but leaving was out of the question. If Neff and Hensman arrived, I wanted to say hello.

I was walking back to my car when Tyson texted again.

> **TYSON:** I might have it.

His message slammed me in the chest, and stopped me in the street. The odds he would have this particular laptop were zero to nothing.

> **ELVIS:** Might?

> **TYSON:** I kept some. How can I tell which one is theirs?

I stared at the building, and pictured him sitting on a towering stack of laptop computers. Maybe I wouldn't wait for Devon. Maybe I'd kick down the door.

> **ELVIS:** You have them with you?

TYSON: No.

A car approached but it wasn't a black sedan. I moved out of the street and watched it pass. A woman was driving. Not two men.

ELVIS: Where are they?

TYSON: Hahaha. Gotta go.

Asking had been a mistake.

ELVIS: What I meant was, can you get them so you can figure it out?

I waited, but Tyson didn't respond.

ELVIS: The faster we ID these people, the faster we stop them.

We, not I. Work with me, son.

Nothing.

I walked back to my car. Tyson was thinking, and thinking was progress. He was trying to figure a way out of his jam, and he seemed willing to cooperate. I wondered how many laptops he kept, and whether he had the laptop the men wanted. He would have stashed the laptops just as he stashed the cash and the Rolex, but not in his room. Devon would have found them.

I was back in my car, watching for black sedans, when Jasmine's parking gate opened, and a bright aqua Mini Cooper nosed up the ramp. The convertible top was down, making the girl at the wheel and her passenger easy to see. Tyson. I started my car, hoping they were off to pick up the laptops.

The Mini turned right, away from me. I waited to see if they were followed, but no black sedans appeared. When their signal blinked at the end of the street, I swung around after them.

The Mini turned south toward the freeway. I turned south with them, and let them pull ahead. I thought for sure they would use the freeway, but they continued south, and turned at Ventura Boulevard. Their signal blinked again after only two blocks, and they parked in front of a Starbucks. I guess this wasn't an expedition to recover stolen laptop computers.

I slid into a red zone, fired off a text to keep Pike in the loop, then strolled up the sidewalk. I photographed the Mini's license plate, then peeked inside the Starbucks.

Most of the tables were taken, and a handful of people waited around the pickup station. The order line snaked past a pastry case to a display stacked with packaged coffee beans, insulated cups, and designer mugs. Amber stood talking to an older woman who sat in an overstuffed chair in the corner. The older woman held a scruffy white dog in her lap. Tyson was across the room in the order line, concentrating on his phone. He finished whatever he was doing, put the phone away, and stood with his hands in his pockets. I hoped he wasn't doing anything stupid.

My phone buzzed with an incoming text, and Tyson's name appeared.

I walked back the way I had come so the people inside couldn't see me.

TYSON: I can get them. How can I tell which one is theirs?

I sent a response, and drifted back to the Starbucks. Tyson was in line with his hands in his pockets just as I left him.

ELVIS: See what's on them. Something on their computer will tell us who they are. Find it.

Tyson glanced at Amber, slipped the phone from his pocket, and casually read the message. He glanced at Amber again, tapped a quick reply, and once again palmed the phone.

Hm.

> **TYSON:** Easy for you to say. I don't know what I'm looking for, and
> I'll have to search all of them. What am I trying to find?

The line shuffled forward, putting Tyson next to order. I fired a quick reply.

> **ELVIS:** Something dangerous.

Tyson glanced at Amber, and eased his phone from his pocket. He was frowning at my reply when Amber stepped away from the woman and her dog. Tyson saw her turn, and jammed the phone back into his pocket. Even from the sidewalk, his mad scramble to hide the phone told me Tyson was keeping secrets.

Double hm.

I went inside as Amber joined Tyson at the head of the line. She grabbed his arm and made a big show of pointing at the dog.

"Isn't that doggie cute? That dog is *sooo* cute. I want a dog just like that."

Amber spoke loudly, and her gestures were broad, the way a stage actor played to the house.

Tyson said, "That's a cute dog."

I had seen Tyson in person only once, and then from a block away. He was a nice-looking kid, but held himself close, as if wary. Amber was the opposite. She was lean, pretty, and her smile was bright with confident energy. A blousy, off-the-shoulder cream top exposed flawless skin, and long, slender legs were revealed by little white shorts that were loose, but not nasty. The Gucci sunglasses looked great on her.

Amber ordered a Grande Skinny Caramel Macchiato with extra foam.

212 | ROBERT CRAIS

Tyson asked for a Venti Vanilla Frappuccino with extra vanilla. Amber draped a hand on his shoulder when he ordered, and grinned at the barista.

"Give him extra vanilla, *puh-leeze*. It has to be sweet 'coz he's so sweet."

The barista and Tyson grinned. So did the people in line and at the nearby tables.

Tyson paid cash and went to wait for their drinks. Amber returned to the dog lady, oo-ing and ah-ing at the dog.

Tyson drifted to the far side of the pickup station, keeping a nervous eye on Amber until he was behind other customers. He made sure she wasn't coming, and took out his phone.

I eased up beside him. Tyson seemed even younger up close, soft and without edges, studying his phone like a twelve-year-old. Here we were in a Starbucks, him looking twelve, the girl oo-ing and ah-ing at a dog with yellow stains on its face, the two of them having committed eighteen felony burglaries.

"Your friend wants a puppy."

He startled, and shoved the phone in his pocket.

I smiled, easy and nice, and glanced at Amber.

"She's cute. Your girlfriend?"

Tyson edged a few inches away, meeting my eyes then looking away, awkward and maybe afraid.

"Thanks."

"You should get her a dog."

"I guess."

"She looks familiar. Like an actress. Has she been on television?"

He watched the barista making drinks, unwilling to look at me, as if he could hide by watching the barista and the stranger would go away.

"Uh-uh."

Amber swirled up from behind him, and rolled over him like a wave.

"We don't have our drinks? What's taking so long?"

She leaned forward across the counter, and spoke so quickly her words mashed together.

"Agrandeskinnycaramelmacchiatowithextrafoam and aventivanillafrap-puccinowithextravanilla. You didn't give them to someone else, did you? We need caf-*feine!*"

Her personality swept over and around him, and defined their dynamic. He stood taller at her touch, held himself less wary, and seemed larger, as if a static *pop!* of her crazy wild confidence had sparked from her into him. Amber fed his fantasies and needs, and made him feel strong in his weakest places. Whatever Amber had wanted, Tyson would have done. Her attention empowered him. Her approval was everything.

Tyson said, "She's making them now. I'm watching the cups."

"Oh, thank GODDDD!"

Dramatic and large. I noticed the scar on the inside of her wrist. Bright and pink, a glossy line. Seeing the scar reminded me of the sad things Rae Bracken and Dick Gurwick had told me. I left, and went back to my car.

Tyson and Amber came out with their drinks a few minutes later, and the bright aqua Mini pulled away.

I told myself Tyson was going to pick up their laptops, but half a mile later they joined the drive-thru line at an In-N-Out Burger. Tyson. Eating was constant. Maybe he needed sustenance before they retrieved the laptops.

A few minutes later they rolled out the exit, and I followed them back to Jasmine's apartment.

No black sedans or men who looked like police detectives were present, but Pike's red Jeep Cherokee idled across the street. When the Mini disappeared beneath Jasmine's building, I drove forward and parked by a fire hydrant.

Pike climbed out of his Jeep, and we met on the street.

"How long were you gone?"

"Forty-five minutes, tops."

"I've been here ten."

Thirty-five minutes. We studied the building and both ends of the street. They could have come, and set up in thirty-five minutes. One could've dropped off the other, who was waiting inside, or they could've parked around the corner, and set up together.

I said, "Let's get it done."

34

We planned the work as we moved.

I said, "Six units. Three on top, three on the bottom. They're on top in the middle unit."

Pike said, "Gate?"

"Opens from the inside. I'll get the garage."

Pike trotted to the entrance gate as I ducked down the ramp to check the garage. Amber's Mini Cooper and a silver BMW SUV were the only vehicles present. The other tenants would be at work.

Pike had gone over the wall and opened the gate. I checked the mailboxes again on my way in. Jasmine's apartment was #5. The apartment below hers would be #2. The name on the #2 box was Steiner.

I slipped through the gate and we moved past the planters. The property was quiet and still as a morgue. The walkway was clean, and immaculately maintained. Each ground-floor apartment had a private entrance, hidden by design with the lush growth sprouting from the planters. Privacy had probably been a sales feature. Floating staircases led to each of the second-floor units.

We climbed the stairs to Jasmine's landing, and listened. Nothing. Pike drew his Python and stood to the side. I smudged the peephole with spit, and pressed the bell. I didn't expect them to answer, but Amber called from behind the door.

"Who is it?"

"Oh, hey, it's Steiner, from downstairs, number two. Water's dripping out of my ceiling. Do you have a clogged toilet?"

Mr. Friendly, couldn't be nicer.

Amber didn't respond. They were talking it over, or Neff and Hensman had guns to their heads.

I knocked.

"Hello? Did you hear me? I'm drowning downstairs."

"Okay. Hang on."

The lock turned, and Amber opened the door. I pushed the door into her, caught her arm, and pulled her with me as I entered. Pike came fast behind me, and moved left into a large living room, gun up and out. He cleared the room, and disappeared as I closed and locked the door.

Surprise lit Amber's face like a flashbulb.

"Hey! Don't come in!"

Tyson stood at the mouth of the kitchen, eating the In-N-Out. He lurched as if hit by a taser, and shouted.

"It's them! The two men! Run!"

He turned, and ran face-first into Pike. Pike pushed him toward me, and vanished back through the kitchen.

I pulled Amber away from the door.

"Wrong men. We're the *other* two men."

Amber tried to pull away, but couldn't.

"Let go! Lemme go! You can't—"

I ignored her and focused on Tyson.

"Is anyone here besides you and Amber?"

Tyson stood mute, eyes unnaturally wide, too scared to answer.

Amber thrashed pretty good.

"Get out. You can't just walk into somebody's home like this. You don't have any right to be here."

Irony.

"I just walked in like this, and now I'm here."

I focused on Tyson again.

"I'm Elvis. The guy your mother hired."

Tyson shriveled, and seemed even younger. His skin was blotched, and he looked like he might throw up.

Amber pried at my fingers.

"I don't care who hired you. Get out!"

I squeezed her arm. Just enough to get her attention.

"Do you see me here in Jasmine's apartment with you and Tyson? You understand I'm real? You're not imagining me."

Amber pulled harder.

"You're talking crazy. What are you talking about?"

"I found you. If I could find you, the men who killed Alec will find you, and they will kill you, so you're not going to be here. We're leaving."

She twisted and squirmed, trying to make a break for the door. I jerked her back hard.

"Ow! You're hurting me!"

Tyson stood spiked to the floor, all big eyes and fear.

I said, "Stop it, damnit."

Amber screamed. I cupped a hand over her mouth, and held tight. She kicked and struggled.

"This is wearing thin."

Tyson said, "Amber, stop. Please. They've got us."

Amber wound down and finally relaxed. I let go of her mouth.

I spoke to Tyson.

"Does she know what happened to Alec?"

"She doesn't believe it."

"I don't know what you're talking about. We didn't do anything."

"Good luck with that in court. In the meantime, let's try to stay alive."

Pike reappeared and returned to the door.

"We're good."

Pike opened the door enough to clean the peephole, then locked up again.

I glanced at Tyson.

"Are the laptops here?"

"No, sir."

Sir. He was terrified.

"Pack your stuff. Not much, but enough for a few days. I'm taking you to a safe place."

Amber looked sullen.

"You can't make me leave against my will. That's kidnapping. You'll be kidnapping me."

"Yes, Amber, I can, but I won't have to. You're coming of your own free will. You *want* to come. You are *begging* me to take you, and you're going to cooperate."

"No, I am not, and I'm not leaving!"

"Because if you don't, I *will* kidnap you. I'll wrap you in so much duct tape you'll look like a mummy, and take you to the police. They'll check your fingerprints against the fingerprints you left in the homes you robbed, and you'll have a fun sleepover in jail."

Amber glanced at Pike, then Tyson, then back to me.

"Tyson will get in trouble."

"You're both in trouble anyway, but Tyson will be safe, and you'll be in jail. If you rat him out to the police, that's on you."

She glanced at Tyson and looked even more sullen.

I said, "They won't be able to find you. You'll be safe. We'll figure out who these people are, and we'll stop them."

I glanced at Tyson.

"Your mother will be there."

I looked at Amber.

"Your mother is traveling. I called her. When she gets back, you and she can do whatever you want. Go, stay, whatever."

She frowned, and suddenly looked younger.

"She's coming home?"

"I left a message. I haven't spoken with her."

Her frown deepened, but now she seemed thoughtful.

Tyson said, "They'll kill us, Amber. Please."

Amber glanced at Pike, and the glance turned into a stare. She finally turned back to me.

"You're really private detectives?"

"Impressive, isn't it?"

She glanced at Pike again.

"He doesn't look like a detective."

Pike's head moved, just enough to acknowledge he heard her. His shades were so dark, they looked like twin doors to nowhere. He considered her, but said nothing. He turned back to the peephole.

Amber grinned.

"This is kinda cool, like we're in a movie."

Amber was cooperative once she got on board, and Tyson was docile. We grabbed Tyson's backpack and toiletries, and Amber stuffed a few clothes and toiletries into a tote bag. I watched what they packed, and checked their bags. Amber moved quickly once she got going, and didn't whine or complain. Tyson said nothing, and avoided eye contact. I grabbed two towels from Amber's bathroom on the way out, and tossed a towel to Joe. He draped it over his gun.

Once we were ready, I collected their phones and keys.

Amber looked unhappy for the first time since we started.

"But why do you want my keys? I need them."

"We're leaving your cars. Tyson's riding with me. You'll ride with Joe."

Amber studied Pike, all arrows and muscles and merciless black shades. She grinned so wide she beamed.

"Oh, man, this is so frickin' cool. I'll take two, please."

I grinned at Pike.

"Isn't this cool?"

Pike didn't grin back.

I drew the Dan Wesson, and wrapped my gun with the towel.

"Joe will go first. You two stay with me."

Amber held Tyson's arm, and huddled behind him. Her eyes were so bright they twinkled.

"How cool is this? I mean, *really*? They could be outside. They could shoot us!"

Tyson didn't share her pleasure, and probably didn't think this was cool or exciting.

I touched his shoulder.

"We'll be fine."

Tyson didn't respond.

Joe opened the door an inch, checked the landing, and stepped out. I hung back, keeping Tyson and Amber behind me.

Pike peered over the rail, and moved to the head of the stairs. He glanced back, nodded, and went down. I stepped out with Tyson and Amber, and locked the door. Pike reached the walk below, signaled, and we followed quickly.

Pike moved ahead to the gate, checked the street, and motioned us forward. We ran to join him, and immediately separated, Pike pulling Amber to his Jeep, and me pushing Tyson. I felt exposed on the open street, like a fly on a plate. I knew the black car was coming. I expected the car to appear, and race toward us. I pushed Tyson harder.

"The yellow Corvette. Move, boy. Run."

He ran. I ran beside him, watching the street.

I shoved him into the passenger seat, climbed behind the wheel, and fired the engine. Pike was already rolling.

I watched the mirror for black sedans as we pulled away, and checked every side street as we drove to the freeway. I looked for their big black beast as we climbed the ramp, and kept looking, even after the freeway swallowed us, a buffalo joining a herd, one hiding among the many, and finally safe.

35

I FELT MYSELF SLOW. For the first time in days, I began to relax. I had him. He was safe. The shrieking wind and creaks from my car were calming.

"You okay?"

He didn't answer.

I glanced over again. He held the backpack tight to his chest. He stared ahead at the freeway, but his eyes were empty, as if the road ahead didn't register. He seemed smaller than before, and afraid.

"Your mom's at the safe house."

He hugged the backpack closer.

"We'll be there soon."

I studied him out the corner of my eye. He probably knew I was watching, but he gave no sign.

"She's been worried."

He shifted a little, and looked out the passenger window.

"Where'd you stash the laptops?"

He didn't answer.

"I didn't hear you."

"The garage."

His voice was so soft I barely heard him. He still didn't look at me.

"How many do you have?"

"Six."

"Speak up."

"Six."

Louder, but he still didn't look at me.

"They're all in the garage?"

"One's in my room. The rest are in the garage."

"Anyone else know where they are?"

"No, sir."

"Did Alec know?"

"No, sir."

This was good. Alec couldn't have told them.

"Does anyone know you have them?"

"Alec knew. Amber."

"Okay. Good. Your mom wants to see you, so we'll let her see you. Then we'll get them."

He nodded, but said nothing. He simply hugged his backpack, and stared out the window.

I glanced over, and wondered what he was thinking. I thought he might be seeing all the many things he could not change.

Nothing about what they did and how they lived had been real, but this was now changing. He was caught, and a man he feared was bringing him back to his mother. He was beginning to understand. There would be consequences.

I stole another glance, and Tyson seemed smaller. I thought of *The Wizard of Oz*, the scene at the end when the Wicked Witch of the West grew smaller and smaller until she was gone.

"You messed up."

He nodded.

"You'll have to answer for what you did. Understand?"

He made another nod, so slight I almost missed it, and his shoulders quivered. He was crying, but he cried so softly I couldn't hear him.

I said, "Tyson."

He lowered his head, and the quiver grew into shaking.

"You'll feel worse before you feel better, but you'll get through this."

He cried harder.

"Now is when you start making things right."

He cried even harder.

After a while I reached over and squeezed his shoulder, but only the once. The tears were his. Tyson had earned them.

We drove in silence the rest of the way to his mother.

36

WE PULLED UP outside the safe house as Pike and Amber climbed out of his Jeep. Devon had already arrived.

The safe house was a furnished two-bedroom rental north of the river in Studio City. The owner lived out of state. A long-term tenant had recently moved, so repairs and improvements were being made so the owner could raise the rent. Devon ran out to meet us. Tyson watched her coming, and looked like he wanted to hide.

I said, "We'll drop off Amber and split. We won't stay long."

"My mom's here."

"Your mom's mad. She has a right to be, so man up. Get out."

Devon threw her arms around him like a linebacker trapping a running back, and sobbed as if he'd risen from the grave.

Pike unlocked the house, but Amber lingered behind. She watched Devon maul Tyson with hugs, and seemed annoyed. She suddenly glanced at the bungalow, and spoke in her loud voice.

"I expected bars on the windows, or really big walls. This is just a little house. It doesn't look so safe."

Tyson squirmed and tried to pull away.

"Mom, would you stop? Please."

Devon grabbed his shoulders, and gave him a shake.

"No *please*. There is no *please*. How could you do this? What were you thinking?"

"I'm stupid."

"You're not stupid. Don't you dare say you're stupid."

I interrupted. Gently.

"Devon, why don't you check the house? Tyson and I will unload the car."

Devon started to say something, but stopped when she realized she was making a scene. She gave me her keys, and stalked up the drive. I steered Tyson to the Audi.

"In case you missed it, I just cut you a major break. You're welcome."

He met my eyes for the first time, but only for a second.

"Thank you."

He watched his mother walking away.

"She won't like Amber."

"No. You can bet on it."

I loaded him down with his mother's bags, and the extra-large plastic trash bag she'd filled with towels, sheets, and toilet paper. It was bulky and awkward to carry, but wasn't too heavy. I took four grocery bags packed with soap, soda, paper plates, and plastic utensils, and the food she scrounged from my pantry. We carried the bags inside, and left them in the kitchen.

The bungalow was small, and the furnishings were bare, worn, and crummy. A small dinette and three spindly chairs. A threadbare sofa and a cheap metal coffee table. Two bedrooms, a bath, and a living room with a dining area off the kitchen. The house had been painted the week before, and smelled like paint thinner.

Devon stood in the dining room as far from Amber as possible. Glaring. Amber circled the tiny living room as if Devon wasn't glaring, taking in the cheesy room with obvious pleasure. Tyson hid behind me, trying to be invisible.

Amber beamed at him.

"This sucks so bad it's kinda cool, isn't it?"

Tyson shuffled uncomfortably, avoiding his mother's eyes.

Amber ran her hands over the walls as if they were the most amazing walls she'd seen.

"It's like we're trapped in one of those creepy houses where people get chopped to death."

Devon snagged my arm, and pulled me aside.

"Does this little bitch have to stay here?"

I pulled her farther away, and lowered my voice. Tyson snuck glances our way, too scared to move.

I said, "Her mother's away. I left a message. When she calls, Amber can stay with her."

"There has to be someone. What about her sister?"

"She's out of town. I told you."

"How nice for them. Maybe they're getting away from *her*."

Pike returned from his tour of the house, and went to the door.

"Toilet works. Locks work. Windows secure. We're good."

I pulled Devon farther away, and lowered my voice even more.

"I know this is awkward, but we have to get the laptops. I need you to handle this."

Amber suddenly spoke up behind us.

"My mother won't call."

Amber was leaning against the wall with her arms crossed. She looked somber, and maybe tired.

"My mother never calls, so don't get your hopes up. She doesn't care."

I glanced at Devon, and felt bad.

"She'll call. If she doesn't, I'll keep calling until I reach her."

Amber shrugged, like I would only be wasting my time.

"You'll see."

Devon's lips were pursed, and her expression was irritated. I arched my eyebrows. *Well?*

She closed her eyes.

"How long will you be?"

"A couple of hours. I'll stay in touch."

Devon managed a nod. She squared herself, and turned toward Amber.

"I'm Devon. Tyson's mother."

"I know. I'm Amber."

Pike left without a word. I grabbed Tyson's arm, and followed him.

Outside, I clapped Tyson on the back.

"That wasn't so bad, was it?"

"It was weird."

I looked at Pike.

"I thought it went pretty well."

Pike said, "It was weird."

We climbed into his Jeep and went to get the laptops.

37

WE CRUISED PAST TYSON'S HOME, looking for the black sedan. If the men had planted a warning device, they wouldn't be watching the property, but we still had to check. We circled the block, and parked in front of a neighboring house.

Tyson craned forward, wondering why we stopped short.

"This isn't my house. Go to the next driveway."

"They planted a device on your house. Pike's going to check it out."

Pike gestured behind his seat.

"On the floor. The black backpack."

The backpack was heavy. Tyson made a little *oomph* when he handed it forward.

"What device, like a bomb?"

Pike dug into the bag.

"Probably something that tells them if the garage opens, or someone enters."

Pike took a dark gray handheld device from the bag. It looked like an oversized walkie-talkie with stubby horns.

Tyson perked up, and leaned forward. Interested.

"Is that an RF detector?"

Surveillance devices used radio frequency signals to transmit data the same way cell phones used Bluetooth to pair with a car phone, or Wi-Fi to connect with the Internet.

Pike's head turned, and Tyson's reflection appeared in his lenses.

"You interested?"

"Yes, sir!"

Pike let him handle the unit.

Soul mates.

"It detects radio signals, and pinpoints the source. That gives you the device location. Then, if you want, it matches the frequency, and jams the transmission."

Pike took the unit back, and turned on the power.

"I'll show you how it works when we get to the safe house."

Tyson was all in, and fired off another question.

"But Bluetooth changes frequency, like if the connection gets weak. What happens if it hops to a different frequency?"

They were having a moment, and I wanted to get the damned laptops.

"Let's save Mr. Wizard until later, okay?"

Pike answered anyway. Maybe I hadn't really said anything. Maybe I only imagined two killers were trying to murder this kid.

Pike said, "No problem. We jam the entire spectrum, all frequencies across the range. Cell phones, TV remotes, Wi-Fi—every wireless device inside twenty meters stops working."

The men in the black car had used a similar device to beat Nora Gurwick's alarm.

Tyson looked awed.

"I thought you couldn't buy things like this."

Pike opened the door.

"You can't."

Pike slipped from behind the wheel, closed the door, and disappeared between the houses. A dog barked, but only once.

Tyson looked at me.

"I thought jammers were illegal."

I grunted.

"Where'd he get it?"

"I could tell you, but I'd have to kill you."

He studied me, then stared at his house.

"What if those men are inside?"

I settled back.

"They'll be sorry."

I angled the mirror to see him, and took out my phone. I showed him the pictures of the two men.

"This is them."

His brow wrinkled as he studied each picture, first the man outside the restaurant, then the bigger man.

"You took this one here, outside my house."

"Joe took it. He was here while I was looking for you. Either of these people look familiar?"

"No, sir."

"How about this guy?"

I showed him the businessman. Tyson shook his head.

"Is the laptop his?"

"We don't know who these people are. If you have their laptop, something on it might tell us."

"Something dangerous. Okay."

I put away my phone, and studied him again. Devon had called him their resident IT expert, and he seemed pretty knowledgeable.

"If they're password protected, can you open them?"

"I reset the passwords when I got'm."

I twisted around to face him.

"You changed passwords?"

"I have reset software I got from a friend. It was easy."

The Carl.

"You didn't delete anything, did you?"

"No, sir. I just wanted to check the RAM and graphics cards."

I grunted like checking the RAM and graphics cards would be my first move, too, and turned back to the house. Pike had been inside a long time.

"The five in the garage, where are they?"

"A box on the top shelf. My mom can't reach. I should get some cables and a drive from my room. We might need'm."

I nodded again. Tyson might be the world's worst student, but he had the IT jargon down cold.

"Your mom says you're a hard-core gamer."

He fidgeted and looked embarrassed. Mentioning his mother probably reminded him how upset she was.

"That why you kept the laptops? To game?"

"The PCs. The Mac's too old, but it's so old it's cool. It's older than me."

"Ancient."

"The PCs have faster graphics, and superfast drives. You can always add RAM, but you're stuck with the graphics card. I like to match the most RAM with the fastest GPUs."

"Meaning you take parts from one to soup up another?"

"Yeah. It's easier with a desktop, but you can play anywhere with a laptop."

"Like when you and Carl played."

"My mom told you about Carl?"

"Yes. I went to see him."

He fell silent, and stared at the house. Thoughtful, and distant, and maybe smaller again.

"Answering my text took guts. Thanks."

He met my eyes in the mirror, and nodded again, but this time the nod showed hope.

Pike reappeared in the neighbor's yard twenty-three minutes later, and climbed in behind the wheel.

"Two devices, one on the sidelight outside the garage, and one in the living room. They feed to a transmitter in the garage. Quality gear."

"Can we get into the garage?"

"Through the kitchen. Once we're behind the motion detectors and camera, I can crash the signal as long as we need."

I glanced at Tyson, and winked.

"You're on deck, bud. Let's go kick some bad guy ass."

Tyson grinned as he pushed out of the Jeep.

We traced Pike's route through the neighbor's yard, climbed a fence, and entered Tyson's house through the dining room. Pike went first, letting the jammer work its magic as we made our way to Tyson's bedroom.

He frowned when he saw his gaming gear and monitors on the floor.

"Wow. They trashed me."

He toed through the rubble and looked under the desk.

"It's gone. It was on my desk, but it isn't here. Somebody took it."

"If they have it, it wasn't the one they want. Get your gear."

He took memory sticks and an external drive from his desk, and cables from the mess on the floor. Pike loaded his gear into the backpack, and we made our way toward the garage. Pike stopped when we reached the living room.

"The fish."

The aquarium stood on its stand, bubbling.

I said, "What about them?"

Tyson said, "We gotta feed them."

We waited while Pike fed the fish, then followed him into the garage. The walls were lined with gray metal shelving units. The shelves were crowded with different-sized boxes and the clutter that accumulates as time passes, and more boxes were stacked on the floor in front of the shelves. Handwriting identified their contents: *Christmas/ornaments, Christmas/lights, Tyson—baby clothes, Mom's lamp.*

Pike pointed out a small black box clipped to the outside of the garage door's track, up high by the ceiling and difficult to see.

"Transmitter."

I nudged Tyson toward the shelves.

"Get'm."

Tyson squeezed past boxes, and leaned an aluminum ladder against the shelves. He reached for a box on the highest shelf. The cardboard was heavy with dust, and striped with peeling tape. *GAMES* was written on the side in faded Marks-A-Lot.

I didn't help. He tugged the box to the edge of the shelf, and eased down the ladder.

The box was a jumble of game controllers, old game carts, keyboards, a monitor, cords and cables, and the five laptop computers. Tyson took them out one by one, and handed them to Pike. Four sleek, expensive PCs and a boxy Macintosh PowerBook that looked like a '58 Ford truck next to four fire-breathing Ferraris.

I said, "This is everything?"

"Yes, sir. These five."

Pike tucked them into his pack, then moved the ladder to the middle of the garage, and removed the cover from the garage door's opener.

Tyson said, "What're you doing?"

"They paired a remote to your opener so they could open the garage. Now their remote won't work."

He snapped the cover back into place, went to the transmitter, and looked at me.

"We can take it, kill it, or leave it, whatever you want."

I thought for a moment, and felt an idea.

"When we stop jamming the signal, will it transmit again?"

"Yes."

I took out my phone, and studied their pictures. Two men with rare skills.

Tyson said, "What are you doing?"

I smiled, and moved to the door.

"Sending a message."

Pike cocked his head, and found some telling sign in my eyes. The corner of his mouth twitched. Pike, dying with laughter.

Two men.

With rare skills.

38

HARVEY AND STEMMS

THE EXTRA-LARGE IN-N-OUT CUP sat in a puddle on Jasmine Reed's kitchen counter. Harvey shook the cup, rattling ice.

"Split less than an hour ago. They won't be back."

"Without their cars?"

The Connor kid's Volvo was parked across the street, and the girl's Mini was in the garage.

Harvey shrugged.

"All the cash they've stolen, they could've bought a Porsche. Question is, why did they leave so fast?"

Harvey and Stemms had entered Jasmine Reed's apartment, and found a half-eaten In-N-Out double-double burger cratered on the kitchen floor. A second double-double and a single sat on the counter by the cup, still wearing their wrappers.

Stemms squatted by the fallen burger, and considered the halo of sauce and lettuce around it.

"I'm not liking this, Harvey. You don't drop a burger, and leave it, not even if you're an arrogant, criminal dipshit. You pick it up."

"As I said, they're gone."

"You leave food on the floor, you're being chased, or you've been grabbed."

They stared at each other for a few miserable seconds, then quickly searched for the laptop.

Stemms was in a foul mood when they left.

Harvey planted a gizmo above the door, but Stemms believed they had lost their advantage. If the laptop had been at Jasmine's apartment, it was gone, and if Jasmine was blown as a lead, they needed a new direction. Stemms was frustrated when they returned to the Chrysler, and annoyed when Harvey's phone screamed with an incoming alert from the Connor boy's home.

Harvey didn't set his phone to beep or buzz or vibrate like a normal person. Harvey's phone screeched with a string piece from the Hitchcock movie *Psycho*, the scene with Janet Leigh in the shower, the knife rising and falling, the string section shrieking with short, staccato stabs, the lone violin slashing through the fermata with discordant glissandos, more violins joining the first, violas adding their teeth, mad strings schooling like orchestral sharks at a blood-drunk feast.

Stemms hated it.

"Turn it off, Harvey. *Please*. We don't need to hear the shower."

Harvey would let the track play if Stemms didn't stop him, the third movement fading to the monotonous sound of the shower, Janet Leigh's blood circling the drain.

Harvey said, "What are you talking about? You love this piece."

"I hate the scene, all right? Hate the scene, hate the score, hate everything about it. I never want to hear it again. *Hint*."

The motion sensor had already alerted them four times that day, so Harvey and Stemms didn't jump to see what triggered the alarm. So far, the Connor residence had been visited by two nicely dressed women who appeared to be Jehovah's Witnesses, a gardener, a guy who read the gas meter, and a Saint Bernard dog who wandered through the yard like it was lost.

Harvey turned to face him, shocked and incredulous.

"But you know this piece by heart. You played it like a boss! What do you mean, you don't like it?"

"Playing it doesn't mean I like it. I played it for the kid."

"I'm having trouble here, Stemms. You were *brilliant!*"

Stemms was sorry he mentioned it. He should've just plugged his ears.

Six years earlier, a job in Albuquerque flipped sideways, so Harvey and Stemms blew south to Ciudad Juárez, three miles down from El Paso. Second night, hungry, they happened upon a run-down cantina out on Highway 2. A dump, strictly for locals, men with dusty boots and women with rough hands, but the cervezas were cold, and the carne asada was smoky with roasted chiles. Had a kid there, maybe nineteen or twenty, playing Mexican cowboy songs for tips. Stemms knew the kid was gifted before their first beer. This Mexican kid, he sat perched on a stool in the corner with only his strings for company: a fifty-cent mandolin, a twelve-string Gibson covered with cigarette burns, and a stained violin so scarred and ugly Stemms would've bet his Tesla the kid used it to kill rats.

Stemms liked the kid's open smile, and the effortless way he pulled off riffs and difficult chord changes while yakking with customers, almost as if the music carried his fingers. Stemms had no idea what they were saying, but Harvey spoke pretty good Spanish, and translated.

Couple of hours and five or six cervezas into the evening, the kid blew his mind. The crowd had thinned, and people weren't so quick with requests. The kid finished off yet another dull ranchera ballad, traded the mandolin for his twelve-string, and finger-picked the opening bars of *Sonatina Meridional*, a complicated composition by Manuel Ponce.

Stemms was so surprised he kicked Harvey under the table.

"Holy shit."

Harvey said, "What?"

"Manuel Ponce."

"The kid?"

"The composer. *Listen.*"

Stemms was on the edge of his chair when the kid finished, and shouted his first request of the evening.

"*Sonata Tres!*"

He held up three fingers, hoping the kid understood. *Sonata Tres* was one of his favorites.

The kid grinned, and opened the *Sonata* like he had played it a thousand times. More couples left, and the drinkers thinned. The kid followed the *Sonata* with another by Ponce, and then a Segovia. Halfway through the Segovia, Stemms walked over, dropped a C-note in the tip jar, and gestured to ask if he could use the kid's fiddle. The kid nodded happily.

Harvey said, "Don't be a douche, Stemms. C'mon."

Stemms plucked softly at the strings, adjusted the tune, and as the Segovia ended, Stemms planted the fiddle under his jaw and swept into Bach's *Violin Concerto in E Major*. The sun sparkled in the kid's glee, and he fell in with his guitar, swooping and flying along with the violin.

Harvey jumped to his feet and applauded.

"Holy shit, Stemms! Are you kidding me? For real?!"

Stemms played the first and second movements, but stopped at the edge of the third, and the kid looked surprised.

Stemms pointed the bow at the kid, the bow saying *your turn*. The kid thought for a moment, then let out a looping maniacal laugh and launched into *Wipe Out*, by the Surfaris.

Stemms kicked Harvey again and applauded. Then the kid finished, and spoke to Harvey in Spanish.

Harvey said, "He wants to request a song."

Stemms raised the bow, saying, bring it, whatever you want.

The kid said, "*In-A-Gadda-Da-Vida.*"

Harvey roared.

Stemms did his best with the Iron Butterfly classic, then threw one back to the kid, Wagner's *Ride of the Valkyries*, after which the kid double-downed with Mike Post's theme for *The Rockford Files*. Stemms saw his raise with Henry Mancini's *Peter Gunn*, and the kid fired back with Lalo Schifrin's *Mission Impossible*.

Harvey, drunk as two fucks by then, got in on the play, shouting at the top of his lungs.

"Talking Heads! *Psycho Killer!*"

The kid owned it.

They went back and forth. Stemms riffed *Machine Gun* by Hendrix, which was a bitch to pluck on a fiddle, and the kid fired back with Metallica's *For Whom the Bell Tolls*, playing his twelve-string all badass and nasty. Stemms brought it low with *Hurt*, the Johnny Cash version, which Stemms dearly loved, a song so filled with pain he cried each time he heard it. He sang the lyrics as he strummed the slow, wounded chords. *What have I become, my sweetest friend? Everyone I know goes away in the end.* Even Harvey cried. Even Harvey.

Harvey said, "Stemms, you're breaking my heart, you bastard. Where'd you learn to play like this?"

"Nowhere."

Then it came back to Stemms, and the kid asked for the Hermann piece from the movie, the movement known as *The Murder*, so what was Stemms supposed to do, after sharing so much music? He bent to the fiddle, and tortured the strings.

Must've been three or four in the morning. Five rough men stumbled in, loud and large, edgy from crank and screaming for tequila. Harvey peeped guns, and glanced a warning to Stemms. Cartel banditos.

The kid quickly began packing his instruments, and the bartender roused the whore. One guy, a tough-looking middleweight with a scrambled nose, swaggered over to the kid and scooped up his twelve-string.

Harvey's chair scraped the floor when he stood.

"Watch this."

Stemms touched his arm, stopping him.

"What's he saying?"

"Something about songs. He's gonna play some songs."

The guy walked back to his friends, strumming the guitar, and the kid didn't know what to do, stood there, empty and scared.

Stemms got up.

"Go on, Harvey. Best you leave."

"My ass."

Harvey reached under his jacket, his big face gone dark.

Stemms picked up an empty Jalisco bottle, and threw it. Hit the dude's head and bounced off his ear. Dude didn't even know what happened, touched the side of his head like he expected to find ants, then he and his friends turned.

Stemms said, "Tell him the guitar belongs to me. I'll let him have it if he sucks my dick."

Harvey passed along the offer, swaying like a rattlesnake.

So the guy, Mr. Cartel, a cold-hearted savage, reared back to swing the guitar. Stemms shot him twice in the chest, flashes like lightning in the tiny cantina, thunder shaking the walls.

The Frito banditos stood frozen like turds, not sure what had happened or why.

Stemms said, "Give'm a pat, Harvey? Please?"

Harvey tossed their guns and knives and wallets behind the bar, but kept their keys. Harvey knew what was coming. He couldn't stop smiling.

Stemms waved his pistol at the door.

"Tell'm to carry the guitar thief outside."

Stemms did not look at the kid or the bartender, nor speak to them.

Out in the parking lot, the pallbearers loaded the stiff into a battered Toyota Land Cruiser. Harvey told them to take their asshole friend, and feed him to the snakes. Happy to get a pass, the banditos piled in and fired the engine. Harvey and Stemms shot them, a double-tap each in the head. Harvey dragged the driver from behind the wheel, loaded him into the back with his friends, and followed Stemms out along Highway 2.

Harvey was covered with so much blood when they finished, he stripped, and rode back to their motel naked.

Harvey and Stemms stayed in Ciudad Juárez for another eight days, but did not return to the cantina. Stemms thought about the kid every so often in the years since, and wondered how he was doing. Wondered if he kept that twelve-string guitar.

Stemms had played the Hermann piece for the kid, but he had hated that scene and the score from as far back as he could remember, and now Harvey had it on his damned phone.

"I was screwing around, Harvey. I wasn't brilliant. I'm begging, change your alert to something else. I hate that fucking scene. *Please.*"

Harvey gaped, flabbergasted. He could just do it and move on. He couldn't let go.

"I don't get it. Every film school on the planet *teaches* that scene. It's one of the best-known scenes in the world."

"Which makes it all the worse."

"Makes *what* worse?"

Stemms felt himself getting a headache.

"She just stands there and takes it, Harvey. Does that make sense, 'cause I'm missing the brilliance?"

Harvey shook his head, confused.

"What are you talking about?"

"You're taking a shower. A knife comes out of nowhere, and some asshole stabs you. Not once, but over and over. You just going to stand there?"

Harvey seemed even more confused.

"She was caught off guard."

"You wouldn't try to get away? You wouldn't jump out the shower, or grab the guy?"

"I'd take the fuckin' knife, and gut the freak, Stemms, but she wasn't us. She was in shock."

"I hate that scene. It's evil."

"You should see your face. It's a movie."

"You have no idea."

Harvey rolled his eyes.

"Oh, okay, here we go. Enlighten me."

"Four Oscar nominations. Golden Globe Award. Edgar Award. *Huge* box office all over the world, and this was 1960, a more innocent time, before people were all fucked up, right?"

"Okay. And?"

"It's the message, is what I'm saying. The subtext. That scene misled a generation of young women. The message was bad."

Harvey gave him the dumb cow eyes. Stemms sighed and kept going.

"The message was, women are powerless. Here's this lunatic, he's stabbing her, what did she do, the chick in the movie? Just stood there. So what's being modeled? Whatever some guy does to a woman, they're supposed to take it. That's the message, Harvey. Don't fight. Don't try to get away. You're helpless. Isn't that a terrible message for all those young women?"

Harvey cleared his throat, and turned to his phone.

"Let's check the alert. Bet you a buck it's another dog."

"Point being, dump the *Psycho* piece. I'm begging."

Harvey tapped away on the phone, ignoring him.

"You could go with *Jungle Boogie* by Kool and the Gang, coming in right at the top where they're singing 'Get down Get down,' or *Magic Carpet Ride* by Steppenwolf, coming in on 'I like to dream.' You like Steppenwolf."

Harvey sighed, and kept tapping.

"Go with the Steppenwolf, Harvey. We'll be happier."

The app finally opened, and Harvey accessed the feed.

"Check it out, Stemms. We've got something."

"What?"

"Lemme wind it back."

Harvey leaned closer, holding the phone so they could watch together.

The image had the hyper-real clarity of high-def TV with a wide-angle bend. A man walked up the drive. Harvey nudged Stemms, and leered.

"The Corvette guy. Dropped by for another slice o' Mom."

Only, the Corvette guy didn't go to the door. He came directly to the camera, looked into the lens, and held up his phone. He held the phone close, showing a photograph.

Harvey tipped forward, his voice turning raspy and soft.

"That's me."

Stemms felt the stillness spread, a kernel of loss that filled his chest and dulled his belly.

Harvey breathed hard beside him, panting like a big dog on a hot day.

"He has my picture, Stemms. *How'd he get my picture?*"

The man lowered his phone and reached toward the lens. His hand grew larger until the screen went black, and Harvey's phone screeched another message alert.

Harvey frantically killed the music.

"System fail. He killed the camera."

The *Psycho* score screamed again.

"System fail. The living room."

Stemms closed his eyes. He took a slow breath, and cherished the stillness.

"The burger."

"What?"

The *Psycho* score screamed a third time. Harvey punched the dash, and read the alert.

"System fail. The transmitter's gone."

"He's why they left the food. He beat us, Harvey. He found them first."

Harvey's face turned purple. Mountain-range veins cut his forehead.

"STEMMS! He has my *PICTURE!*"

Stemms fired the engine, and pulled into traffic.

"Relax, Harvey. Breathe."

Harvey took a breath, and straightened himself.

"We're compromised. We should tell the client, and let him bring in a new team."

"Let's think it through."

"What's to think? The client's at risk. This isn't about us, Stemms. Client service comes first."

"Think. The guy didn't just happen by. He knew the place was bugged, and found the gizmos without tripping a sensor. He saw us go in."

"Excuse me. That was *me* in the picture, not us."

"Think. We went to the Connor house, so he knew we would go to Jasmine's. He yanked them before we got there, and now he's showing us up."

"Don't personalize this, Stemms. It smacks of hubris."

"If these little shitbirds are with *him*, then *he* has the laptop, and, excuse me, Mr. Client Service, the client would like it back. So we ain't saying shit until we deliver."

Harvey stared, his mouth as slack as a plastic bag.

"Have you lost your mind?"

Stemms patted Harvey's leg.

"Not yet, but I will if I hear the *Psycho* piece again. Go with the Steppenwolf."

Harvey stared out the window, and shook his head.

"He has my picture, and you're talking about Steppenwolf."

Harvey stared out the window for a while, but finally turned back.

"I wonder what happened to that kid, the one in Juárez. You ever think about him?"

"Thinking about him now."

"Here's this kid in a nowhere cantina, and he was amazing. A truly special person. Where do these people come from?"

"Same place as you and me."

Harvey fell silent, and turned back to the window.

"You, maybe. I'm nothing special."

Stemms looked at the back of Harvey's head, wondering what he was thinking.

"You're the most special person I know, Harvey."

Harvey looked over with sorrowful, basset hound eyes, then suddenly grinned and wiggled his eyebrows.

"I know. I was screwing with you."

Stemms burst out laughing. Harvey had always been able to make him laugh.

PART IV

THE GIRL WHO GOT
WHAT SHE WANTED

39

ELVIS COLE

PIKE DROPPED US OFF, and went back to Devon's. The rest of us worked on the living room floor, surrounded by power cords, pizza, and paper plates. Devon had taken Amber for takeout. Cassett called twice while we worked, but I let her calls go to voice mail.

Tyson lined the laptops against the wall, plugged them into a power strip, and powered them up. The ancient PowerBook took forever to load, and made clickety noises like a windup toy.

Devon eyed the laptops doubtfully, watching their screens fill with folders, photos and documents, and inexplicable icons. MOM'S WILL. CONTRACT-REVISION2. KENNY. CONTEST RESULTS. LAKE ARROWHEAD.

"How are we going to figure out who these things belong to?"

"Open whatever you find on the desktop. Start with documents, letter files, whatever you think will show a person's name. If you see the same name enough times, you'll figure it out from the context."

Devon seemed uncomfortable.

"This is like reading someone's mail."

Amber seemed fascinated by the PowerBook.

"OhmiGod, I want this one. What's this little ball?"

Tyson showed her how the ball rolled in its socket.

"A trackball. Roll it with your finger, and the cursor moves."

She moved the ball, and beamed.

"This is so cool! I *love* it!"

Identifying each laptop's owner was surprisingly easy. We came up with likely names, and Devon checked the police reports for a match. The PC I searched belonged to an Emmy-winning costume designer named Clara Pearl Schiltzen. Tyson's PC belonged to an eighth-grade student named Harrison Hardy Franks, whose parents owned a discount shoe store chain. An interior designer named Steven Joyce owned the laptop Devon checked. Joyce seemed as unlikely a suspect as the others, but I knew of a lighting dealer on La Brea who was a former KGB sniper.

Amber still hadn't found a name, and looked unhappy as she twiddled the trackball.

"This sucks. There's only one stupid folder, and nothing but pictures of some stupid kid."

I sat beside her and studied the desktop.

A folder named DEREK contained the pictures. DEREK and a hard drive icon were alone on the otherwise empty desktop.

"Hey, Tyson. What's the deal here? No files."

Tyson wedged in beside me to study the screen.

"Might be something in the drive, but I dunno. It's old. Maybe they were gonna get rid of it, so they erased their files."

I reopened DEREK, and scrolled. The greenish, monotone photographs of boys, babies, and young men were all of the same person at different stages of his life, alone or with friends, at schools and ballparks and on ski slopes or at the beach. The pictures seemed to be arrayed in no particular order, and labeled with meaningless numbers.

Tyson said, "Okay. Why is this creepy?"

Amber said, "Self-love, much."

Devon moved closer.

"It's a photo album, all this one boy."

A baby in this one, a young man sporting a tuxedo in the next, a teenager wearing the garish white face, scraggly hair, and bloody, maniacal leer of the Joker. Cassett called again, and another one went to voice mail.

Tyson suddenly touched the trackball.

"Let's see something."

A list of the picture files appeared, showing the date each image was scanned.

Tyson said, "Dude. This stuff has been here forever."

Devon said, "As long as you. Seventeen years."

We scrolled, and a second folder appeared. The new folder was labeled TRIAL.

Amber said, "I have to pee."

The new folder contained PDF scans of nine news articles from the *Los Angeles Times,* the L.A. *Daily News,* and the *LA Weekly.* The first bore a simple headline: *HOOP FREED.*

Devon was suddenly excited.

"Hoop. That's one of our names."

She turned to her files.

Tyson and I read the article while Devon searched the police reports.

> Derek Hoop, 23, convicted last year for the murder of Adele Silvani, 25, was freed yesterday after the District Attorney submitted a brief asking Judge Eloise Wallace to vacate Hoop's conviction.
>
> The District Attorney said, "Based on newly discovered evidence proving his factual innocence and directly supporting Mr. Hoop's testimony, we believe him innocent of the charge, and we asked Judge Wallace to order his immediate release."
>
> Marquis Nelson, 25, has been charged with Silvani's murder, and is currently in custody.
>
> Hoop, the son of prominent businessman Ivar Hoop,

served eight months of a fifteen-years-to-life sentence.
He has maintained his innocence since the night of his
girlfriend's murder.

Hoop's attorney, Carlos Philippe, has asked the court
to expunge Mr. Hoop's record once his conviction is va-
cated.

Hoop, speaking through a family representative, said
he feels vindicated, and bears no ill will toward the police
or prosecutors.

"The same people who convicted me are the people
who freed me. I'm sad that it happened, but happy it's
over."

Devon found the report.

"Here it is. Lillian Hoop, in Holmby Hills. Officers summoned to the
residence by Ms. Lillian Hoop. I Googled her—"

She paraphrased as she read.

"Married to Ivar Hoop, president of Hoop Technologies. They own
nine privately held companies valued at two-point-two billion dollars."

Tyson said, "Wow."

The next story was a *Daily News* piece about Derek's arrest. I had just
started to read when my phone sounded again. Devon, Tyson, and Amber
jumped. I jumped with them. This time it wasn't Cassett.

Nora Gurwick had finally returned my calls.

"It's your mother."

Amber's mouth turned down at the corners.

I got up and went to the far side of the room. As if an extra twelve feet
could shield Amber from what I would say.

Nora Gurwick said, "What are you, the new boyfriend?"

"I'm a private investigator. Thanks for returning my calls."

"Rick called, and Rick never calls. What's she done this time?"

I told her I was employed by the parent of one of Amber's friends, and explained that Amber and her friends had been involved in a series of burglaries. I told her the police were closing in, and Amber would have to surrender, or she'd be arrested. I actually said 'closing in.' Nora Gurwick cut me off.

"I get it. You want someone to take her off your hands."

"Yes. And she needs an attorney."

"Everything is always about her. Can't I have five minutes for myself without something happening?"

Five minutes in Banff. Mother of the Year.

"Maybe her father can help."

"Worthless. Where's Jazzi?"

"Away. Amber shouldn't be alone, Ms. Gurwick. She needs an attorney, and she needs someone to help her through this."

Amber sat hunched across her legs, watching me like a lip-reader.

Nora heaved a dramatic sigh.

"All right, all right. I get it. I'll come home. Rick might help with the lawyer. I'll call him. Maybe she can stay with him."

"The sooner the better."

"You ever been to Banff? I'm in the middle of fucking nowhere."

"Give Rick my cell. He can call me directly."

"Is she there?"

I walked back to the others, and handed my phone to Amber. She sounded six years old when she spoke.

"I'm in trouble."

Her eyes lost their gleam, and her face seemed to empty, as if the parts that made her Amber were fading.

"I know, I'm sorry, I was stupid, I'm just—"

I wondered if Nora heard her, or ever had.

Amber began to rock.

"Rick's fine. I don't care. You don't have to leave your retreat."

Devon glanced at me, and edged closer to Amber.

Amber rocked faster.

"All *right*! I messed up, okay? I mess up everything. Oh, like you would know? Look at your shitty life!"

The rocking stopped, and Amber shouted.

"You're a *disaster*, and you talk about me? I *hate* you. *Jazzi* hates you. You're a disgusting JOKE, and *everyone* hates you!"

Devon touched her arm, and took the phone.

"This is Devon Connor. I wanted to introduce myself. My son is involved in this, too."

Devon's voice was low, and soothing. A few minutes later she ended the call.

I mouthed 'Thank you.'

Devon nodded, and gave me the phone.

"She'll book the first available, and let us know when she's arriving."

Devon turned to Amber.

"You okay?"

"That didn't go so well, did it?"

Tyson reached out. His eyes were filled with a heartbreaking sadness. Amber took his hand, and squeezed before letting go.

I used the bathroom, then went outside, and listened to messages. Cassett had called five times since she'd seen me that morning.

"Cole, it's Sergeant Cassett. Call me ASAP."

"I talked to the Crenzas. They're working with a sketch artist right now, and I have more questions. Call. This is important."

"Cole, do you ever answer? These men are impersonating police officers. I need to talk to you, so call me. Let's straighten this out."

"All right, Cole, you want to play? If these people killed Louise August, you are aiding and abetting after the fact, and I will hang your ass on a hook."

Cassett sounded calmer in her final message. Maybe I was wearing her out.

"I'm thinking you're dead. Neff and Hensman killed you, which is the only possible reason you haven't called. You know what the old lady told them. You know who these kids are, don't you? You should've told me before you died, Cole. I'm the only chance they have."

I deleted her messages, then checked in with Joe. The bug men had not returned. I wanted to think they'd quit, but I knew better.

The night was dark, and the air was crisp. A nearby hiss marked the freeway. I took deep breaths, and enjoyed the chill. I looked up. A starless black canopy. Being outside was good. The cold air was good. I enjoyed it for as long as I dared, then went back inside.

"Get to work. Someone is trying to kill you."

40

THE SAFE HOUSE WAS QUIET. Tyson and Amber worked at laptops in the dining room, searching for reasons someone would kill for them. Devon combed through her victim files, and I skimmed the PDFs. The *LA Weekly* provided the most detailed coverage of Derek Hoop's trial with a three-part feature capped by a potboiler headline: *LESS THAN HERO: HOW WEALTH, DOPE, AND ENTITLEMENT LED TO MURDER.*

Lurid.

Hoop was described as a bad-boy scion of wealth, trailing a history of private-school expulsions, DUI arrests, and multiple stints in rehab. Adele Silvani was presented as a drug-dealing party girl who bragged her billionaire boy toy wiped himself with hundred-dollar bills.

Classy.

On the night Silvani was murdered, Hoop ran into an all-night convenience store, covered in blood and screaming that he and his girlfriend had been attacked.

Amber said, "I miss television."

I told her to keep searching.

Hoop led responding officers to Silvani's body in nearby Elysian Park, telling police an unknown black male had robbed them at knife point, taking Hoop's watch, wallet, and cell phone, as well as Silvani's purse, which contained several packets of heroin. When Silvani resisted, their assailant stabbed her, and fled.

Amber piped up again.

"Can we play music, at least?"

"No."

Officers began to question Hoop's story when they learned Silvani had been supplying drugs to Hoop, who ran up a tab he never paid. On the night she was murdered, Silvani and Hoop were seen arguing about the money he owed at a nearby bar. Silvani threatened to collect from his parents unless he paid, and announced she would do so that night. Hoop followed her out, and the couple was seen departing in Hoop's black-on-black Porsche. The knife used to murder Silvani was not recovered. No evidence of a third person was found at the scene, on Silvani's clothes, or on her person, and the only DNA found on Silvani other than her own was Derek's. The ending felt anticlimactic. I knew from earlier stories that Hoop had been convicted, only to be released eight months later and cleared of all charges. Spoilers ruined everything.

Amber sighed loudly.

"I'm bored."

I grabbed waters for everyone from the kitchen. On my way back to the living room, Tyson closed his laptop.

"I'm hungry. Can we go for sushi?"

I dropped a bottle into his lap.

"Eat some water."

Devon and Amber laughed.

The next article caught me off guard. Three years after his release from prison, Derek Hoop once again checked into rehab. Ten weeks later, he was found on Mulholland Drive above the Hollywood Bowl, dead in his car from a heroin overdose.

I sat back and rolled my neck. Tyson wanted sushi. I wanted a beer. I wanted to strip down, work out, and run hard for miles.

I studied Devon, swiping and tapping her phone, then her son and the girl beside him. They looked like everyday teenagers living everyday lives. They weren't, but they might be when this was behind them. I didn't want them to die in a car above the Hollywood Bowl.

"He's dead."

Devon was making notes, and didn't stop.

"Who?"

"Derek. He died of an overdose."

She glanced up.

"That's so sad."

She went back to work, but suddenly tensed. She studied her phone, reread the page, then glanced at her phone.

"It's him. It has to be Ivar Hoop."

She held out her phone.

"Look at number five. This is the downtown address. Those men went to this address!"

Tyson heard her excitement.

"What'd you find? Mom?"

Tyson and Amber hurried into the living room.

Devon had found the nine companies Ivar Hoop owned on a business networking site. The fifth company on the list was called Hoop Security Group, whose offices were located at the DTLA address.

Tyson said, "What's going on?"

Devon flipped more pages.

"I have a tenant list. Here! Hoop Security Group, floors thirty-six and thirty-seven. This is the building! It's *him*!"

Tyson dropped to the floor beside me, and peered at the PowerBook like he expected something dramatic.

"What'd you find?"

I stared at the same dull screen with the same dull pictures.

"Pictures of Derek. Stories about what happened. Nothing."

Devon said, "There has to be something."

Amber sat cross-legged behind Tyson and looked over his shoulder.

"Maybe these pictures are all he has left of his son."

Tyson rolled the trackball and studied the drive.

"They're scans. People scan pictures, and have all the copies they want. These aren't the last pictures on earth of this kid."

Amber shrugged.

"We don't know. Maybe they are. Maybe his parents are heartbroken."

Devon tossed the tenant list aside, and pushed to her feet.

"Nobody murders people for an old memory book. Something's here. It's right in front of our noses, and we just haven't found it."

She glared at the old PowerBook, and gave me an idea.

"Maybe they don't want the pictures, but something inside the pictures."

Tyson sat back and looked at me. Surprised.

"Encrypted?"

"Encrypted, embedded, however you hide something. Can you tell?"

Tyson pushed back from the keyboard.

"We'd need special software. I wouldn't know where to start. I don't have the skills."

"Does Carl have the skills?"

Tyson glanced away, probably flashing on the scene he'd made, bragging to Carl about his smoking-hot porno freak girlfriend.

"Carl's really smart."

Devon said, "You're smart, too, honey."

Tyson flushed, and Amber bumped his back.

"Ty, that's so sweet! Don't make a face."

Devon stared at me. Hard.

"Ty?"

Tyson twiddled the trackball, and managed a nod.

"Carl has mad skills."

Amber said, "Do we still have to look for stuff on the other laptops?"

"No. You did good. Thanks."

Tyson and Amber wandered back to the dining room, and sat against the wall. I watched them talk, and thought about Amber.

Devon said, "We can't just sit here and do nothing."

"We're not. I'm thinking."

"What are you thinking?"

"Thoughts."

"*So* not funny."

"Will you phone Carl's mother again? See if he'll take a look."

"Right away."

"In the morning, first thing. I should find out what the Hoops know, and whether someone at his company wants this computer."

"Okay."

"The problem is how."

"Of course. You can't just walk in and ask."

I watched Amber and Tyson some more.

"Do we have an insurance claim from the Hoops?"

"Yes! Absolutely!"

Devon found their file, and we went through their claim. The Hoops listed eighteen stolen items. The PowerBook was not listed among their losses, but they claimed five antique rings, two antique bracelets, a brooch, and an antique necklace. A description of each piece of jewelry was included, along with documentary photographs.

I studied Amber.

"What are you thinking now?"

"That I can walk in, and ask without asking."

I got up, and showed the pictures of jewelry to Amber.

41

TYSON CONNOR

TYSON STARED into the grocery bag, and called to his mother.

"I thought you brought food. All I see is cereal, but we don't have any milk."

His mother called from the living room.

"The other bag. Look."

"I *looked*. Where?"

Amber giggled, and whispered so his mother wouldn't hear.

"Eat the pizza box. Maybe you'll like it."

Tyson made a face as his mother entered the kitchen and went to a bag by the stove. She took out packages and jars, and stacked them on the counter.

"Here, Mr. I Looked. Chips. Fig bars. Dried apples. Nutella. Salsa. Trail mix. Try not to bite off a finger."

Tyson felt a wave of relief, and tore the wrapper off a fig bar.

His mother glanced at Amber, and her face seemed to soften.

"How're you doing?"

Amber made one of her little shrugs.

"My mom kinda stresses me out."

His mother touched Amber's arm.

"I'm sure she does. Maybe we can talk later, if you'd like."

"About the police?"

"That, and whatever else."

His mother went back to sit with Elvis.

Amber said, "Your mom's kinda nice."

Tyson swallowed the fig bar, and opened the bag of tortilla chips.

"Yeah. Considering how much trouble I'm in. I hope we don't go to jail."

"We're too pretty for jail. Only ugly people go to jail."

She smiled so he'd know she was joking, but Tyson didn't think it was funny.

"I'm serious. What happens if the men who killed Alec find us?"

Amber made her eyes wide.

"Have you seen that guy Joe? With the arrows? He's a beast. He's kinda hot, too."

Tyson opened the salsa, and scooped with the chips. Joe was definitely a badass beast, and Elvis looked kinda tough, but Tyson kept thinking about Alec, and seeing himself in prison. Even juvie was bad. He was small and chicken, and he'd be trapped with gangbanging rapists and killers. Tyson shoveled in chips and salsa. He tried to think about something else, but couldn't.

"We can't afford a fancy lawyer. Your mom has money, but my mom's gonna go broke paying for this."

"You worry too much."

"Amber. This is happening. We could've been killed like Alec, and we would've been caught anyway. We're lucky Elvis found us. This is our chance to turn things around."

Amber nudged him, and whispered.

"We're going to be famous. They might even make a movie about us."

Tyson coughed, and sprayed bits of tortilla chips.

She nudged him again, and glanced at Elvis and his mom. They were huddled over the PowerBook.

"You think that's the one they want?"

"What?"

"The laptop those men are looking for."

"I dunno. I guess so."

She nudged him again.

"It belongs to a *billionaire*. If he's killing people and doing all this to get it back, it's worth *millions*. We could sell it back to him."

Tyson thought she was joking, but this time she didn't smile. Amber was serious.

"You're crazy."

"We can help the cops arrest him for killing Alec, and we'll be heroes. We can get an agent, someone really good, and have him pitch us to a studio. We'll be stars."

Tyson studied her face and the way her eyes were bright and excited.

He was thinking up something to say when Elvis came over to them and showed Amber pictures of jewelry.

"Recognize these?"

Amber deflated like a popped balloon.

"Uh-huh."

"Do you have them?"

Amber made an awkward shrug, like she was embarrassed.

"The necklace and the bracelets. I didn't keep the others."

"Where are they?"

"My sister's. In my closet."

"Hidden? So your sister couldn't find them?"

Tyson wondered why he was asking.

"Uh-huh."

Cole seemed to be thinking, and Tyson wondered what he was thinking about. Cole finally nodded.

"Okay. That's good. That's very good."

Cole snatched the bag of trail mix and a fig bar, and went back to his mom.

Amber whispered again as soon as Cole left.

"Celebrities don't get into trouble, you yo-yo. They only get more famous. We'll be the burglars who turned out to be heroes, and everyone will love us."

Tyson stared into the bag of chips, and felt queasy.

"That isn't going to happen."

Amber frowned.

Tyson searched her pretty eyes, but now they seemed watchful and hostile.

"We broke into houses. We stole stuff, and Alec is dead. We're the bad guys. Bad guys aren't heroes. Don't you get it?"

Amber stared at him for the longest time, and then she stepped away.

"You don't get it, and you never have."

Amber walked out into the living room, and sat on the floor against the wall. Tyson felt anxious and scared, and knew she was right. He didn't get it. He had never gotten it, but now he was beginning to understand.

Amber was crazy.

42

ELVIS COLE

THE NIGHT CRAWLED past between fitful naps, the lullaby hiss of the freeway broken by rumbling trucks and the burping roar of drilled-out choppers. I gave up on sleep at four-fifteen and drifted into the kitchen. The floor was dirty. I hadn't noticed before.

I Googled the Hoop Security Group on my phone. HSG provided specialized security services for the other eight Hoop companies, as well as their clients and business partners, ensuring cutting-edge protection against data loss, cyber attacks, and external security threats. Job applicants with experience in law enforcement, the military, and those with security clearances were given preference.

The man had his own police force.

I called Pike, and sketched out my plan. Pike had been awake for almost sixty hours, but he answered on the first ring. All Pike, all the time.

Pike said, "Maybe you shouldn't do this alone."

"What, you think I'm not tough enough?"

Pike hung up in his usual way, but something about this familiar act made me smile.

I grabbed the last fig bar, and sat with the PowerBook while I ate it. Derek's mother or father or both had made this little machine their son's resting place, but nothing of Derek's true nature or joys or interests had been included, as if the sum of their love had not been Derek's life, but on those events leading to his end. The single short piece reporting his death felt like a period ending a sentence.

I crept into the bedroom where Devon slept with Tyson and Amber. I touched her arm, but she was already awake. She rose without a sound, and followed me to the kitchen.

"I'll talk to Cassett, and make sure Tyson and Amber are safe. If I can't get back to the safe house, you'll have to take them in without me."

"Are we going to surrender?"

"I'll let you know after I talk to her, but yes. She'll go for it."

"What if she doesn't?"

"She will, so have your lawyer ready to go. Call her first thing. We'll want to deliver the kids fast, so these bastards won't have time to react. They'll be thinking about me."

"Why you?"

"I'll set it up that way. Be ready."

She gazed at me in the dim kitchen light, and suddenly kissed me. A quick peck on the lips, nothing more.

"That fucking woman is a fool."

Tyson and Amber slept until I woke them, and staggered through their morning as if nothing unusual was happening.

Devon phoned Carl's mother at ten after eight. I spoke to Carl, explained about the PowerBook, and asked if he'd try to help.

The Carl's voice was a sneer.

"Do. Or not do. There is no try."

Hyuk-hyuk-hyuk.

Star Wars fan. Of course.

The Carl didn't drive, so I'd have to bring the laptop to him. He also wanted six hundred dollars. I agreed, and told him when to expect us.

"Us? Is Tyson the King of Dickland coming?"

"Yes. There a problem?"

Hyuk-hyuk-hyuk.

Tyson looked sick when I lowered the phone.

"Do I have to go?"

"Man up."

Amber told me the jewelry was in a bright red shoe box at the back of her closet in Jazzi's apartment. She wanted to come, and accused me of gender bias when I refused.

I took Devon aside.

"Is she nervous about her mom coming back?"

"We talked a little last night. That family has serious issues."

Nora had promised to call when she booked a flight, but still hadn't called. Neither had Rick.

I checked the time. There was nothing more to ask, or do, except deliver the PowerBook to Carl, get Lillian Hoop's jewelry, and talk my way into the Hoop Security Group. The trick would be talking my way out.

Tyson looked miserable as we drove to The Carl, and neither of us said much. We each had our reasons, but our reasons were different.

He said, "Are you scared?"

Maybe our reasons weren't so different.

"Yes."

"Please be careful."

I wanted to touch his head, but didn't.

I walked him up Carl's drive and through the gate. The Carl was waiting outside, dressed in his business suit and bow tie. He glanced at Tyson, and fidgeted. He looked awkward and uneasy, and barely made eye contact. Tyson wasn't much better.

Tyson said, "Hi, Carl."

The Carl said, "Hi."

I gave him the PowerBook.

"Tyson knows what we're looking for. Do. Or not do. There is no try."

The Carl didn't laugh, and neither did Tyson.

I drove to Jasmine's apartment, and let myself through the gate with

Amber's key. The bright red shoe box sat at the back of her closet exactly as Amber described, but finding Lillian Hoop's jewelry took several minutes. The shoe box contained so much jewelry it looked like a treasure chest. I finally found the pieces I wanted, tucked them into a Ziploc bag, and let myself out.

43

HARVEY AND STEMMS

HARVEY EYED the snapshot of Jasmine, and glanced up with sneering contempt. His face was twisted with revulsion.

"What's wrong with you, Stemms? You're disgusting."

Stemms was surprised.

"See those calves? C'mon. She's hot."

"She's a *child*, you pervert. A little girl playing soccer. Jesus. My skin is crawling."

Stemms had copped the pic from Jasmine's old room at her mother's place, the freak with the incense and weed and creepy lips. The snapshot caught Jasmine as she planted to deliver a downfield kick during a soccer match. Big deal. The little shorts, sweaty, the curve of her muscular calf.

Stemms put the picture away, sorry that he shared.

"You're being dramatic. She's gotta be what here, fifteen, sixteen?"

"You disgust me."

"It's an old picture, Harvey. She's grown now. A legal adult woman."

"You cop her panties, too?"

Harvey made sniffing sounds. Sniff-sniff-sniff.

Stemms gave him a nasty grin.

"The panties from her apartment were fresher."

Harvey tried to keep scowling, but finally laughed.

"She gets home soon enough, you can enjoy those calves for real."

Stemms slurped his lips.

"More than her calves, brother."

Harvey suddenly sat taller, and squinted ahead.

"Here we go. Exit."

Stemms guided the Chrysler off the 405 at the top of the Sepulveda Pass, and turned toward Mulholland Drive.

Stemms patted the dash.

"I like this car. Gonna miss it."

Harvey squinted ahead, searching for the drop.

"On the left. Swing around, and come back."

A tiny Park & Ride lot sat across lanes on the opposite side of the street. Stemms continued up to Mulholland, swung around, and guided the Chrysler into the entrance. He parked in the first available space, but left the engine running. They studied the surrounding cars.

The Park & Ride was built so freeway commuters could leave their cars when they hooked up for carpools, but being isolated, unguarded, and next to a freeway ramp, the little lot was mostly used for dope drops, middle-aged make-out sessions, and gardeners needing a convenient place to change their oil.

Harvey said, "Your side?"

"Couple in the Prius, man and a woman. Male in the pickup. They're nothing."

Harvey got out first, three-sixtied the area, and slapped the roof, letting Stemms know he saw nothing suspicious.

Stemms turned off the engine, checked around his seat a final time, and got out.

"Gonna miss you, car."

He tossed the keys onto the floorboard, and closed the Chrysler for the last time.

They had been told to be in this place, and given a time frame, which meant people knew where they would be, and when they would be there. This left them vulnerable, and neither man liked it.

Stemms walked along the row of parked vehicles to a clean, new, white-on-black Mercedes S-class sedan. Harvey trailed ten feet behind, hand on his gun, head on a swivel.

The Mercedes was unlocked.

Stemms slid in behind the wheel, found the key, and immediately backed out. Harvey swung inside the instant Stemms braked, and Stemms hit the gas. Neither relaxed until they were up on Mulholland, and certain they weren't being followed.

Stemms took a moment to feel the ride.

"Not bad. This is kinda nice."

"I liked the Chrysler."

Harvey always grumped when they changed cars. Attachment issues.

Stemms parked at an overlook so they could adjust the mirrors and seats, and figure out the controls. Stemms was flipping through the owner's manual when Harvey's phone filled the big car with a bouncy, familiar tune. *Who's peeking out from under a stairway? Calling a name that's lighter than air?*

A motion alert from Jasmine's apartment.

Harvey pasted Stemms with a nasty grin.

"Sounds like your girlfriend, pervo! Let's see if she's naked!"

Harvey bent to open the video feed from Jasmine's apartment, but Stemms stopped him.

"The song, that's The Association."

"Yeah."

"I thought you were sticking with *Psycho*."

"Don't be a douche. We're partners."

"I *love* this song."

Harvey glanced over and smiled again. His smile was peaceful, and his voice gentle.

"I know."

Stemms was so moved he teared.

"Jesus, Harvey."

Harvey tapped his phone, filling the car with the cheery, upbeat music.

Who's peeking out from under a stairway? Calling a name that's lighter than air?

Stemms taught himself to play the opening bassline when he was seven years old, the first time he held a string instrument. The lady in the next apartment listened to an oldies station. Stemms heard the song playing, the bassline intro, the bright happy bouncy melody, and even when the song stopped playing on the radio, *Windy* played again in his head, and played over and over like someone had hit the replay button, the rest of that day and all night and the next day, and the joy he felt filled him like magic. *Windy*. Written by Ruthann Friedman. Produced by Bones Howe. Recorded by The Association in 1967, a long-ass time before Stemms was born. The first music he played. The first time he was touched by joy.

Harvey just sat there, smiling the gentle smile, eyes kind.

Stemms reached out, and touched Harvey's face. Harvey kissed his finger, just the once, then pulled himself together and turned to his phone.

"Let's see who's under the stairway."

Harvey brought up the feed, and watched for a moment. Then he held the phone so Stemms could see.

"Who IS this guy?"

The man who killed their bugs came out of a bedroom, crossed the living room to the entry, and let himself out.

"Run it back, Harvey. Real time."

Harvey reset the video. The apartment was empty, then the door opened, which was when the sensor was triggered. The man stepped inside, and turned to close the door—

"Stop."

Harvey froze the feed.

Stemms looked closer.

"Keys. He has keys."

"The girl. If she's with him, he would have her keys. Her, and the Connor kid."

THE WANTED | 273

The video resumed.

Having closed the door, the man crossed the living room and entered the first bedroom. Amber's room.

Stemms noted the time. Three minutes and fifty-five seconds later, the man came out, and started across the living room. Harvey froze the image.

"Hands are empty. If he took something, it's small."

"Keep going."

The video resumed.

The man walked directly to the entry, and let himself out. Once the door closed, all motion within the apartment ceased.

Harvey said, "Entered with purpose. Straight to the bedroom, did whatever he did, bailed. He's here for a specific reason. What do you think?"

"I think he wasn't wearing gloves."

Harvey looked surprised, like this hadn't occurred to him, which it hadn't. He reset the video, and they watched it again. The man closed the door after he entered. When he left, he opened the door. Both times, his bare hand gripped the knob. Harvey and Stemms gloved up everywhere.

Harvey grinned. He positively beamed.

"Oh, dude. Prints."

Stemms turned out of the overlook, and headed toward the freeway. Harvey started laughing, just out of the blue he was laughing. Stemms smiled, and he began laughing, too.

44

ELVIS COLE

Hoop Security was one of two hundred eighteen tenants, occupying two floors in a skyrise running thirty-three elevators. Total employee population among the tenants probably hit three thousand. Hourly visitors entering and leaving the lobby added a thousand more. The more people the better. Safety in numbers.

I parked three blocks away, wedged my pistol under the seat, and called Cassett.

"Morning, Sergeant. Was that you leaving all those messages?"

"You asshole. Where have you been?"

"Solving your case. Meet me in an hour, and I'll tell you about it."

"I have a better idea. Meet me in my office, and bring your lawyer."

"Grand Central Market in an hour, and forget the big talk. Come alone. I'll answer your questions."

I hung up, and took deep breaths. Long and slow in, long and slow out. Back in my army days, they sent us to find the enemy in jungle so thick the helicopter couldn't land. The pilots would pull to a hover, we'd step on the skids, and slide down ropes through beautiful green leaves into places we could not see. We could not see what was waiting below. We never knew if hard men with rifles were watching. Each time I stepped on the skid, I was scared. I felt like that now, but, as then, I stepped out, and walked the three blocks to their building.

The lobby was as big as an airline terminal and even more busy, sporting escalators to a shopping level, marble floors, and a guard station blocking entrance to the security floors. I stopped in front of the guard station, and studied the directory. I already knew the floor, but I wanted the guards to see me. The elevators to the thirty-sixth floor required a security card. Visitors had to sign in with the guards, who would check a visitor's list to confirm an appointment, then issue a magnetic pass. No appointment, no pass.

When they'd seen me enough, I went to the desk.

"Is there a phone I could use to call Hoop Security, up on thirty-six?"

"Is someone expecting you?"

"No, sir. I have something to drop off, but I don't know who to leave it with."

"You can leave it with me. I'll send it up."

"Thing is, I'm not sure who should get it. I'll find out, write a little note, and leave it with you. Sound good?"

The guard motioned me to the end of the desk, called up to thirty-six, and gave me the phone.

"Here you go."

The woman who greeted me was the receptionist.

"This is Elvis Cole. I'm investigating the burglary at the Hoop residence. I recovered a couple of items might belong to Mrs. Hoop. I'd like to drop them off, if that's okay."

"Mr. Hoop's office is in Long Beach, at Hoop Industries. He isn't here."

"Thing is, I'm here, not in Long Beach. I can leave them with you as long as Mrs. Hoop gets them."

She asked for the guard. The guard listened, then asked for a photo ID. He logged my DL, gave me a pass card, and directed me to an elevator. I pressed the call button, and waited. My shoulders tightened worse than before, and my pulse slammed hard in my ear. I breathed deep again, but my pulse raced.

The elevator opened. I stepped in, and swiped the pass.

The receptionist might know nothing about the burglary, but Mrs. Hoop's name would get her attention. She would be on the phone, asking what she should do, saying a man was coming up with something that belongs to Mrs. Hoop. She would mention the burglary.

I told myself Neff and Hensman wouldn't be waiting when the doors opened. Hoop Security was a large company, with many employees doing legitimate work. Men like Neff and Hensman lived between raindrops and worked under eaves. Only one or two people would know them or know what they were doing, and whoever employed them would limit their exposure. I told myself I wouldn't be shotgunned when the elevator opened, but cobblestone knots still cramped my shoulders.

The reception area was sleek, modern, and corporate. Instead of Neff and Hensman, a young woman with a friendly smile greeted me from behind a sleek, modern reception desk. A tall man with curly blond hair and large hands smiled along with her, and offered his hand.

"Mr. Cole?"

"Elvis Cole. Good to meet you."

"Steve Kleiner. Which agency you with?"

"None. Freelance."

I gave him a card. The one with a smoking .45 in the corner, and my name spelled in bulletholes. He didn't like it. He frowned.

"Not a LEO?"

Law enforcement officer.

"Freelance. Insurance recovery. Things like that."

I held out the Ziploc, letting him see the bracelet and necklace along with another business card.

"I think these belong to Mrs. Hoop. Would you see she gets them?"

He looked surprised when I gave him the bag.

"Is she expecting these?"

"No. I just thought she'd like them."

He fingered the pieces through the plastic, and asked me to follow him.

Kleiner led me to a nice square office with a clean desk, neat shelves, and a view of the skyscraper next door. The skyscraper blocked his view. Middle-tier manager.

He told me to make myself comfortable, and settled behind his desk.

"Why do you think these belong to Mrs. Hoop?"

"They match photos and descriptions on her insurance. I've seen the police report and the claim."

He fingered the necklace again, as if feeling it made it real.

"But you're not a police officer."

"Like it says on the card, freelance. Eighteen rez-burgs in the string, I've been nosing around."

He nodded again.

"And how did these come into your possession?"

"Sources, contacts, elbow grease. It's the grind, Steve. Freelance. We can't afford to sleep."

Kleiner laughed, but the Pinkerton reference flew past his ear. He set the bag on his desk, and nudged it toward me.

"I hear you. Listen, I can't say these belong to Mrs. Hoop, but even if they do, you shouldn't give them to us. Take them to the police."

"I don't work for the police. Freelance, remember?"

He spread his hands, giving me helpless.

"If they do, in fact, belong to Mrs. Hoop, they're evidence. See what I'm saying?"

"The police don't cover my rent. See what I'm saying?"

He laughed again, like he was seeing the light, and laughing for not seeing it sooner.

"Okay. I get it. What do you want?"

"I wouldn't turn down a recovery fee, but that isn't why I'm here."

I nudged the bag back to him.

"These pieces belonged to her mother. I thought she'd like knowing they're safe, and having them back."

Kleiner scooped up the bag, jiggled it as he studied me, and suddenly stood.

"Mind if I take these for a minute? Only be a minute."

"Sure. Whatever you want."

"Let's find out if these do, in fact, belong to Mrs. Hoop. That okay?"

"Absolutely. But, hey, if it turns out they don't, I want them back."

"Goes without saying. Want coffee? Water?"

"I'm good. I'll enjoy the view."

He strode away with the bag, off to spread the word.

I crossed my legs, and stared at the building across the street. The reflective glass skin was like staring into a metallic blue mirror. My phone vibrated, but I ignored it. I didn't want anyone to see me take a call or hear what I would say. Every office and hall on the floor was probably bugged.

Kleiner wasn't alone when he returned. The businessman from Pike's picture was with him. I hadn't expected to see the man, or meet him, or even learn his name, but I stood as they entered, and gave him a card.

"Elvis Cole. Good to meet you."

"Kenneth Loan, Deputy Head of Security. Please. Sit."

If Loan knew who I was, he covered it well. He hitched his pants, sat on the edge of Kleiner's desk, and parked the bag by his leg. Neff and Hensman were killing people like they were nothing, and this guy was as relaxed as a Shriner at a Friday night buffet.

"Lillian will be thrilled. Thank you so much."

"You'll see she gets them?"

"Of course. I'll phone her as soon as we're finished."

"Could I get a receipt? For my records."

I thought he might balk, but he didn't.

"You bet. Hang on—"

He scooped Kleiner's phone from its cradle, and touched a button.

"Draft a receipt for Mr. Cole. Two pieces, that would be items thirteen and fourteen on the claim."

He dropped the phone in its cradle.

"He'll bring it right down."

"Great. Thanks."

He crossed his arms, and considered me.

"Just so you understand, the Hoops will tell the insurance company and the police the items have been returned."

"Sure. I understand."

"The police will have questions."

"Fine by me. Happy to help."

"They'll want to know how you found something an awful lot of people have been looking for."

"I know a fence who knows a fence."

"That probably won't fly."

"I don't give up sources. Bad for business."

"They could jam you. Hit you with obstruction, interference, maybe even accessory."

Shrug.

"Be a shame for the Hoops. I have a line on some other things they lost."

A tiny smile played at the corner of his mouth. I couldn't tell if he was trying to figure my angle, or if he was deciding to kill me.

Loan slid off the desk.

"We're finished, Mr. Cole. My bullshit meter hit the red line."

I stayed seated, and nodded at the jewelry.

"What's in the bag isn't bullshit. Ask Mrs. Hoop."

He didn't react. He also wasn't calling the guards, so I kept going.

"The crew who ripped the Hoops and all these rich people are kids. They've been laying off stuff at a flea market, if you can believe it, but something happened, I'm not sure what. What I'm told, they hooked in with a professional. Guy I know, a gentleman who owes me way more than a favor, claims he has access."

"Access to the crew."

"Claims, I said. Can't swear for a fact, but these—"

I glanced at the jewelry again.

"These are facts. Other items are available."

"Items belonging to the Hoops?"

A slender young man in a dress shirt and tie leaned through the door and handed a page to Kleiner. Kleiner glanced at the page, and held it across his desk.

"Here you go. Receipt."

I folded it, and tucked it away in my jacket.

Loan said, "These items, they were stolen from the Hoops?"

"Didn't say. I might be able to find out. Want me to ask about something specific?"

The businessman's eyes melted into the distance. I had danced to the edge, and maybe I'd fallen.

I winked at Kleiner, trying to save myself.

"For an appropriate finder's fee, of course."

Kleiner grinned, like he'd been waiting for me to say it.

"You shaking down anyone else?"

"I'm talking to people, but this isn't a shakedown. It's an opportunity."

I waved at the bag.

"My gift to the Hoops, gratis. Something comes up in the future, maybe they'll pick up the phone. See what I'm saying?"

Kleiner said, "I get it."

Loan slipped the bag into his pocket, and wet the edge of his lip.

"This source, the one who says he's in with the crew—"

"No promises."

"You want a finder's fee? Deliver the crew. Give me the crew, we'll work something out."

I stood, and stuck out my hand like he was making my day.

"You got it. I'll see what I can find out."

He left without shaking my hand. I stared hard at his back as he walked away, thinking about Alec, and thinking about Louise August. Please be kind.

I must have smiled. Kleiner saw, and looked uneasy. It was a nasty, tight smile. He didn't know why I smiled. He didn't understand what it meant.

45

CASSETT MET ME at Grand Central Market, two blocks from the Police Administration Building. The market was crowded but Cassett had staked out a table between a Thai food stall and an old-school vendor slinging *lengua* and *carnitas* by the pound. Cassett wasn't alone. Rivera saw me first, and nudged her, his expression somewhere between curious and amused.

I dropped into the chair across from them.

"I asked for alone time, Sergeant. Scared I won't come across?"

"Neff and Hensman. Sixty seconds. Go."

She wanted it fast, so I gave it fast. The cop version of speed dating.

"A young man named Alec Rickey was murdered in Pacoima three nights ago. He was chased off the freeway, and shot to death. Neff and Hensman did the shooting."

Rivera flipped open a notebook and began scratching notes.

"You know this how?"

"The day after his murder, Neff and Hensman showed up at his apartment, identified themselves as police officers, and questioned his roommate."

I pushed a slip with Claudia's name and address across the table. Rivera copied them into his book.

"They searched her apartment for laptop computers. Rickey was one of your burglars."

Cassett leaned back, but Rivera wrote harder. The scratch of his pen across paper was so loud I heard it above hundreds of milling people.

I showed them the picture of Hensman.

"Know this man?"

They hunched together to see.

Cassett said, "No."

"Maybe he's been to your briefings."

Cassett looked annoyed.

"No."

"Rickey's roommate identified this man as Hensman. That won't be his real name, but it's the name he uses. Show his picture to the Crenzas. They'll say the same."

Cassett pulled the phone closer and studied the picture.

"Send it to me. Email."

She gave me her LAPD business card with her LAPD email address. Nobody spoke while I tapped her address and sent the picture. When I looked up, she was waiting.

"How do you know Rickey was in with the crew?"

"He was one of the couple selling stolen goods at the flea market."

"The kids who sold the camera?"

"That's it. Neff and Hensman asked the Crenzas if they were selling laptops. They didn't ask about cameras or anything else. They asked about laptops."

Rivera glanced up from his notes.

"You have a name for the girl?"

"I do."

"I'm waiting."

"Enjoy the rest."

Rivera tapped his pen to the page.

"How many obstruction and withholding charges you want? Aiding and abetting. Conspiracy. Accessory. I'm getting excited."

Cassett touched his arm. The tapping stopped, and Cassett leaned back.

"Gotta hand it to you. We've been grinding this case for weeks, and here you are. Wow. How in the hell?"

"The mother of the second male burglar found a watch in his room. She hired me to find out how he got it. I caught a gimme, Cassett. Luck."

Rivera's pen tapped, but this time he smiled.

"The watch belonged to the Slausons."

I nodded.

"Jesus, man, how much do you have?"

I showed them the picture of Kenneth Loan.

"How about this guy? Know him?"

They recognized Kenneth Loan the instant they saw him, and stared to buy themselves time to think. Rivera broke first when he glanced at Cassett. Cassett looked up, and the tip of her tongue tasted air.

"Sure. Kenny Loan. I've known him for years."

Rivera seemed more careful with his answer, as if he knew something bad was coming.

"He attends our briefs. What's it matter?"

I adjusted the picture.

"See what he's holding? Under his arm."

"I see."

I adjusted the picture again.

"His back is to us, but the shoulder here is Hensman. We followed Neff and Hensman from the Valley to the building where Mr. Loan works. Hensman delivered this particular laptop to Loan a minute or so before the picture was taken."

I flipped to the next picture.

"Not a great shot, but you can see Hensman a little better. The black Chrysler is their car. You can't see Neff, but he's the driver."

Cassett's mouth puckered, and her eyes narrowed to slits.

"You're saying Neff and Hensman work for Kenneth Loan? I want to be clear here. Is that what you're saying?"

"I'm saying they've been hunting for a particular laptop. They killed Louise August and Alec Rickey to find it, and here they are delivering a laptop to Kenny Loan. An astute detective might see a connection."

Rivera leaned back.

"Is this the laptop they've been after?"

"Uh-uh. I have the laptop they want."

They stared at me.

"And why would Ken Loan want that particular laptop?"

"Dunno. All I found on it were pictures of Derek Hoop. Ivar Hoop's son. Loan's boss."

Cassett seemed nervous.

"We know who he is, Cole. Do you?"

"He's rich."

"Mr. Hoop is a *huge* supporter of law enforcement. The money he gives, you can't count. Lets us use buildings and properties for training, helps raise money for special—"

I cut her off with a picture of the PowerBook.

"I have an expert checking it. Seeing if we can find something besides pictures of Mr. Hoop's son. Something is in this box, Cassett. You don't send animals like Neff and Hensman to find a lost memory book. You send them to make sure no one else finds what you're trying to hide."

I didn't tell her the expert was a bow-tied teenager who spoke in third person and hacked video games.

The three of us stared at each other until Rivera broke the silence.

"Ken Loan used to be on the Sheriffs. You know how he came to work for Mr. Hoop?"

"No idea."

"Arrested a dude named Marquis Nelson. It was Loan found the murder weapon in Nelson's house. That's how the boy got free. Loan found some things in Nelson's house."

He glanced at Cassett, and made half a shrug.

Cassett took a breath and stared at the table. When she tired of staring she cleared her throat.

"What else do you have?"

"A lot. Not everything, but enough to close two murders and the eighteen burglaries. I can give you the kids, their testimony, and whatever stolen items remain in their possession. The kids will cooperate."

"You trying to cut a deal for these kids?"

"Both suspects are with the male's mother at a secure location. She has a lawyer standing by to arrange their surrender. I want them off the street, and protected until this is over."

"Over how?"

I told them about my meeting with Loan, and the jewelry, and the move I'd set into play.

"I want you to let me run with it. Doesn't matter whether it's Hoop or Loan calling the shots, they'll want their laptop, and they'll send their killers to make sure I don't keep it."

"They'll make sure with a .45, Cole."

"I want these kids safe. They'll surrender to you, under the proper terms, and you will not blab to the rest of the department. No briefings."

Cassett nodded, and her eyes looked milky.

"Nobody knows but us."

"That's it. Keep them safe, and I'll give you everything."

Cassett gave me another card, and this time she wrote her personal number.

"Give this to their lawyer. If they have a D.A. they're dealing with, they should tell me."

I tucked her card in my pocket, and started away.

Rivera said, "Cole."

He offered his hand, and we shook.

I felt tired as I walked back to my car, and kept looking over my shoulder. I called Devon before I started the engine.

"She's in. Let me give you her number."

I read off Cassett's contact info.

"Call your attorney, give her Cassett's number, and have her get started. I'll pick up Tyson, and we'll come to the house."

"Thank God this is finally over."

I hung up, and started my car.

46

DEVON CONNOR

Nora Gurwick called from the Calgary Airport twenty minutes or so after Elvis and Tyson left. Amber jumped when Devon's phone rang, as if she somehow sensed the call was her mother. Amber's reaction was so intense, Devon wondered if the girl suffered from post-traumatic stress.

Nora said, "It was the only seat left, all the way back at the ass end of the plane by the toilet, one of those awful center seats. Coach."

Amber watched as Devon listened, so Devon kept her expression pleasant.

"That's lovely, Nora. When will your flight arrive?"

"Rush hour. The worst possible time. Where's Amber?"

"She's taking a shower."

Amber placed her hands together like she was praying, and mouthed, 'thank you.'

"I hope she appreciates the sacrifices I'm making."

"I'm sure she will."

Devon ended the call. Pleasant.

"She'll be home this evening."

Amber rolled onto her back and stared at the ceiling.

"I wish she wasn't coming."

Devon couldn't bring herself to offer up platitudes about a mother's love when she knew nothing about this girl's life.

"I'm sorry."

"I think she did drugs when she was pregnant. That's why I'm messed up."

Jesus.

"I don't know about you, but I could really go for a cup of coffee."

Amber rolled upright and brightened.

"Coffee!"

They ate Cheerios with nonfat milk and bananas, and drank coffee brewed at the little neighborhood market three blocks away. Since they were without a coffeepot, they bought four large coffees so they'd have plenty for refills. The coffee turned out to be bitter, and tasted like bark.

Amber took a sip, and made a sour face.

"Yuck."

Devon sipped, and wrinkled her nose.

"I wish we had chocolate. Chocolate would help."

Amber closed her eyes and looked dreamy.

"Chocolate makes everything taste better."

Devon said, "Yum."

Her phone rang again, but this time Amber didn't jump. It was Elvis.

"She's in. Let me give you her number."

Devon gave Amber a thumbs-up, and jotted the number. Elvis filled her in, and asked her to call their attorney.

"Okay. I'll call right away. Thank God this is finally over."

She hung up, and breathed an exaggerated sigh of relief.

"They agreed. The lawyer has to work out the terms, but Sergeant Cassett understands the situation. It shouldn't take long. Maybe later today."

Amber seemed thoughtful.

"Will I get to go home, you think?"

Devon wasn't sure, and didn't want to lie.

"I don't know. I'll ask when I talk to the lawyer."

Devon had been worried about the same thing. She didn't want Tyson to spend the night in a juvenile facility. She wanted to take him home.

Devon said, "You can come home with us if they'll let you."

Amber looked surprised.

"That's really nice."

Her surprise became thoughtful, and maybe confused.

"Do you hate me?"

Devon wasn't sure how to answer, and less sure she could describe her feelings. She didn't want to elaborate on Tyson's struggles, or on the soul-searching she had done these past few days, but she wanted to be real with this girl.

"I believe with all my heart Tyson is a good person. I raised him to know better, but he did what he did, and I can't help but feel the failing is mine. I wish none of this had happened, but I'm his mother. I keep asking, what did I do? How did I fail? I don't hate you. I don't even blame you. I'm trying not to hate myself."

Amber stared at Devon, but her eyes seemed distant, as if the girl were looking at something farther away. Then Devon realized her lips were moving. Amber was saying something. She was speaking so softly, Devon couldn't hear what she was saying.

"I can't hear you."

"I was saying, I wish I was you."

Devon smiled, and touched her arm.

"You can talk to me."

"Really?"

"I'd like that. I mean it."

Devon remembered Cassett's number, and glanced at the time.

"I'd better call the lawyer. They'll be here soon."

"Do I have time for a shower?"

"Sure. They won't be here *that* soon."

Amber got a bottle of water from the kitchen, and took it with her into the bathroom. Devon sat on the floor against the wall in the living room. She gathered her notes, made sure she was clear on the particulars Elvis described, then made the call. She spent almost twenty minutes on the phone with her attorney, at which point her attorney was ready to speak with both the D.A. and Sergeant Cassett. When they finally hung up, Devon heard the shower. All this time, the water still ran.

"Amber?"

Water.

The bathroom door was closed, in plain view from the living room, right there in front of her.

"Amber?"

Devon hurried to the door, and knocked hard three fast times.

"Amber!"

Pike had fixed the doors so they couldn't lock. The knob turned, and Devon opened the door.

The shower rained on the cheap plastic curtain, but the bathroom window was open.

Devon ran to her phone.

47

ELVIS COLE

I WAS WITH TYSON AND CARL, thinking the smell of failure was pickles and body odor. The pictures of Derek Hoop flashed on the PowerBook's screen, almost as if he were winking at me.

"You didn't find anything?"

The Carl huffed at my choice of words.

"I *found* there is nothing to find, which is, in fact, finding the fact that no encrypted or hidden data is present."

The PowerBook was wired to Carl's computer, which sprouted external drives like pumpkins from a pumpkin vine. The video game commando on the oversized monitor had been replaced by multiple windows. Each window showed the results of software used to detect digital image compression loss and steganographic signatures, both sure signs of hidden files.

"You checked all the pictures?"

"Pictures are data. The total binary data on this device was examined."

The images of Derek Hoop scrolled past, one followed by another. I didn't want to believe they held nothing.

"Are you positive?"

The Carl drew himself up.

"I am The Carl."

Tyson said, "Carl knows what he's doing. He encrypts everything."

The Carl grunted.

"Only way to protect my work. The legacies would steal my ideas and loot my code."

The legacies were the big gaming software companies.

The Carl made a dismissive wave at his monitor.

"Trust me. This isn't rocket science. Pedophiles and terrorists use these same techniques."

Maybe the FBI would find something.

Devon called as I stared at the PowerBook, her voice tight with strain as she told me Amber was gone.

"How long ago?"

"Ten minutes, maybe. Fifteen at the most. I thought she was taking a shower."

Tyson read the edge in my voice.

"What happened? Is it Amber?"

I nodded, and motioned him silent.

"I'm with Tyson at Carl's. We'll leave now, and we'll find her. She hasn't gone very far."

"She took my car. She must've snuck my keys before the shower, and now my car is gone."

The car made it bad. I told her to hang on, and turned to Tyson.

"Amber took your mom's car. Where would she go? Is there a friend, maybe?"

Tyson answered immediately.

"Jazzi's. She'd want her car. Maybe money, but she'd definitely want her car. She'll go to Jazzi's."

I left Tyson with Carl, and ran to my car.

48

HARVEY AND STEMMS

STEMMS TOOLED THE MERCEDES down Beverly Glen to the Valley, and turned toward Jasmine's apartment. He ran his fingers over the dash and his seat, admiring the stiff German leather. Excellent quality. Beautiful appointments. The vehicle drove like a dream.

Harvey said, "You and this car should get a room, Stemms. Keep stroking, you'll give it an orgasm."

Stemms was trying to think up an insult when the *Pink Panther* theme blasted from Harvey's phone, the original recording with Plas Johnson on sax.

Harvey held his phone at arm's length like it smelled bad, and gave it the finger.

"Answer it, Harvey. C'mon."

Their client. Harvey had chosen the *Pink Panther* theme for his ringtone, the music bringing to mind the cartoonish, bumbling Inspector Clouseau. Stemms thought the choice was brilliant, Harvey being Harvey.

Stemms pulled into a parking lot, popped an Adderall, and offered the bottle to Harvey. Harvey waved him away, listening close to the call.

"Uh-huh, uh-huh, okay. Yeah, we're going there now. He was there. How about I put you on speaker? Yeah, with Stemms. We're in the car."

Harvey rolled his eyes, and flipped off the phone.

"Whatever you want. Got it."

Harvey lowered his phone.

"Asshole."

"What's up?"

"Got our ID. The dude in Jasmine's apartment? He's a private investigator. Elvis Cole."

"Wait. What's his name?"

"Elvis Cole."

"For real? Elvis?"

"The client says he's Elvis, he's Elvis. Who gives a shit what he's
named?"

"Take it easy. What's the big deal?"

"The deal is, Inspector Clouseau wants us to drop everything and find
the guy. Lives up in Laurel. Has an office in Hollywood. He's sending the
address."

Stemms didn't like it.

"He just left Jasmine's. We should figure out why he was there before
we go chasing around, don't you think?"

"I think the client wants what he wants, and I want my picture."

The bright, happy sound of *Windy* suddenly chimed again. Stemms
beamed, and punched Harvey's arm.

"Maybe the a-hole came back."

Harvey opened the video feed, but this time it wasn't Cole. Amber
stepped through the door, and hurried into the bedroom.

Stemms looked at Harvey.

"We're five minutes away."

Harvey said, "Let's get her."

The big white Mercedes powered out of the parking lot.

49

AMBER REED

AMBER DROPPED into a spindly rose bush beneath the bathroom window. The bush raked her legs, but she didn't slow. She walked directly to Devon's car, and threw open the door. The Audi beeped so loud when the door unlocked, Amber freaked. Devon had heard, for sure, and would come flying out of the house.

Amber jumped in behind the wheel, and freaked even more. The Audi was totally different from her Mini. She fumbled with the fob and frantically searched for an ignition button, certain that Devon was racing down the drive.

"Don't look, don't look, don't look—"

The Audi woke with an even purr. Amber pulled away, and did not look back. Hands at ten and two. Her eyes burned. She forgot to breathe. Amber drove to the end of the block, put on the blinker, and left the safe house behind. Going to jail was not part of the plan.

Amber wasn't familiar with the east Valley, and felt kinda lost. She studied the dash map to get her bearings, then pulled over to adjust the seat and the mirrors. Once she was on the freeway, Amber was fine.

Ninety-two thousand dollars in cash and a spare key for the Mini were waiting in Jazzi's apartment. Devon would call the police and Elvis, and Elvis would look for her at Jazzi's. She didn't have much time. She needed to grab her cash and car, buy a new phone, and disappear into Amberland. The possibilities made her smile.

Amber parked the Audi half a block from Jasmine's building, and hurried to the gate. She jabbed the call buttons, but nobody answered. Assholes. She punched the call buttons again, jabjabjab-jabjab, but wasted no time by waiting. She gripped the bars, put her foot on the knob, and climbed over the gate. This wasn't the first time Amber came home without a key.

Jazzi kept a spare in a black magnetic box under the first step on the stairs leading up to the apartment. Amber found the box, hurried upstairs, and let herself in.

Amber was so close to getting away she giggled, but she did not slow. She grabbed her spare keys from the kitchen, and ran to her bedroom.

Amber shoved pants and tops and bras and underwear and shoes into an oversized beach bag. She grabbed clothes without thinking about them, packed only enough to get by, and didn't care. She dragged the bag to the closet, and went for the cash.

The ninety-two thousand dollars was spread between a rain boot, two shoe boxes, and a pink brocade box she stole from a house in Brentwood. Handfuls of cash went into the beach bag with her clothes, and each handful brought her closer to waving bye-bye. She upended the shoe box of jewelry, decided it would take too long to pick the pieces she liked, so she scooped handfuls of jewelry into the bag.

Amber opened more boxes, checked inside shoes, and turned pockets inside out for the last of her money.

Almost finished.

Almost had everything.

She stuffed the last pack of hundreds under the clothes, thought for a moment to make sure she wasn't forgetting a secret stash, then zipped the bag.

Amber was so focused on gathering all of her cash, she did not hear the entry door open.

50

ELVIS COLE

I IDLED PAST DEVON'S AUDI, checking the street for the black sedan. Amber's Mini was in the garage, and Jasmine's building appeared quiet. I turned around at the end of the block, drove back, and called Pike.

"No reason to watch the Connor house now. Pick up Tyson, and take him to the safe house. I'll meet you with Amber. Once the surrender goes down, you and I can set up for Loan."

"Once they surrender."

"Yeah. Cassett will take the kids, and we'll deal with Kenny Loan."

"You've been a target since you gave him the jewelry. I should be watching your back."

Pike didn't like it.

"I'm here. I'll get Amber, and we'll meet at the safe house. First things first."

Pike was silent.

"Joe?"

Pike hung up, clearly unhappy.

I wanted to get in, get out, and leave as quickly as possible. I opened the gate with Amber's keys, and crept up the stairs. I listened, and the keys worked again. Scrapes and bumps came from the bedroom, and Amber shuffled sideways through the door, an enormous beach bag catching the jamb. When the beach bag pulled free, she saw me and shrieked.

"You scared me! Jesus, I wet myself!"

"You'll dry. C'mon."

I hooked her arm, and pulled her into the living room. She pulled back, and tried to twist away.

"I don't want to go."

"Tough."

"I'll pay you. I'll hire you to let me go."

I stripped the bag off her shoulder, tossed it aside, and dragged her toward the door.

"That's my money! I'm not leaving my money!"

"You're not safe here, Amber. We have to leave."

"I was leaving. I would be gone if you'd let me go."

She twisted, and squirmed, and pried at my fingers.

"You're going to surrender like we planned. You want to jump bail after that, and play Bonnie Parker, knock yourself out."

"Who's Bonnie Parker? Just kidding. I'm kidding!"

I got her to the door, managed to get it open, and that was as far as we got.

Two men with guns filled the space. One big, one bigger, both bigger than me. Nice-looking jackets and ties. Nice-looking pistols.

I said, "We were just going out. How 'bout you catch us later?"

The smaller man tipped his gun.

"How 'bout you put your hands on your head and lace your fingers?"

I put my hands on my head, and laced my fingers.

"Five steps back, stop."

I took five steps backward, and stopped.

They came inside, and immediately moved apart. Professional. Alec Rickey's roommate told me the larger man was Neff, which made the smaller man Hensman.

Neff closed and locked the door. Hensman's eyes never left me. They were rawboned men with broad shoulders, blocky hands, and tight collars. Early thirties, or younger.

Hensman's pistol tipped down.

"Do not remove your hands from your head. Turn around."

I turned.

"Kneel."

I kneeled.

"I'm going to take your hands, and lower you forward onto your belly. Clear?"

"I know how it's done."

He lowered me to my belly, told me to release my fingers and extend my arms above my head. When I was stretched on the floor like Superman flying, he took my pistol and wallet, slipped them into his pocket, and stepped away.

"If you move your hands to your body or try to get up, I'll kill you."

I twisted my head enough to see him.

"Is your name really Hensman?"

The larger man took out a phone.

"Is your name really *Elvis?*"

Turd.

The larger man called someone, and backed away mumbling.

The smaller man circled Amber, and stopped directly behind her. He tapped his thigh with his gun.

"Hello, Amber Reed. Do you like music?"

Amber said, "Excuse me? Who's Amber Reed?"

The bigger man finished his call, and gave the finger to his phone.

The smaller man grimaced.

"Don't tell me."

"He's coming. Ten out, twelve tops. We gotta wait."

The taller man took a seat on the couch, scowling.

The smaller man finished circling Amber, and stopped in front of her. He looked down the length of her body, tapping his leg with the gun.

Amber didn't like it, and I didn't like it either.

Amber said, "Stop it. You're creeping me out."

"You look like your sister."

I twisted enough to see him. Smaller than the larger man, but tall as a tree.

"What about me? Who do I look like?"

The smaller man kicked me in the ribs, then kicked me again. He kicked me so hard I heard them break.

He said, "You look like someone in pain."

The bigger man laughed, and the smaller man moved back to Amber. She glanced at me, but I couldn't tell if her eyes held pity or fear.

Pike had been right. Waiting to deal with Loan had been a mistake. I felt bad for Amber, and me, but mostly for Amber. I wanted to live long enough to tell Pike he was right.

51

JOE PIKE

PIKE RAN TO HIS JEEP, checked the time, and called Devon. Her phone rang seven times before her voice mail answered.

"Call Pike."

He killed the line, and immediately tapped out a text.

CALL NOW

Devon returned his call in less than a minute, and sounded afraid.

"Is anything wrong?"

Pike's voice was calm.

"Just checking in. Everything okay?"

"So far so good. I've been on the phone with the lawyer. I spoke with Detective Cassett. There's so much to consider, but she's trying to help."

"Feel good about it?"

"Yes. Considering the situation, this is something I can live with."

Pike checked the time again, and figured the travel time from Devon's home to Jasmine's apartment.

"Good. Is Tyson okay?"

"He's still with Carl. I guess you or Elvis will bring him home."

"Elvis says they didn't find anything."

"I don't understand it. How can these people be doing all this for nothing?"

"Maybe an expert will find something."

"I don't even care. I just want Tyson safe, and this horrible mess behind us. If the police find something, fine, but I just want him safe."

"Me, too."

Pike put the Jeep in gear, and rolled away from her house.

"I have to hook up with Elvis, but I'll pick up your boy after. That okay?"

"Of course. Did Elvis find Amber?"

"Yes. And your car. One of us will bring it."

Pike pushed the Jeep faster.

"I'm getting a call. The lawyer."

Pike said, "We'll see you later."

So calm, he might have been taking a nap.

Pike knew exactly how long it would take to reach Jasmine's apartment, and pushed the Jeep harder. He screamed through the streets, racing to make up the time he had lost, racing to get there in time.

52

ELVIS COLE

WE DIED when Kenneth Loan stepped through the door. Amber didn't know we were dead, but Loan wouldn't leave us alive to testify. The bigger man let him in. The smaller man pulled me to my feet. Lightning flashed from the ribs, but I swallowed the scream.

"This is the thanks I get, Kenny? Didn't Mrs. Hoop like her jewelry?"

Loan ignored me, and spoke to the smaller man. He seemed anxious, like a man in a hurry.

"You got it?"

"It isn't here. We checked before."

Amber said, "Are you a billionaire?"

Loan glanced at Amber as if she didn't exist, then came over, and faced me. He stood with his fists on his hips, a slim little .38 Snubby clipped to his waist.

"Be straight, and we'll work this thing out."

The bigger man was on the far side of the room. His partner hovered to my left, closer, but out of reach. Kenneth Loan was close. The ribs would slow me down, but I might be able to get his gun. I might get me and Amber shot to death, but our choices were limited.

"What would this thing be?"

"Who are you working for?"

"The boy's mother. She found a watch in his room he couldn't explain. Hired me to find out where he got it."

Amber pooched her lips.

"She messed up *everything*."

I said, "How about you, Kenny? Who are you working for, yourself or the Hoops?"

Loan glanced at the bigger man.

"Harvey."

Harvey walked around behind me, and punched me in the back. He hit me so hard I stumbled and fell to a knee.

Amber shouted.

"What is *wrong* with you people? Are you *ill?*"

Loan flicked a hand, irritated.

"C'mon. Pick him up."

Harvey started to lift me, but I pushed his hand away and got to my feet. The ribs grated, and hurt even worse.

Loan said, "We won't discuss Mr. Hoop. The Hoops are off limits."

"Sure."

"All right, then. I believe you. The boy's mother hired you, and one thing led to another."

"That's it."

"I'm not here for more jewelry. You know what I want?"

"Hard not to know, what with Dr. Doom and Lex Luthor here asking half the city about a laptop. And since these animals are killing people, I'm thinking it's worth plenty."

"Fair enough. And I'm thinking you have it, which is why you came to my office. You'd like to sell it."

"Jewelry. They sold off the laptops they stole at a flea market."

Harvey shook his head.

"No way. Stemms and I compiled an excellent accounting. Alec and Amber here sold many things, but never a laptop."

Compiled. I wondered what they compiled from Louise August.

I focused on Loan, trying to stall.

"I'd love to sell it to you, Kenny. As bad as you want this thing, I could retire, but it's gone. They sold the electronics."

Loan frowned, and seemed to be going for it when Amber spoke up.

"He's lying. We have it. What's your best offer?"

I glanced a warning at her and tried to laugh it off.

"They dumped the electronics. The boy told me. She's confused."

"Do I look confused, Mr. Sexist? The thing with the trackball, with the pictures of Derek Hoop. Make me an offer."

Derek's name hit them like a hand grenade. Derek's name told them we had it. Loan smiled. Stemms flashed dimples so deep they could swallow a Buick.

"You are blowing my mind."

"Rock my world. How much?"

I tried to stop her.

"Amber."

Amber bugged her eyes at me.

"I *so* totally know what I'm doing. Trust me."

Loan left me, and went to Amber.

"I'm buying. Where is it?"

"They took it to this hacker guy. They think secret stuff must be on it, and he's like a genius, The Carl. He's checking it right now."

Loan flushed bright red, and the smile stiffened to a stricture. He breathed so loudly the two men stared.

"Where?"

I interrupted, trying to draw him away.

"She doesn't know. He's my contact, not hers. But my guy has it, and he's probably found whatever you're trying to hide."

Stemms backhanded the pistol at my head. I caught most of it on a forearm, and stepped in close to roll his arm, but Harvey came out of nowhere and hit me again.

Amber shoved herself between us.

"The Carl is Tyson's friend, okay? I don't know where he lives, but Tyson was staying here until his *mommy* found us. His things are still here. I don't know for sure, but The Carl's address or phone number or *something* might be here. Let me look."

She pointed at the bedroom, waiting.

Loan glanced at Stemms, and Stemms nodded.

"Yeah. They were shacked up."

Loan motioned at Harvey.

"Go with her, and let's get the hell out of here. This is taking too long."

Harvey swaggered past Stemms with a big leering grin.

"Guess who's hitting the rack-shack with Jasmine's baby sister? Not you."

He made a sniffing sound as he followed Amber into the bedroom.

Loan moved away, and took out his phone. Stemms stayed by me, and Harvey was gone. The odds were as good as they would get. Stemms was big, and fit, and looked like a guy who could handle himself, but he was staring at the bedroom. The gun dangled alongside his leg, and his grip wasn't firm. Amber was talking, but I couldn't make out what she was saying.

I edged closer, and lowered my voice.

"Stemms."

His eyes were calm, and maybe sad.

"Were you kind?"

"What?"

I edged closer. Not much, just a little. I knew what I needed to do.

"When you killed Louise August, were you kind?"

I saw the play in my head like a dance straight from hell, but a single loud BANG exploded behind me, followed by a second BANG. Kenny Loan stumbled backward onto the couch. Stemms dived sideways, and tried to raise his pistol, but froze in mid-motion, and dropped it. Then I saw why.

Amber stood in the bedroom door behind me, clutching Alec Rickey's pistol with both hands. A small silver pistol with a white plastic grip.

Her eyes were wild and bright.

"Get his gun! Get his gun!"

Then Harvey reared up behind her, and pulled Amber down.

53

JOE PIKE

PIKE SLID OUT OF HIS JEEP, and three-sixtied the area. He saw Cole's car and Devon's car, but no black sedan. Turning, he noticed a gleaming white Mercedes, so clean it had to be new. Something about it bothered him. Pike drifted closer, and saw a temporary registration fixed to the corner of the windshield. Closer, he saw the dealer card, and touched the Python under his sweatshirt. Ekezian Motor Craft, same as the black sedan, a dealership that didn't exist.

Pike ran for the gate. A muffled but unmistakable gunshot *cracked* from the building. One second later, a second.

Pike hit the gate at a sprint, and hoisted himself over.

ELVIS COLE

Harvey's shirt glistened red when he appeared behind Amber, and he fell into her like a collapsing bear.

Stemms shouted.

"Harvey!"

I hit Stemms hard from the side, and drove him away from his gun. He rolled with the hit, and tried to spin free, but I locked his arm close, and moved with him, keeping the fight on the floor. My pistol was in his pocket. Stemms clubbed me with his free hand, and I clawed at the pocket with mine.

Amber's pistol cracked again, and then again. She still had the gun, but Harvey held her hands away, and the bullets slapped the wall.

Behind us, Kenny Loan clawed at the wound on his chest, shouting as if the rest of us weren't fighting for our lives.

"I'm shot. Call 911, for Christ's sake. Look at my blood."

He fell off the couch, and crawled toward the door.

Stemms hit me again, and then Amber shouted.

"Help! He's getting the gun! Help!"

She was kicking and thrashing, but Harvey had her wrists and was working his way to the gun.

I pulled Stemms closer and shouted.

"Amber!"

Amber pushed her gun toward me.

I punched Stemms three hard, fast times, then released him, and went for her pistol.

A single loud gunshot froze the scene.

Kenneth Loan sat propped against the wall, burping red bubbles, and holding the Snubby. He tried to aim at me, but his gun swayed like a reed in the wind.

"You bastard. You bastard."

The Snubby dropped, and Ken Loan tipped over.

Stemms scooped up his pistol, pointed it at me, and scrambled to his feet.

"Harvey?"

"I'm fine."

Harvey reached inside his very nice jacket, and took out a pistol.

Stemms checked Kenny Loan, and made a face.

"He's done. Asshole."

Harvey said, "Fuck'm."

Stemms kept his gun on me, and hurried to his partner.

"Get up, Harvey. C'mon. Let's go."

I glanced at the silver pistol on the floor, and wondered if I could reach it before I died. Stemms would shoot me, but maybe I could save Amber.

When I looked up, Stemms lifted his gun. He smiled.

"I'll give you a shot. Go for it. You never know."

I glanced at the gun again, and thought maybe I should, and I did. I dove for the little silver pistol, and braced for a bullet that never arrived.

The front door crashed in as if it were hit by a locomotive, and splinters peppered the room.

Pike shot Stemms twice in the chest.

Harvey put his gun to Amber's head, and I shot him once in the face. The bigger man fell over dead.

I cleared their guns quickly, and pointed at Loan.

"Gun. Get 911."

Pike took the Snubby, and called emergency as I rolled Harvey off Amber.

"You okay? Are you shot?"

She rolled onto her back, and took deep breaths, and finally sat up. Her thin top was wet with Harvey's blood.

Pike was talking with emergency services.

I checked Stemms, then pulled off his jacket, and pressed it to Kenneth Loan's chest. He was alive, but he was dying.

"Hang on. Paramedics are coming."

He pushed my hands, maybe because he didn't want to be saved, but I held the compress to his wound.

"Was it Hoop? You? Why was it so important?"

His lips moved, but I couldn't hear him. I leaned close, and put my ear to his lips.

". . . didn't trust . . . didn't trust . . ."

I didn't know what he was saying, and he probably didn't know, either.

Climbing to my feet took forever. I saw Pike. I went to him, and hugged him. I held him for a very long time.

He whispered.

"You okay?"

I nodded, but I held him tight, and he held me.

After a while I stepped away, and called Dani Cassett. She told me she'd arrive as fast as possible.

I walked over to Amber, and sat on the floor beside her.

"Okay?"

"Feels weird, like I'm inside a really big can and everything echoes. Even the lights look weird."

I didn't know what to say, so I thanked her.

"Thank you. For what you did."

"I was really scared."

"Yeah. That's how it is."

She was quiet.

"You know what's really weird?"

I shook my head. I heard sirens. Coming closer.

"When they make the movie, I'll be the hero."

I had nothing to say. I put my arm around her, and we sat together until the police arrived.

54

TYSON CONNOR

CARL'S SISTER BROUGHT them swiss-and-pickle sandwiches with English mustard from England on rye bread from Art's Deli in Studio City. If the rye bread wasn't from Art's Carl wouldn't eat it. She also brought a phone from the house because Tyson's mother had called.

"Elvis will pick you up in about twenty minutes."

"Okay."

"I'm sorry you didn't find anything."

"Okay."

Tyson wanted to get off the phone. Carl was next to him, and listening to every word. Carl thought everyone was crapping on him behind his back because he didn't find any secret documents.

Tyson said, "I gotta help Carl. I'll see you soon."

She finally signed off, and Tyson put down the phone. They had spent the past four hours in the pool house, and looked each other in the eye maybe twice. Mostly they looked past each other or at the monitors.

Carl said, "You're not helping. You're just standing."

"I wanted to get off the phone."

"You didn't have to be a dick and say you were helping. Now she thinks I can't do it myself."

"Carl."

"What?"

Carl had been like this all day.

"I'm sorry. All those things I said. I'm sorry. I was a dick."

Carl fitted the motherboard into the base frame, and snapped the cover onto the frame. The old PowerBook was almost back together.

"The King of Dickland, that's what you were. Like, one day you're up with this smokin'-hot porno chick, and I'm just a dweeb?"

"Amber didn't do porn."

Carl stepped away from the bench as if he were thunderstruck.

Tyson said, "She isn't a porn star."

"*Dick!*"

"I lied, okay?"

"*DICK!*"

"Can we please get past this? I'm going to jail."

The Carl stared at the floor, then put the finishing touches on the PowerBook.

"Maybe you'll get probation or something, and pick up trash on the freeway."

"I miss gaming with you."

"I totally kicked your ass."

"I miss—"

Tyson stopped, and held so tight to the bench his elbows hurt. His eyes filled, and he began to cry, and he didn't know what to say, and even if he did he couldn't.

Carl looked at him, and glanced away, and looked back, and glanced away again, and then Carl held him, really tight, even though Carl didn't look at him, and Tyson cried harder.

After he finished, Tyson stepped back, and blew his nose, and Carl booted up the old PowerBook.

"You should come play. The new hacks I did, they kill."

"I don't know if they'll let me. I might have to wear one of those ankle things."

Carl looked embarrassed.

"You want to play, we'll figure it out."

The PowerBook's screen came to life, and the two lonely icons appeared. Carl rolled the cursor around the desktop, seeing if everything worked. The little trackball scratched when it rolled in its socket.

Carl leaned close, and rocked the ball back and forth.

"They haven't cleaned this thing in forever."

"What's wrong?"

"It drags. A trackball does not drag. It isn't designed to *drag*."

Carl unscrewed the collar, and lifted the ball from its socket. He peered in the hole.

"Jeez Louise."

"What?"

The Carl snatched up a pair of tweezers, and lifted a tiny golden microchip from the socket. He held it under a light, then examined it under a magnifying glass.

He smiled, and showed the chip to Tyson.

"Do, or not do."

"What is it?"

The Carl smiled even wider. Hyuk-hyuk-hyuk.

"Evidence."

PART V

FATHER'S DAY

55

I WAS ABOARD a jet bound for Louis Armstrong New Orleans International Airport when they arrested Ivar and Lillian Hoop. I was renting a car when the news broke in Los Angeles, and did not learn of their arrest until I reached the hotel in Baton Rouge. One of those national cable news channels was playing when I got out of the shower. The anchor finished a piece about salmonella, and segued to the shocking arrest of the Hoops. I didn't want to see it or think about it. I didn't care. I turned off the news, finished dressing, and met Lucy and Ben at a lovely restaurant overlooking the Mississippi River. We had a wonderful time.

Ben flew back to L.A. with me two days later. I didn't have to pick him up in Baton Rouge, but I wanted to see Lucy, and spend time with Ben where he lived. Baton Rouge was a great little town. Seeing it through Ben's eyes made it special.

Detectives from LAPD and senior prosecutors from the D.A.'s office interviewed me for seven hours over two days following the events at Jasmine Reed's apartment. Dani Cassett sat with me during all seven hours. Jasmine flew home to be with Amber, and I had a chance to meet her. I liked her a lot.

The case against Mr. and Mrs. Hoop was made by Carl Riggens. The memory chip he found contained a detailed account of a conspiracy between Ivar Hoop, an attorney named Sheldon Fitz, a since-deceased employee named Dennis Ng, and a young Sheriff's investigator named Kenneth Loan to identify and frame a credible suspect for Adele Silvani's murder. The research detailed by Ivar Hoop was shocking in its scope, and horrifying to read. Marquis Nelson had died of cancer in prison, an innocent man no one believed.

I avoided all news about the Hoops until their confession, which came as a surprise. It was Lillian Hoop who convinced her husband to detail their conspiracy. Ivar had thought it a silly and dangerous idea, but Lillian insisted, believing Fitz, Ng, and Loan could not be trusted. She felt a record of their involvement could be used as a weapon if one was needed. Kenneth Loan did not learn of the chip until the PowerBook was stolen. This explained what he tried to say when he was dying. I liked knowing, and once I knew, I stopped thinking about it.

Eleven days after the events in Jasmine's apartment, the glass sliders were open to my deck, a fresh breeze stirred the air, and I felt relaxed and content as I answered the phone.

"Hey, it's Dani. Get this—"

Sergeant Cassett.

"What's up?"

"Three weeks ago, Chippies found a stiff on an on-ramp in Eagle Rock, young male, strangulation, evidence of an assault—"

"Sex crime?"

"Uh-uh. ID'd as a Jesse Guzman, twenty-two, on parole. Worked as a busboy at a club called Jade House."

I'd never heard of it.

"Uh-huh."

"Disappeared during a shift one night, no one knew why, the next day he's on the ramp. Guess what?"

"Is this a trick question?"

"We got a hit from the DNA under his fingernails. Floyd Ranson Harvey. You believe those guys? All the bodies they dropped?"

Cassett had called to share her excitement, but the news felt like an intrusion.

Then she said, "How about we grab drinks and dinner tonight? My treat."

"Thanks, but I can't. Got plans."

It occurred to me Cassett had been calling a lot.

I said, "How about next week?"

She brightened.

"I thought you were giving me the brush."

"No way, Sergeant. Busy tonight, but I'd love to see you next week."

"I'd like that, too. But not if you call me Sergeant."

The guest room door opened, and Ben Chenier thundered down the hall. He was bigger now, and moved like a horse. He saw me on the phone, and pulled up. I held up a finger, and finished with Cassett.

"Deal. Gotta go, but I'll call."

I put away the phone, and joined him. Ben had pulled on shorts and a faded LSU T-shirt. He tanned golden-dark like his mother, and he was almost as tall as me. He would be taller.

Ben grinned.

"Don't hurt me."

I laughed, and we walked out onto the deck. A red-tail floated high over the canyon.

"We'll start slow, then go as slow or fast as you want."

Ben was studying martial arts, and had become a dedicated student. We'd been playing with close-in Wing Chun moves, a fighting art where opponents were only inches apart, and in constant contact.

I placed Ben in position with his feet spread and hands up, then stood very close with my hands at my side.

"Ready?"

He grinned. Ready.

I said, "Touch my nose."

As he reached for my nose, I rolled his arm gently toward his body.

"Again, opposite hand, and keep it going."

He reached for my nose with his other hand, I rolled him again, and he reached again, and we picked up speed. Our arms rose and fell, twining and flowing like kelp in gentle swells.

Ben grinned and picked up the pace. I grinned, and nodded.

"Show me whatcha got."

His hands and ours were a rolling blur, faster and faster, and then he tried to surprise me. He came in low to poke my belly. I rolled him down and away without missing a beat.

"Saw it coming yesterday."

"No way!"

"I'll show you."

I showed him, and sometimes he listened, and sometimes he didn't. Those moments we shared were precious. They filled me with joy, and hope, and a belief I had done something lasting and real.